HER CELTIC
CAPTOR

ASHE BARKER

Published by Stormy Night Publications and Design, LLC.
www.StormyNightPublications.com

Cover design by Korey Mae Johnson
www.koreymaejohnson.com

Images by Period Images and 123RF/Galyna Andrushko

1st Print Edition. August 2017

ISBN-13: 978-1974564620

ISBN-10: 1974564622

FOR AUDIENCES 18+ ONLY

This book is intended for adults only. Spanking and other sexual activities represented in this book are fantasies only, intended for adults.

PROLOGUE

Skarthveit, Norseland
1095

"I will help you."

The woman whirled, her blonde plait swinging wildly as it loosened itself from its binding. She swept the stray locks, streaked with the beginnings of grey, away from her face and glared at the unknown youth who had emerged in silence from the shadows of the surrounding trees and now stood before her. "Who are you? What are you doing here? Spying on me? My warriors are close, I shall have you flogged—"

"You need help. I am offering my aid, lady." The intruder bowed his head in affected subservience then stepped forward to assist.

She stood her ground and glowered at the young Celt as he lifted his chin and met her gaze. He schooled his expression to ensure his features remained steady, unmoved, despite the gory presence of the body of a man, dead for just a few moments, who lay sprawled at this Viking noblewoman's elegant feet.

Her hands on her hips, she panted from her recent

1

exertions. Even in the inky blackness of the night he could discern her flushed features, the residual rage etched there, now mingling with fear of discovery. Her initial fury spent, the consequences of her actions now beckoned. She was frightened, shocked perhaps, but still she tilted her head back, eyes narrowing as she regarded him. Her expression was haughty despite her predicament. "Why? Why are you here? Where did you come from?" she demanded. "Have you dared to follow me?"

He shrugged. "I can leave you, if you prefer." He made no move to do so however. She had no choice. He knew it, she knew it. He waited in silence.

"Very well," she capitulated. "Can you lift him?"

"Aye, I can. Where—?"

"Anywhere. He must not be found. Ever."

The youth nodded. He understood perfectly well. The cliffs then. He would toss the body into the churning waves below. If the dear Lord looked kindly upon his endeavours this night, the remains would be dashed to pieces on the rocks, then sink, never to surface again. Good riddance, and if he could extract some advantage for himself from the situation so much the better.

The woman watched him come forward, her agitation evident in the rapid tapping of her booted foot on the ground and in the stiffness of her spine.

He dropped to his haunches then bent to roll the dead man over onto his back and noted with grim satisfaction the blood still oozing from the single stab wound to his chest. The body was still warm, pliant, alive but moments ago. He had witnessed the altercation, heard the vicious accusations, seen with his own eyes the cold, hard fury of a vengeful woman. He had seen the flash of the blade as she struck, heard the death gurgle as the man crumpled, his final breath churning in his throat as he fought frantically to hang on to a life soon to be extinguished. It had been quick, he would grant her that. He glanced up at her, nodded his approval. This woman killed with ruthless efficiency.

2

"Get on with it. I need him gone."

"Of course, though I will require something from you in return."

She appeared unsurprised. "What?"

"Food. Two days' supply. Warm clothing, in the Viking style. A weapon. And your silence. No one should know I passed this way." On that last point he had no doubt that he and his unlikely accomplice were in perfect accord. Neither would wish to revisit this night's work.

She considered his request for barely moments, then nodded. "So be it. You will dispose of... of... that," she gestured with distaste to the bloodstained corpse in the flattened grass, "then meet me by yonder stand of trees in two hours' time. I shall meet your price."

He had no real cause to trust her, but did so anyway. The bargain was struck, and they both had much to lose. He quashed any lingering doubts and bent to his task. It was a simple enough matter to heft the dead weight onto his shoulder, legs to the front. The torso, arms, and head dangled down his back. He shifted a little to adjust the balance, then turned to stride away.

"Wait."

He turned at the imperious command. "Yes?"

"Do you know why?"

He did. He had seen and heard enough of the fierce and vicious quarrel that had preceded the flash of the woman's knife to know exactly why this vile piece of shit was dead. There were some who might regret the disappearance of this man whose corpse he now bore to a watery grave, one or two who might mourn his loss and wonder, but he suspected not many. The world was no less a place without such as this one. Still, it was not for him to say what the rights and wrongs were.

"How would I know? I am not from here, I am no one..."

She nodded, not disputing his assessment. "You will say nothing, ever. No one must know of this."

"Of course." He inclined his head, his obeisance a given. "You will never return. Ever."

He bowed his agreement and turned away once more. This time she did not call him back.

Ten minutes later he stood at the top of the cliff, his weight tipping forward infinitesimally, just enough to be able to glimpse the rocks below and the boiling waves that lashed them. He could hear the roar of the sea from here, greedy as it sucked in the meal he offered. The pale shadow of the cadaver bobbed for a few moments on the waves, then disappeared below the frothing, foaming surface.

It was done. He turned and walked back the way he had come, his mind mercifully blank as he sought a safe haven in which to wait out the agreed two hours.

CHAPTER ONE

The North Sea
1106

"Heave, one, two. Heave, one, two." The rhythmic roar paused for a second, then, "You! Yes, you. Pull. *Pull!*" The final word was accompanied by the shrill hiss of a whip slicing the air, then a shriek as the lash found its mark.

"Bastards," muttered Taranc under his breath as he leaned in to drag on the huge oar again. "Just shut up and row," he rasped to the men on either side of him in the crammed hull of the Viking dragon ship. "Our chance will come, but for now *they* have the whips."

Murmurings of resentful and fearful discontent surrounded him and the occasional scream rose up as yet another of his Celtic countrymen attracted the vicious displeasure of their Nordic captors. Taranc allowed none of it to distract him as he bent his body back and forth, each powerful stroke of the huge oar ploughing the unrelenting waves. He fought to retain his temper, to not react to the bullying and swagger, the belligerent crowing of the victorious Vikings as they pressed their newest slaves into the hard labour required to carry them back across the

North Sea to their home in the cold and frozen North.

Many of Taranc's friends and neighbours had perished in the swift and violent Viking raid on their villages. Taranc recalled with vivid accuracy the sight of Dughall, Lord of Pennglas weeping over the body of his slain son. Adair was ever a foolish and headstrong lad, but he had died seeking to defend his home and Taranc could not help but admire the young man's courage. It was a waste, though. A bloody stupid waste.

The Norsemen had swooped on them without warning, killing all who resisted and herding the rest into a circle to be taken as slaves. Taranc had been among those rounded up and had surrendered without much in the way of apparent protest. He was but one man, and their Viking attackers were many, and heavily armed. Taranc might privately admire Adair's determination to put up a fight, but did not share his suicidal tendencies. As chief of the village of Aikrig, Taranc saw his duty in seeking the survival of his people rather than a glorious death. Under his leadership they would await their moment, retaliate if and when an opportunity arose. Dead Celts were of no use to anyone.

"Heads down. Just row and keep quiet," he commanded. He glanced from one side to the other, his stern glare calculated to quell any lingering dissent. Taranc expected to be obeyed, and his people did not disappoint him now. They bent their backs in unison, succumbing to the roared commands of their cruel captors who seemed to believe they controlled the situation.

Taranc knew better. At a word from him, the oars slaves would rise up and attack the Vikings, but to what avail? Better to choose their moment, when the odds were more in their favour.

As he rowed in silence he relived those awful moments when he had realised what was happening, and with that understanding had come recognition of the utter futility of resistance. Taranc had been at Pennglas when their attackers struck, having gone there to seek out Fiona, his betrothed.

She was daughter to Dughall, sister to the hapless Adair, and herself now also a prisoner of the Vikings.

Fiona was every bit as courageous and foolhardy as her brother and had sought to repel the invaders with her slingshot. An excellent markswoman, she had felled two or three Norse warriors before being apprehended by no less than the Viking chief himself. She was now his captive and Taranc feared for her. As men, the fate of those who shared the dragon ship with him was clear enough. They would be expected to work, and the labour would be hard. For women, the future might be much more uncertain. All knew the vile reputation of these vicious Norsemen, their cruelty to female captives.

Taranc's feelings regarding his betrothed were somewhat complex. Informally promised to one another since childhood, they had grown up together. The pair had played in the meadows that lay between their villages, climbed trees, and roamed the surrounding moors in search of autumn berries. He had taught her to swim; she shared with him her skill with the slingshot. They were friends, playmates, comrades, but as they approached maturity they had both come to the realisation that they were not destined to be lovers. Taranc adored Fiona, and he knew she shared his affection, but neither considered the other in a remotely lover-like way. If pushed he would describe their relationship as more akin to that between sister and brother. They loved each other but were not in love and never would be.

And now, Fiona was in grave danger and he cursed his own helplessness to assist and protect her. He did not even know for sure where she had been taken, only that she was no longer in the company of the Viking warlord who had seized her.

He knew that because that man was in this very dragon ship, arrogant and tall at the prow of the vessel, gazing ahead across the frothing waves. Ulfric, Taranc recalled. The Viking chief spoke their Gaelic tongue and he had told them his name when he announced that they were to be taken as slaves, or thralls as the Vikings preferred to term such lowly beings. Taranc rowed with his back to the direction of travel so he could not see the Viking leader, but he was acutely aware of his presence. The tall, blond warrior exuded power and authority, but he exercised uncommon restraint too. Back at Pennglas, Taranc had fully expected Fiona to be slain on the spot for her resistance to the Viking assault, but Ulfric had prevented that, instead taking her as a slave. He had no need to spare her, and Taranc could not help but be grateful. And puzzled.

There was another, also. The chief was supported by a second warrior, one clad entirely in black, as dark as the leader was blond. They were friends, it had seemed to Taranc as he watched them, and though the dark one spoke only the guttural Nordic tongue, Taranc recognised that he displayed a less respectful attitude to the leader than did any of the other raiders. If anything, this one had seemed amused by the exchange between Ulfric and Fiona. It was he who had supervised the loading of the slaves, the selection of the females who were to be taken, and the dark Viking now commanded his own dragon ship that sliced through the waves not a hundred feet from their stern. Taranc could discern his tall, powerful figure marching back and forth, the long wolf skin cloak flapping in the brisk offshore wind.

Murdering, thieving bastards. They would pay for this, Taranc promised himself. They would pay dearly.

A muffled sob from his left caught his attention. Taranc leaned forward and peered along the row. A small boy huddled at the very end of the bench, pressed against the outer hull of the ship. His thin fingers gripped the oar and he tugged ineffectually at the unrelenting beam. As the Viking oars master passed by, his lash dangling from his hand, the boy shrank back as though he sought to crawl into the very planks that made up the sleek vessel.

Taranc recognised the boy, or at least he knew him by

sight. The lad had moved to Aikrig perhaps a year ago, with his mother who had married a fisherman from his village. The man was dead, drowned at sea some months ago, and now the boy had been enslaved by the Vikings. The dear Lord alone knew the fate of the mother.

"Pass the boy along here. He shall sit beside me," Taranc instructed the man to his side. "Have a care, do not let the Vikings see him move."

The Celts obeyed, surreptitiously shifting the boy along the bench until he was pressed between Taranc and another burly Celt called Iain. Taranc never broke his rhythm as he leaned down to speak to the boy. "Place your hands beside mine and move with the oar. I shall row, you just hold on."

The boy nodded and did as he was told. Taranc saw that tears still glistened in his eyes. He would have liked to offer words of comfort but such would be hollow in the circumstances. Instead he settled for what he knew to be true. "Remain close to me. I shall do all I can to aid you."

The lad nodded, chewing on his lip. "Thank you, sir," he whispered.

"What is your name, boy?"

"I am Donald, sir."

"It is nice to meet you, Donald. I am Taranc."

"I… I know, sir."

Of course he knew. Such was the reality of rank and privilege. Taranc spared the lad a final reassuring grin and bent to his task.

· · · · · · ·

The journey was mercifully swift, aided by a buffeting wind that filled the sails and carried the dragon ship lightly across the sea. After just two days afloat and one bitterly cold night they sighted land to the north. The dragon ship drew closer, then skirted the rocky coast as they continued on. They passed towering cliffs where the sea churned and boiled at the foot, and narrow inlets where the water was forced between two sheer rock faces. There were tree-lined coves and sloping beaches. Here and there Taranc could make out settlements, the occasional isolated farm, and fishing vessels bobbing closer to the shore whose occupants waved a welcoming greeting to their Viking captors as they sped past.

At last the man at the helm turned the dragon ship to the right and they made straight for the squat harbour that protected a settlement rather larger than any they had passed thus far. As they drew alongside the rough wooden jetty, willing hands flung out ropes, which the Viking sailors grabbed and used to haul the ship in. The hull bounced against the planks with a horrendous bump and a deafening grating sound.

Donald slithered from his seat with the impact, only to be grabbed and pulled back by Taranc. "Grab a hold of me, lad. Stay close."

The boy nodded and grasped Taranc's tunic.

The ship remained motionless when the ropes were secured tightly, and the Vikings swarmed ashore, led by their blond chief. The Celts stayed where they were, panting from the exertion of the last several hours and the sudden, shuddering halt. There was another resounding clatter as the dragon ship carrying the dark Viking slid into the space alongside them at the jetty, and that, too was tied off.

The blond and the dark one greeted each other on the quay, exchanging congratulatory slaps to the back before turning to regard the captives in both ships. Brief words were exchanged, then Ulfric strode away. The other Viking called to several others, issued commands in rapid Norse, then gestured to the Celts in Taranc's ship to clamber up onto the jetty.

They were a sorry crew, reflected Taranc as he surveyed his miserable countrymen. They had been offered no shelter on the voyage, and little enough in the way of food or water so they were cold, hungry, dirty, and exhausted. Donald would be asleep on his feet were he not so frightened.

Taranc shoved the lad behind him and signalled others to cluster about them. It would do no good to attract unwelcome attention to one who was clearly unable to work. The longer they could conceal Donald, the better the lad might fare.

Using the points of their drawn swords, the Vikings herded the Celts together on the jetty, then ushered them along the planking and onto the quayside. They were led to a small enclosure where they were permitted to sit down on the ground and given a few hunks of not quite stale bread. A pail of water was deposited in the middle of the exhausted throng, a metal cup dangling from a chain attached to the handle. Clearly this was all they were to have in the way of a drink, but Taranc was pleased to discover the water was fresh, clean, and deliciously cool. He took a drink himself, then handed the cup to Donald. One by one the men relieved their thirst then lay back to rest and to wait.

Hours passed and dusk started to fall. More bread was offered, and some cheese. The water bucket was replenished. The dark Viking made occasional appearances, no doubt to check that all was quiet and under control, then he made himself scarce again. When darkness descended it became clear there was to be no shelter again, though it was still the summer and the night was less chilly now that they were ashore.

Taranc thought they might manage well enough, but was relieved when the dark, leather-clad Viking returned again, this time accompanied by three other men each bearing a pile of blankets. These were dumped in the compound for the thralls to help themselves. Taranc made sure Donald had one and they all settled in for the night.

• • • • • • •

As dawn broke, the busy harbour sprang rapidly back to life. Fishermen launched their small craft; traders set up stalls offering wares such as fruit, vegetables, oils, and other goods. A forge close to the thralls' compound was opened up and soon a strong blaze crackled in the fire pit there. A huge man wearing just leggings and a charred leather apron rattled a ferocious array of metal implements as he prepared for his day's labours.

The dark Viking returned, and this time Ulfric was with him. They strode among the thralls who remained seated, huddled in their rough blankets. Taranc made sure Donald did not show himself, no easy feat when Ulfric paused to gaze down at him.

"I trust your voyage was not too rough, Celt. The crossing was speedy and the seas kind to us."

Does he seriously expect a response? Taranc glared back at his captor as Ulfric dropped to his haunches to better meet his eyes. "I see the fury blazing in your face, Celt, and I understand the reasons for it. However, do not let your anger get you killed. Heroes do not last long in my slave quarters."

Taranc had little doubt of that, but did not choose to dignify the Viking's remark with an answer. Instead, he had a question. "Where is Fiona? What have you done to her?"

"You mean your lovely little betrothed? She is safe enough, for now."

"If you hurt her, I shall kill you myself, I swear it." Taranc ground out the words, meaning every syllable of the threat.

Ulfric grinned, unrepentant and not apparently unduly alarmed. "Then let us hope that it does not come to that, Celt, for I am loath to needlessly squander good thralls in pursuit of discipline. She is mine now. Accept it." He straightened, offered Taranc a brief nod, and moved on.

"He frightens me," whispered Donald, the words muffled beneath the blanket that concealed him from the Viking chief's notice.

Taranc regarded the Viking's retreating back. His own feelings toward the Nordic warlord were more complex, but did not, surprisingly, include fear. Were he pressed, Taranc might better describe his attitude toward Ulfric as one of grudging respect.

"Do as you are told, cause no trouble, lad, and you will be all right." Taranc hoped this was true as he handed the boy the last of the bread he had hoarded from the previous night. He did not suppose he was alone in wondering what this day would bring.

• • • • • • •

During the course of the morning the thralls were ordered from the main group ten or so at a time and escorted across the flagged courtyard to the forge. There, each was fitted with a heavy metal shackle around their right ankle. When it was their turn to make the short trip, Taranc could no longer hide Donald. The smith raised his bushy blond eyebrows in surprise when he caught sight of the diminutive figure quivering in his forge. He had no shackle small enough so the boy had to wait while the man fashioned a miniature version just for him. Taranc remained beside Donald and no one seemed to object. He was proud of the lad's fortitude when the iron band was at last secured about his ankle and they both made their way awkwardly back to the main group.

Hours passed, with nothing else to break the monotony of the wait. More stale loaves arrived, more water, and a large pot containing a broth of some description. Taranc did not believe it contained much meat, but it was palatable all the same and they were happy enough to dip their hunks of bread in it.

At last, darkness fell again. Once more Donald bundled himself inside a blanket as he huddled beside his new protector and they settled in for their second night on these foreign shores.

• • • • • • •

"Get up. All, up." A small, squat individual marched between the sleeping Celts, using his foot to nudge those who still slept. He was not gentle and most rose grumpily to their feet. For the benefit of those not quick enough, the pugnacious little man held a switch that he cast about him with enthusiasm. "Get in line, everyone. Three, then three, then three. Like this…"

He grabbed two men and shoved them into the formation he desired, and pushed a third alongside. He arranged three more behind them. "Face front," he commanded, stabbing his finger in the air. "That way."

The smith moved between the men now assembled in rows of three, looping a length of chain through the shackles to secure them together. It was no longer possible to conceal Donald, and the Viking slave master eyed the lad with undisguised distaste. "Too small, no use," he announced, but still had Donald chained along with the rest, two rows back from Taranc.

It was no longer possible to sit comfortably on the ground so the men shuffled in disconsolate confusion as they awaited the Vikings' next move. They did not have long to ponder this. A group of women were bundled along the quay, clearly having just disembarked from a ship. Taranc recognised several familiar faces, including Donald's mother who was heavily pregnant and appeared ready to drop.

Do these Viking bastards have no compassion at all?

The women were ushered into the forge to be shackled like the men. He could not see Fiona anywhere among them but as soon as Donald's mother came within earshot he called out to her.

"Is Fiona with you? Did they harm her? Are you well?"

A woman standing beside the pregnant one responded. "We are fine, considering. Fiona too, though she required aid to get off the boat."

"Bastards," muttered Taranc, just as Fiona came into view. She walked beside the dark Viking, her eyes blazing with a familiar anger. Taranc hoped she would manage to curtail it for he had no doubt that retribution would be swift should she fail.

The women were shackled like the men, and added to the formation at the rear of the group. The slave master strutted up and down the line yelling his orders in a near incomprehensible broken Gaelic. He used his switch freely as though convinced that a sharp blow to the shoulders or hip would aid his victims in deciphering his garbled words.

"All. Go now. Walk fast, no slow."

Muttering and exchanging bewildered glances, the group shuffled forward, uncertain what they were meant to do. Suddenly a shrill cry rang out. Donald's mother had caught sight of her son.

"Donald! Donald, it is me. Donald…"

Taranc turned, and saw that Donald had, too. The boy saw his mother and his little face lit up. She called a reassuring greeting to him before the slave master brandished his switch at her and she shrank back into the line of women.

Slowly, with much clanking and stumbling and chafing of already bruised ankles, the sorry convoy got under way. The slave master urged them on, his switch swinging freely as he barked orders at the prisoners. "You walk now, two days. No slow down, no stop. All must work, all will walk, yes."

Time would tell, mused Taranc. Were he pressed, he would not wager much on all of them completing the journey. A two-day forced march, on minimal rations, and in chains—impossible. He feared for those not strong enough to meet the vicious Viking slave master's demands.

The first couple of hours were hard but not gruelling. The slave master insisted on setting a brisk pace, but most could manage it, more or less. Taranc looked back frequently to check Donald's progress and was relieved that the lad was being aided by his new companions. Neither man was known to Taranc, presumably they had been seized elsewhere on the Vikings' murderous voyage. He would be sure to thank them when he had the chance.

By the time the sun neared its height, Taranc was feeling the strain of the march and he could only guess at the struggle for those weaker than he was. The shackle left his ankle bruised and battered, and the shambling, uneven gait of the men hobbled together ensured that every step jarred and jolted. Several times he stumbled but managed to right himself.

The Vikings allowed them to stop for a few minutes every hour or so and they were given water to drink, but that was the only refreshment offered. The day was warm and shade nonexistent, and by the time the miserable convoy halted for the midday meal all were exhausted. Despite the discomfort of their chains, all the slaves sank to the ground to take what rest they might as the Vikings handed out yet more stale bread and dry cheese. Taranc was coming to loathe the stuff but he ate it anyway. There was no other reasonable course if he was to retain the strength he needed to see this ordeal though.

Fiona was too far away from him to allow for any conversation, though he succeeded in catching her eye. She offered him a reassuring nod as she, too, chewed on the unappetising fare.

Too soon they were ordered back onto their feet and the march was under way again. Taranc lost track of time as they trudged on, and he even succeeded in disregarding the shrill ranting of the ugly little slave master who strutted up and down the line. The man was a bully and Taranc found him ridiculous, though dangerous too. It did not do to underestimate the destructive potential of conceit and an overblown sense of power and importance.

At some point in the midafternoon the clatter of hooves disturbed their monotonous progress. The line of slaves edged to the side of the track to make way for the horses that caught up and passed them. Taranc recognised Ulfric and the dark Viking among the riders cantering alongside. The horsemen overtook the slaves on foot and as Taranc watched, the dark one leaned across as though he intended to speak to the blond. Any conversation was forestalled by the piercing shriek from the rear of the slave line.

Taranc did not need to turn. He recognised that voice. It was Fiona.

The horsemen turned their mounts and cantered back at the same time as the slave master charged along the line brandishing his ever-present switch. "What happens? Why stop? Why all this din?" He yelled at the slaves and cast about him with the crop as though they all bore equal responsibility for this reprehensible state of affairs.

Taranc could hear the cries of pain and alarm emanating from the rear of their column, but could see nothing of the cause. He only knew that his betrothed was at the centre of it, and that she was hurt.

"Fiona? Fiona, what has happened? Where is she? Let me go! *Let me go!*" The restraint and fortitude of the last couple of days was abandoned now as he fought to escape the chains that held him fast. He had to reach her; she needed him.

There was some sort of commotion, a rattling and clanking of chains, then a slight figure was dragged from the mass of thralls by two of the Viking guards and dropped unceremoniously on the verge at the edge of the track. Taranc could see Fiona clearly now as she lay writhing in the grass, the odious slave master bending over her. She cried out as he reached for her, and even at this distance Taranc could make out her ashen features.

She seemed unable to stand, though he could not discern why. Whatever the cause, the slave master was utterly averse to this turn of events and it would not be tolerated. His appalling solution was at once cruelly apparent when he drew his dagger and grasped the front of Fiona's tattered tunic.

"No!" Taranc cried out, hurling his weight against the chains that held him back. Other Celts, too, saw the horror that was unfolding and rushed forward with him. A riot was erupting in the slave ranks and the Vikings were quick in their determined efforts to quell it. Their swords and war-axes drawn, the Norse warriors surged to surround the men who now squirmed and fought against their chains. A rock was hurled, then another. The confrontation grew angrier, uglier, more deadly by the moment.

Ulfric and the dark Viking arrived in the middle of the melée and slithered from their horses. Words were exchanged and the slave master relinquished the disposal of the stricken Celt female to his chief and rushed to lend his aid to the rest of his men.

Taranc found new breath and raised his voice above the growing babble that surrounded him. He screamed at the Viking warlord. "Let her be, you animals. I shall carry her. I will—" His words were but briefly interrupted by a vicious swipe from the slave master. The switch caught him full across the face and shoulders but he was not to be deterred. The men around him, too, found renewed anger and outrage at the assault on their leader and the din rose to a roar.

Suddenly, unexpectedly, the Viking guards stepped back. Taranc found himself facing just the leader, Ulfric, who had abandoned Fiona to stride across to where the rebellious slaves mounted their incensed protest. Fearlessly he stepped among the angry thralls to plant himself before Taranc. The thrall boiled with rage but the Viking was unmoved.

"You, listen to me and heed me well. What is your name, Celt?"

"I am Taranc." It was all he could do not to fly at the Nordic warrior, chains and whips forgotten. Every sinew bristled, Taranc was ready to do murder, and to die for it. The slave master made as though to step in and restore order and authority. *Let him fucking try*, thought Taranc and he glowered at the vile little thug. Ulfric seemed to share his view and dismissed the Viking karl with one upraised hand. The man fell back obediently.

Ulfric stepped closer to the unruly slaves showing not

the slightest trepidation. He stopped less than a foot's length from Taranc. "She is mine now. I told you this. My property."

"You will not harm her! I—"

"No, I will not. I take care of what is mine. She will be safe." Ulfric paused as though considering, then continued in a lower tone, "You have my word on this."

"Your word? What is that worth? The word of a murdering, robbing savage impresses no one." Taranc spat his response at their captor, who straightened and narrowed his eyes. Still the Viking did not raise his voice though all about heard his words clearly enough. He stood his ground, his steady gaze unwavering.

"I have offered you the word of Ulfric Freysson, Jarl of Skarthveit. You may rely upon it."

Taranc returned his glare as waves of frustrated fury rolled from him. Despite their dire situation, his instinct told him he could trust this man. If Ulfric Freysson gave his word, he meant it. Fiona would not be harmed. The pair stood almost nose to nose as Taranc considered what he had heard. At last he allowed his shoulders to relax and he offered the Viking a wary nod. He had a warning of his own to deliver though, before he was done. "If you harm her I shall kill you. *You* may rely upon *that*. This is *my* promise to you, Viking."

Now it was Ulfric's turn to consider. He did so, and seemed to find their peculiar bargain satisfactory. He nodded, his lip quirked in what might have passed for a smile in less fraught circumstances and he turned away. He paused to say something to the slave master, and strode away to where Fiona still lay on the grass.

As the Viking lowered himself to his haunches beside the injured woman, Taranc should have been overwhelmed by jealous impotence. He wondered why such finer emotions eluded him as he returned to his position in the line and the convoy of slaves lurched into motion again. Fiona was no longer his. He had lost her. He knew that, and at some level he regretted it though he did not begrudge the Viking his gain, provided the man understood the value of his prize. Taranc believed he did. Now, he just had to hope that Ulfric would prove worthy of Fiona, and that she might find it in her to accept him. If not... he preferred not to dwell on that.

What the...?

Another furious shout went up from the slave master and again he dived in among the female captives. This time he emerged dragging Donald's heavily pregnant mother behind him. Once free of the line the woman hugged her distended abdomen with her one free arm and sank to the ground. The column of slaves watched in disbelief as the slave master again drew his dagger. Red-faced, he was babbling in broken Gaelic, something to the effect that the woman now cowering at his feet was too slow, too clumsy, too useless.

Taranc again opened his mouth to roar his protest. Was this what Viking mercy amounted to? The callous murder of defenceless women and unborn infants? His intervention was not required. The dark Viking beat him to it.

"*Neinn!*" The sharp command from the leather-clad Norseman halted the slave master's descent into butchery, though not before a sharp swipe of the switch landed across the woman's shoulders. The karl shrank back, open-mouthed as the tall chieftain towered above him, dark eyes flashing with pure menace. The slave master made no protest at all when the switch was snatched from his grip. Taranc believed for one glorious moment that the dark Viking intended to acquaint the little bully with the fiery bite of his own weapon, but instead he settled for a rapid exchange in their harsh Norse tongue. Taranc could not understand the conversation, but it was clear that the slave master had come off the loser and he retreated back to the waiting column of slaves, his features puce with rage. Impassive now, the dark Viking watched him go, then extended his hand and assisted the woman to her feet.

"Get moving. We have wasted enough time here. Onward. Now!" The angry thrall master brandished a whip he had commandeered from one of the guards as he passed and he cracked it at the heels of the slaves closest to him. They danced back into line and the column started forward again.

But even now the drama was not concluded. The pregnant woman struggled to escape her rescuer, screaming at him as she sought to wriggle free and pursue the slave convoy.

"My son! My boy! He needs me. He is but a baby. Please, let me go! I have to remain with him. I can manage..." Her efforts were completely ineffective. The dark Viking restrained her with ease, though he appeared bemused at her determination to leave his protection. The column halted again and Taranc made a rapid recalculation. Whatever the final outcome, surely the boy was better off with his mother. He could not be worse off, certainly...

"Show him. Show them the lad. He should stay with her." The men on either side of Donald understood and obeyed. They pushed the diminutive figure to the front, in full view of the slave master who peered at him with undisguised loathing.

Ulfric and the dark Viking exchanged a few words, and, incredibly, the dark one untied a purse of coins from his belt and tossed it to Ulfric. The Viking chief laughed and issued an instruction to the slave master. Seconds later, Donald was free of the chained slaves and staggering away from the convoy. He appeared confused, disoriented, utterly terrified.

His mother shrieked again and this time succeeded in escaping the grip of the man who held her. No, she did not escape, concluded Taranc. The dark, enigmatic Norseman had released her, permitted her to rush across the rough ground that separated the captive Celt from her son and take the boy in her arms. She sank to her knees, sobbing.

They made an unlikely tableau, reflected Taranc as the remaining thralls were once more ordered to form up and move out. As they shuffled away along the rough track he glanced back over his shoulder at the tall, leather-clad warrior who now stood over his latest acquisitions. Taranc found the expression of the Norseman's harsh visage difficult to define as the Viking studied the small boy he had paid such a generous price to purchase. The closest he could come to a description would perhaps be 'resigned.'

CHAPTER TWO

"Hilla, be quick now. The turnips will not peel themselves." With a groan and a hand pressed to her aching back, Brynhild Freysson straightened from stirring the huge pot suspended above the fire pit in her brother's longhouse. The broth was bubbling well. It would make a fine meal for when Ulfric returned, and according to the news from Hafrsfjord he could be expected within hours. It was her responsibility to ensure that all was in readiness, not least a nourishing meal on the table to welcome him home.

"I am coming, mistress." The breathless tones of a small maidservant reached her through the open door. Brynhild stepped over to see what was causing the delay. A slender girl of perhaps fourteen summers, though Brynhild was not entirely certain, struggled toward her threshold dragging a large sack. The bag was almost as big as the wench, and put up quite a fight as the servant sought to drag it across the rough earth beyond the longhouse. Brynhild rushed to aid her.

"What are you doing? I told you to leave the grain where it was until one of the men was free to help." Together they managed to pull the load into the longhouse, Brynhild shouldering most of the strain.

The girl was unrepentant. "We need to get on with grinding it, mistress. There is bread to make, and—"

"Even so, it was too heavy for you. Go and sit down, peel the turnips for the pot and get your breath back." The girl might have protested, but a glower from her mistress was sufficient to quell such foolishness. It usually was. Brynhild had been chatelaine of this settlement for long enough now to be able to command her house thralls with ease. Satisfied that the lass was more appropriately occupied, Brynhild glanced up as a male thrall entered. "Harald, this sack needs storing with the rest. Could you see to it, please?"

The man, a blond-haired Saxon of perhaps twenty or so hoisted the sack of grain onto his shoulder and strode across the longhouse to the store at the far end. He whistled as he went about his work, and winked at Hilla as he sauntered from the low dwelling.

"Where is he going now?" Brynhild wondered aloud as the door swung behind the slave.

"I think he has a sweetheart, mistress," confided the girl at the table who now wielded a sharp knife and was peeling vegetables with a deft skill.

"I know full well he has," muttered Brynhild. She would let the matter ride, as long as Harald's dalliance did not interfere with the smooth running of her domestic arrangements. She had learnt from an early age that contented thralls served their masters well. As long as he did his portion of the work, Harald could sow his oats with any willing female of his own class.

Brynhild took a seat beside Hilla and set to on peeling the vegetables. The work was soon finished and the turnips added to the pot.

"Go bring that fleece we are combing, Hilla. We shall use the rest of the daylight to tease out wool for dyeing." The girl ran to fetch the bale of unwashed, tangled wool, fresh from the sheep, and they settled themselves by the open door to drag their sharp metal combs through the oily strands. The longhouse had been constructed, as was customary, with no windows in order to preserve warmth and keep out the damp, so the open doorway and the fire pit provided the only illumination. The fire was never allowed to go out, whatever the season, but natural light was preferred for close work such as this.

The pair worked in quiet companionship for the next couple of hours, and Brynhild enjoyed the gentle warmth of the late summer afternoon. A soft breeze played about her ankles, lifting the hem of her loose woollen over-tunic. As a woman of the Jarl, the noble class in Viking society, Brynhild was well-dressed, her clothing fashioned of brightly coloured linens and soft wool. She had woven the fabrics herself, her skill at the loom something of a legend among those who knew her. Most of the blankets and other woollen items at Skarthveit, her brother's thriving settlement on the Nordic coast, were her work and she took great pride in it. None would be cold or hungry here. Not under her management.

For the last three years she had been in charge of her brother's domestic arrangements, including the care of his young son, Njal. The boy was just five summers of age, and had been motherless since Ulfric's wife, Astrid, succumbed to a fever some three years previously. Brynhild's own betrothed had perished at around the same time, the victim of an ill-fated raiding assault on Orkney. Her own future in tatters, it had seemed natural enough that she would return to Ulfric's household to take her sister-in-law's place. She had lived almost her entire life at Skarthveit and here she remained.

Brynhild's thoughts turned to the new influx of thralls expected in the coming days. Her brothers, Ulfric and Gunnar, had led a raiding expedition to the land of the Celts in search of fine, strong slaves. She had no doubt of their success. The new thralls would arrive a day or so after her brother, having made their journey from the port at Hafrsfjord on foot whereas Ulfric would ride. She sighed, and wished she might have been successful in convincing them to seek their new workers elsewhere. Anywhere but Scotland.

Brynhild loathed Celts. She found them untrustworthy, dishonest, duplicitous, and frankly dangerous. None of her house thralls were from the land of the Celts; she would not tolerate such worthless individuals within her home and she would have preferred to have none of them anywhere at Skarthveit. Still, she supposed the location of the slave quarters at the foot of the lower meadow would provide sufficient distance to separate the vile creatures from her. It had better be.

Ulfric required the extra labour to build a new granary. Brynhild well understood the necessity; they needed to store food over the winter and many hungry mouths depended on it. The existing one was too small and overrun with vermin. She had no quarrel with the project, nor with the seizing of slaves to accomplish it. This was the Viking way, it served them well and the thralls would be well-fed and cared for. They would resent their captivity, that was inevitable, but such was the way of things and Skarthveit was better than many settlements. Her brother was a decent, fair-minded Jarl. He had been taught well by their father, as had she. They took care of their own.

But not Celts. Celts did not count.

Brynhild had pleaded with her brothers to sail further south, to the English shores. Saxons made good workers, biddable, diligent. They were worth the extra day's sailing. Ulfric would have probably heeded her advice, but Gunnar was having none of it. He had raided this particular Celtic village before, a few months previously. The slaves they needed were to be found there and he was determined that this was the right target. Brynhild's protests fell on deaf ears and the raid was planned according to Gunnar's wishes.

Tomorrow, she would go down to the slave quarters to ensure that all was in readiness. Celts or not, that was her responsibility, to ensure that their accommodations were weatherproof and supplied with the necessities required—firewood, basic food and drink, a few blankets. She preferred to do her final checks before the new occupants arrived, and from there on would endeavour to avoid them as best she could.

"Lady, they are here." Harald yelled at her from across the settlement, pointing to the hills to the south. "See? Coming through the pass, there?"

Brynhild stood and shaded her eyes against the lowering sun. She could just discern the movement in the distance, several horses picking their way down the coastal track leading from the mountains that divided the upper slopes of their land from the lower plains.

"Ready the stables," instructed Brynhild. "Hilla, make sure the broth is ready, and put new loaves in the ovens now. They shall have fresh bread when they get here. Where is Njal?"

"Here, Aunt Brynhild. I am here." The small boy bobbed beside her, dancing from one foot to the other in his excitement. "My father is home. I see him."

"Yes, I do too." Brynhild bent to hug the little boy. "You can show him how well you have done with your swordplay whilst he has been away."

"I shall go with him, next time he goes raiding."

"Aye, perhaps," acknowledged Brynhild doubtfully. "Though maybe he will need you to look after things here at his home. He trusts you more than he does anyone else, you know that."

"I know, but…"

"Good lad. Would you like to wait indoors? Maybe you should have your sword ready to demonstrate your progress when he arrives."

"I must go and look for it." The lad grinned and charged back into the longhouse as Brynhild turned her attention to the approaching convoy.

• • • • • • •

Ulfric and his party clattered into the village less than an hour later. Her brother was surrounded by a dozen or so of his trusted karls, but it was the small figure seated before him on his stallion who held Brynhild's attention. She peered at the odd sight from her vantage point just within the longhouse.

The girl was beautiful, in a wild and vaguely barbarian sort of way. Her hair was dark, darker than any Brynhild could ever recall, and she was slender. It was difficult to see how tall the wench was, though Brynhild thought not overly so. Her brother's arm was wrapped around the woman's middle in a manner Brynhild found disconcertingly possessive. The female was not a Viking, that much was obvious, not even of the karl class. A thrall, surely, so what, then, was she doing seated upon Ulfric's stallion and riding right into the heart of Skarthveit with him?

She was still contemplating this unexpected twist in affairs when Njal rushed past her with whoops of joy. The boy burst from the longhouse and charged at his father, who had now dismounted and aided the woman from the horse too. She clung to Ulfric as though she might fall over were she to let him go. Ulfric, too, seemed to share the sentiment and did not relinquish his grip on her as he bent to hug his son one-handed. He lifted the boy high and laughed as Njal's arms clamped around his neck. Ulfric spoke to the lad, and Njal glanced at the pale-faced woman standing at his father's side. The little boy bestowed one of his gap-toothed grins on the newcomer, and she managed a tremulous smile in return. At once Brynhild was seized by an unfamiliar wave of bitter resentment. *Who is this foreign wench and what is she doing at my door?*

"Ulfric, you have returned. I am so pleased to see you back, safe and well." Slowly and with all the dignity she might summon in such circumstances, Brynhild emerged from the sanctuary of the longhouse. She stood on the threshold, her hands folded at her waist and assumed an air of bemused curiosity as she regarded her brother's companion. "Who are you?" Brynhild directed her question at the stranger but the inquiry was met with a blank stare.

Ulfric answered for the wench. "She does not speak our tongue, Brynhild. This is Fiona, a captive taken from the land of the Britons."

Of the Celts, more like. Her brother knew of her aversion to that race and sought to soften the blow. It would not work.

"A thrall? Then I shall see to it that she is taken to the thrall's hall at once. When will the rest be arriving?" Brynhild did not speak the fluent Gaelic which her brother had mastered, but could manage a clumsy rendition of that tongue, which she had picked up from servants when she was a child. She switched to this now to ensure that the interloper was left in no doubt as to her status at Skarthveit.

Ulfric's features did not slip. "She is to live here, with us."

"What? Why?" Astonished and horrified in equal measure, Brynhild lapsed into her own tongue once again.

"Because she is mine. My slave. She will serve me, and assist you in the care of my son."

"Our boy has no need of the services of a Celtic whore." Brynhild delivered this insult in Gaelic, and took pleasure in the start of shock that swept the other woman's ashen features.

"Watch your tongue, Brynhild." The admonishment from her brother stung, and Brynhild's anger seethed even more. Ulfric continued. "Fiona is to be treated well under our roof. And now, she is injured and has need of rest, food, and water in which to bathe. I trust I may leave those details to you?"

He expected her to actually serve this creature? Despite her resentment, Brynhild was left with little option at that moment. She snorted in disdain and turned on her heel. "Follow me, thrall."

The girl did not move, and suddenly Ulfric picked her

up and carried her past Brynhild into their home. He marched through the main hall of the longhouse and past the trailing woven curtain that divided his own sleeping quarters from the rest of the dwelling. He did not stop until he reached his own bed, where he laid the Celtic wench as though she were the finest Jarl maiden.

Brynhild followed, and paused by the curtain. Foot tapping, she watched in mounting irritation as Ulfric settled the wench among the blankets and furs. Her brother turned to glance in her direction.

"You will bring food, and have a bath brought in here."

"I am to fetch and carry for a worthless Celt now, am I? You insult me, brother."

"You are to do as I ask, and at this time that means providing my property with food and seeing to her comfort. I shall return soon, when I have made certain that the new slave hut is ready."

It was on the tip of Brynhild's tongue to inform him that he had no need whatsoever to check on the slave quarters. Had he not left that matter in her own capable hands? Did he imagine that she had become derelict in her duty whilst he was away seizing Celtic whores and bringing them back to install in *her* home? Her eyes narrowed but she held her tongue… for now.

Ulfric rose. He spoke to the girl on the bed. "My sister will see to your needs. She runs this household so you will obey her as you would me. You understand the consequences if I have cause for complaint?"

At least this was something. The girl would soon learn her place, Brynhild would make sure of it. And if she had anything to say on the matter, the wench would soon be gone.

Brynhild Freysson was *not* about to share her home with a Celt, and if her fool of a brother thought otherwise, he had much to learn.

Ulfric strode from the sleeping chamber, Brynhild at his heels. He marched outside, accompanied by a chattering

Njal.

Brynhild paused for a few moments to collect her thoughts. A Celt? Ulfric had taken a Celt as a house slave. What was he thinking? Surely he realised how dangerous they were, how unreliable. That could none of them sleep safe in their beds as long as such vile creatures lived among them. It was too much, just too much...

In a near daze, Brynhild set Hilla to collecting the necessities for a crude meal. At her instructions a bowl of broth was drawn from the simmering pot then left to cool and congeal on the table, carefully devoid of any meat or decent chunks of vegetables. A lump of stale bread was retrieved from the bottom of the bag where offcuts were stored.

Brynhild was tempted to have Hilla carry it into the bedchamber, but decided to do so herself. She dumped the unappetising fare beside the bed. "You will eat," she announced in a curt Gaelic, but she did not remain long enough to see if her instruction was obeyed. She had no desire to so much as look at the girl.

Back in the main hall she sank onto the bench beside the long table that ran the length of the central portion of the dwelling.

"Lady, shall I take in the bathwater?"

"What?" Brynhild twisted in her seat to regard Harald. The young man stood before her, his expression puzzled.

"The Jarl said that the new thrall is to have a bath. Shall I carry the water into the chamber now, lady? I have some heating, down there..." He gestured to the fire pit where a second cauldron now hung, light wisps of steam starting to rise above the brim.

"Oh, yes... No!" Brynhild straightened on the bench and scowled at the curtain that concealed the object of her anger as an idea formed. If Ulfric could not be convinced that the wench should rest elsewhere, then maybe the girl herself might be brought to that conclusion. She could have a bath, but not one she would enjoy overmuch. Brynhild promised herself that it would not take long before this Fiona was demanding to be allowed to reside with the other Celts in the slave quarters. She would be out of Brynhild's way soon enough.

"Yes, take the bathtub into my brother's sleeping chamber and fill it with water. But not from there. Take the water from the river."

"The river, lady? But it will be too cold…"

"It will be absolutely fine. Just right, in fact. Do as you are told, Harald. You will need help; get a couple of others to aid you or you will be at it all evening." She knew that Ulfric would not be more than an hour or so at the slave quarters so she really needed to get this done quickly.

Harald frowned at her, obviously troubled by her unusual instructions. She did not blame him. Even thralls were treated well here, he would not be able to comprehend her reasons for behaving otherwise now. She could barely comprehend them herself, but was not about to start examining her motives and certainly she would not be questioned by her servants.

"Get on with it. Do as you are told or your next dunking will be equally frigid."

Brynhild watched in haughty silence as Harald and two other thralls trooped past her carrying buckets of cold water drawn direct from the river that skirted their village. Once or twice one of the servants would slide her a sidelong glance of reproach; thralls tended to stick together, after all. Brynhild met their impotent protest with a narrow-eyed scowl.

"The bath is full, lady."

"Thank you, Harald. Now, would you please bring me some ice from the cooling pit, if we have some." She knew full well they did. Every winter she would have her thralls cut large lumps of ice and drop them into a deep pit at the rear of the village. Even in the summer the ice store remained chilled and the ice did not entirely melt. The cold pit offered a good way of storing perishable food, and this evening would deliver up the final flourish for her intended treatment of this intruder in her home.

As Harald left to do her bidding, Brynhild returned to her brother's chamber.

The wench still lay on the bed. Her deep grey eyes darkened as Brynhild entered. This was good, it showed she did at least possess the wit to fear her. As she should.

"You will undress and bathe. We have no use for a filthy Celt here." Brynhild spoke in her halting Gaelic, but had no doubt that the wench took her meaning clearly enough.

She perched on the edge of the bed and looked up at Brynhild as though expecting to be left in privacy to go about her ablutions. She would learn.

"Thank you. I... I believe I can manage." The wench had the temerity to seek to dismiss her.

Brynhild's lip quirked. "I know that you can. Get on with it."

"You must be busy. I would not wish to delay you..."

"I said, get on with it. Now. Or would you prefer I take a whip to you?" Brynhild could not quite recall the last time she had taken a whip to a thrall, probably never, but the Celt was not to know that.

"A whip? But..."

"You are nothing but a dirty little slave. A whore-thrall. Do not think I would hesitate to show you what happens to worthless little sluts who disobey their betters."

"Ulfric would not—"

"You heard what my brother said. I run this home, you will obey *me* or become acquainted with the whip." Brynhild was not entirely certain where the menace in her tone came from, nor the vile words she hurled at this hated Celt. At some level Brynhild knew she was acting unreasonably. The girl was injured, after all, and had offered her no harm. Irrational hatred was proving to be a potent motive, however, and Brynhild found she was unable to mitigate her resolve. She would see this through, and with luck the wench would soon beg to be allowed to live with the other

33

slaves.

She watched as the girl struggled to remove her clothing. First the loose smock, then the linen shift. The girl wore no shoes, so soon stood naked before Brynhild apart from the bandage that bound her injured ankle.

How had she been hurt? Ulfric had not said. It was of no consequence in any case. Brynhild shrugged. "That too." She pointed at the bandage and was gratified by the ready obedience that met her command.

"In the tub," she ordered, gesturing to the frigid water. The wench had not yet realised the temperature and rose unsteadily to her feet to approach the bath. Brynhild could have almost felt pity for the Celt when the awful truth hit her. The girl leaned forward to dip her fingers in the water then turned to face her.

"No, I cannot. It is too cold and—"

Brynhild felt a momentary flutter of sympathy at the girl's stricken features but quashed that hard. A cold bath was unpleasant, but would do her no real harm. "Get in or I shall have my other thralls come back and help you. My brother wishes you to be clean, and we will not disappoint him, will we?"

"He did not intend this…"

"Of course he did. Do you imagine we treat our slaves to a hot bath? You are fortunate not to be made to wash in the river, you filthy little slut."

Brynhild scooped up Fiona's discarded clothing and determined that this matter had better be concluded quickly now. "These will be burnt. I shall count to five, then if you are not submerged to the shoulders in your bath I shall summon thralls to ensure your obedience."

The wench protested, reaching for her filthy clothing and declaring it her intention to wash the garments herself. Brynhild stepped back out of reach and started to count. The girl continued to plead, but Brynhild detected the resignation and defeat now permeating her words. The Celt knew when she was beaten, and Brynhild watched in silent satisfaction as she slowly lowered her shivering body into the frigid water.

Brynhild winced, but did not relent. The wench perched in the tub, her back to Brynhild.

"Lower. I want your shoulders under too."

"I c-c-cannot. The tub is not big enough…"

"Maybe you need more water. Shall I have more brought in?"

This was sufficient encouragement for the girl to slide further into the tub until her shoulders were also submerged. Brynhild flung a rough cloth into the water and ordered her to wash. She even insisted that the girl rinse her matted hair, though she did not offer her any soap.

A movement by the curtain caught her eye. Brynhild turned. Harald stood there, his eyes fixed on the shivering form in the bath. He bore a pail in each hand. The ice. She had nearly forgotten that. She dismissed the thrall with a curt nod and picked up the first bucket.

"Sit up now," she ordered. The girl complied, her shoulders hunched and her head bowed. She knew what was coming, and that she was powerless to resist. Brynhild lifted the pail over the Celt's head and slowly, deliberately, she deposited the icy contents over the narrow shoulders. The girl sucked in a sharp hiss of breath and went rigid. Brynhild set down the empty pail and lifted the next one. That, too, she emptied over the shivering girl.

"You may get out now."

Her work here was done. Brynhild turned on her heel and left.

• • • • • • •

What had she been thinking of?

Brynhild sat at the table, a hank of rough wool between her fingers. She dragged her comb against it ineffectually, painfully aware of the shocked, accusing glances of her house thralls. Hilla sat in silence, her horror at the treatment of the newest thrall near palpable. Harald, too, was sullen and responded in monosyllables when she spoke to him. Brynhild could not blame either of them. Now that her fit of malicious spite was over, she was ashamed of her vengeful cruelty to a defenceless slave.

Regrets were pointless; what was done was done. She could not undo her actions, but would try to be more rational in her future dealings with the girl. She hoped those dealings would not be prolonged. Surely Ulfric would soon see that this situation was impossible, intolerable in fact. This was *her* home, *her* longhouse. She was his sister, his family. Ulfric loved her, he *needed* her. A bed-slave was nothing, worthless, dispensable. The sooner her fool of a brother stopped thinking with his dick and saw the truth of that, the better.

She muttered an exasperated curse and left the longhouse. She needed to get some air.

It was not many minutes before Harald arrived, panting at her heels. "Lady, the Jarl has returned. He wishes to speak with you. He is… I mean, he did not…"

"Thank you, Harald." Brynhild had little doubt what her brother would be thinking, and she knew she had to face him sooner rather than later. He would have plenty to say regarding his precious little Celt and he was not alone in that. She, too, had matters she wished to air and there was no time like the present. She followed Harald back to the longhouse, her chin tilted high.

He made her wait. Ulfric was closeted in his sleeping chamber with the wench, and had left instructions that he was not to be disturbed. The sounds of lovemaking, unmistakable and sensuous, drifted from behind the fluttering barrier. Brynhild gritted her teeth. The wench might have been less than happy at the start of this encounter with Ulfric, but matters had clearly taken a turn for the better. Left with no option but to bide her time until her brother was finished, Brynhild simmered with resentment as she resumed her distracted combing of the unwashed wool, then moved to work at her loom. Weaving usually soothed her; she loved the colours and the soft feel of the wool between her fingers, the magic as the pattern formed under her skilled hands. Not this day. This day she snapped her weft and tangled her yarns, and eventually tossed her spindle away with an impatient curse.

At that moment Ulfric chose to emerge from his chamber. Brynhild looked up from her mangled work, looked past him to the bed where the slave still lay. Their eyes met, the grey darkening in fear. Brynhild should be more satisfied at the trepidation she had caused; this was, after all, what she had set out to achieve. Instead, she just felt bitter anger and disappointment at her brother's insensitivity, coupled with an awful sense that her ordered little world was no longer the safe haven she had thought it to be.

Ulfric stepped forth and allowed the curtain to drop behind him.

"What the fuck was that about?"

"She... I—" Rarely was Brynhild lost for words, but she could find no ready explanation. Exasperated, she signalled for the reproachful house thralls to leave the dwelling then turned to face her brother.

"I do not want her here." Inadequate, she knew. It was all she had.

"But I do, so the matter is settled." Ulfric folded his arms and leaned back against one of the central pillars that ran the length of the longhouse. "What possessed you, sister? This is not like you, to ill treat those weaker than yourself."

"She is a Celt. I do not like Celts, and I will not have one here. This is my home, and—"

"Enough." Ulfric halted her protests with one upraised hand. "The girl is harmless, and she has done nothing to you. I will have your word that she is not to be mistreated further, and that will be the end of it." He waited, an eyebrow raised in determined expectation. Never given to deliberate falsehood, Brynhild merely shook her head and turned away, refusing to offer any such undertaking.

"Brynhild, you will not ignore my command. I shall have your word."

"No, you shall not," she spat back. "This is my house, my servants. I shall run the household as I see fit."

"Where has this callousness come from? I cannot believe this of you, sister. It makes no sense."

"Then you are more stupid than I imagined." Anger and defiance loosened her tongue. "You know how I feel about those... those..."

"Celts?" Ulfric offered the word quietly but Brynhild knew his tone belied a growing anger. "And this is my house, not yours. You will do as I say, run it according to my wishes. And you will keep a civil tongue in your head when you speak to me."

"Or what?" Outrage and indignation drove her now and she flung caution to the winds. "What will you do, brother?"

"Do not test me, Brynhild."

"If I am to run this house with the efficiency you set such store by as a rule then discipline is my responsibility."

Ulfric shook his head in disbelief. "You know my wishes on this matter and you would do well to heed them. Treat the wench well from now on."

"But—"

"Leave her alone," he warned. "She is mine, and I will not have her harmed."

Brynhild tried another tack. "Why? Why is she here? If you do not care for me, what of Njal? What of Astrid?"

"This does not concern Astrid—"

"Your wife, the mother of your son. How can you say it does not concern her?" Brynhild had been fond of her sister-in-law and she was reasonably certain that Ulfric had cared deeply for his late wife. Had Astrid lived, there would have been no interloping Celtic bed-slave brought to their home.

"Astrid is gone. I loved her, but she is dead and we must move on."

Why? Why must anything change?

Even as she harboured this ridiculous notion, Brynhild sought to convince Ulfric of the error of his ways. "You should wed another, provide Njal with a mother, more brothers and sisters. Not move some… some worthless Celtic slut into our home."

"I prefer it if you do not refer to her thus." Ulfric sounded tired, and Brynhild knew she was dismissed. He had not heard her, did not see why this matter was of such concern.

Why are all men such unfeeling pigs?

"I do not want her here. It is not right, not… not…"

He rounded on her, his expression exasperated. "Why does it matter so much to you? She is just a wench to fuck. Not important. I am warning you, leave her be, Brynhild." He slammed the door as he left.

Brynhild sank into her usual seat at the table, and she wept.

CHAPTER THREE

Ulfric rose late the morning after his return from the land of the Celts.

As was her usual habit, Brynhild was out of her bed at first light, stirring up the fire to restore the blaze to cheery life, and setting the pot above the flames to provide hot water for the household. The thralls were stirring as Brynhild fed the livestock in the pens outside the longhouse, collected eggs, and set to drawing a pail of warm milk from their heifer. She sent Harald to collect more water from the river while Hilla set about preparing the porridge that Njal usually enjoyed with a spot of fresh honey. The lad himself appeared beside her as she flung grain down for the poultry, his hair still tousled from his bed.

"Aunt, who is that with my father? There is someone in his bed, and he is still there, too, even though it is already late and everyone else is working."

Brynhild straightened and wondered what to say. She settled for something innocuous. "I expect he was tired after his journey yesterday. Shall we let him sleep a little longer this morning?"

Njal shook his head. "He is awake. I heard them talking. Who is that lady, Aunt Brynhild?"

Brynhild drew in a deep breath. "She is a new thrall who has come to live here. Your father likes her."

"I like her too. She is pretty."

Brynhild snorted, a most unladylike sound that attracted a puzzled scowl from Njal.

"You do not like her?"

The child's guileless question caught her by surprise. Brynhild shrugged and reached into the pouch at her waist for another handful of grain. She flung the seeds before the pecking, chattering chickens and forced a smile for the boy. "I do not really know her. Come, we should take these eggs inside."

The day passed in awkward, acrimonious silence. The usual chatter and merriment between mistress and thralls was absent as Harald and Hilla tiptoed about their duties in a reproachful, sullen hush. Brynhild hated the tense atmosphere and became more irritated with every passing hour. It was all the fault of this troublesome wench, and she glared balefully at the girl as Fiona took a seat next to Hilla and began to peel vegetables. Brynhild sought to busy herself with her weaving but it was no use. Soon, unable to bear the tension another moment, she told the servants to continue with their allotted tasks, excused herself, and left the longhouse.

Once outside she took a turn about the settlement, nodding to villagers as she passed. Did their honest, familiar faces betray their knowledge of what had transpired the previous evening in her longhouse? Brynhild was under no illusions that her house thralls would not have talked to others. Word would get around and by now all would consider her an ill-tempered shrew.

It was unjust. Brynhild Freysson was a decent, respectable woman, a woman of the Jarl, someone to be held in high esteem, not the stuff of common gossip. This bothersome Celt had turned her neat little existence on its head, and the wench had not even been here one day yet.

Brynhild returned to the longhouse, determined to assert

some measure of control in this situation. Her best intentions scattered when she entered to find the hateful wench meddling with her precious loom.

How dare she? How dare she touch my work?

Brynhild let out an angry shriek and the girl spun on her injured heel, only to send flying one of the rods that separated the strands of wool in the pattern. Fiona started to apologise, bent to retrieve the dropped stitches, but Brynhild was beyond reason. She flew at the smaller woman.

"How dare you? Who gave you permission to touch my work? You were trying to sabotage it, I know your tricks, filthy little Celtic whore."

Fiona backed away, her hands upraised in surrender. "I was not. I just—"

"Silence. I will have you flogged for this. Indeed, I shall deal with the task myself..."

"I can help to repair it. I did not mean any harm."

The wench was babbling now. As if this Celt could repair the damage she had caused. She had probably never so much as laid eyes on a loom before. "You will not touch my loom again, slut. Do you not know yet what we do with disobedient slaves here?"

A gleam of defiance appeared in the dark grey eyes that glittered mutinously at her. Fiona was already making for the curtain that separated Ulfric's sleeping chamber, as though to seek refuge there. "I do not care. I am not your slave, nor anyone else's. I was only looking at the weave, admiring—"

"You will be silent, girl. Harald, fetch me a strap."

The young man muttered something under his breath and it did not escape Brynhild's notice that he made no move to obey. Was her authority to be undermined at every turn?

Intent upon restoring order, Brynhild made a grab for the girl. Fiona was quick despite her injury but Brynhild was stronger and seized her arm in a vise-like grip.

The wench was terrified but still she fought like a

cornered vixen and screeched her hatred at her captor. "Let me go, Viking. I do not answer to you, I shall—"

"Silence!"

All heads turned to face Ulfric, who chose just that precise moment to return to his longhouse. He assessed the scene before him in moments, and Brynhild had the grace to flush. How had her calm, orderly household descended into such unruly chaos? His tone low and ominous, Ulfric instructed Harald to go and fetch him a switch.

Brynhild should have felt a greater measure of satisfaction as the Celtic girl paled, her fate now obvious. Fiona's protests died in the face of the Viking chief's implacable features and she obeyed his curt command to take herself into the sleeping chamber and await him there. Brynhild applied herself to restoring her weaving to good order once more, and steadfastly refused to meet the reproachful gaze of her startled house thralls as Hilla and Harald returned to their duties. She flinched at the sound of the switch rending the air, and closed her ears to the high-pitched squeals of the punished Celt as she bore the whipping Brynhild had earned her.

· · · · · · ·

Brynhild shaded her eyes as she viewed the sorry convoy of thralls descending the southern hillside in the direction of Skarthveit. They had made good time, she calculated. Dagr, the slave master, had no doubt forced the pace and the thralls would be exhausted. Brynhild disliked the arrogant little karl and usually managed to avoid his company, but she had to allow he was adept at managing slaves.

She could not be certain from this distance, but believed she could make out a handful of women among the shambling column. The females would not be quartered in the slave barn since they would be set to work as house thralls and would live with the families they served. She had better see to allocating tasks and accommodations.

Brynhild made mental notes as she strode across the settlement. Torunn, recently widowed and with three young children to see to, could do with some help so she would have one of the new wenches. Old Olaf and Gudrun could also do with an extra pair of young hands about their longhouse since their eldest daughter had wed so that would take care of another. As for the rest, she would see what seemed needful once she had taken stock.

"Harald," she called, catching sight of the young thrall. "Can you find a barrow, if you please, and meet me by the weaving shed?"

He nodded and scurried away, and Brynhild headed for the stables. There she quickly procured the services of two lads and a horse-drawn cart and issued instructions that the vehicle was to be loaded with firewood and driven out to the slave quarters at once. The fire pits in the barns would require stoking and tending if the new slaves were to have warmth and light this night, so the sooner they had the fuel the better. This matter settled, she and Hilla rounded up a half dozen hens whose finest laying days were behind them and secured the birds in a wooden crate. The thralls could slaughter them as needed. The meat would keep them going for a while, supplemented by bread that she would provide, and anything the Celts might forage for themselves from the surrounding fields. She would not coddle them, but neither would she see them starve.

Harald was waiting for her at the weaving shed. Brynhild strode past him and started to select rough blankets from the selection stored there. Most were her own work, though not her finest. Not one to waste anything, Brynhild used rough offcuts of poor wool to make these basic things. The wool was plain, undyed, but the fabrics warm and thick enough to keep out the winter chill. They were not pretty, but the Celts would probably appreciate them.

"I counted about fifteen in the convoy, I think. Collect enough blankets to go around and load them onto the barrow." Harald hurried to obey while Brynhild and Hilla hoisted the crate of chickens onto the top of the pile. Between the three of them they started to make their unsteady way across the meadow toward the slave barn.

· · · · · · ·

Taranc narrowed his eyes as he took in his new surroundings. As soon as their Viking guards removed the chains securing their shackles together, the other Celts sank to their haunches in silent, exhausted misery. Not Taranc. He remained standing, assessing the condition of their bedraggled ranks. The four women were utterly spent, and the men hardly any better. Ever one to dwell on the bright side, Taranc took comfort in the knowledge that at least they had arrived, no one had perished on the journey despite the best efforts of the short Viking with the long switch. Now they could rest.

"You, all stand. All up, now!"

For fuck's sake...

Taranc had never loathed anyone the way he had come to detest the little slave master. The man was called Dagr, he had learnt, and he was a bully. Never satisfied, always complaining and ready to lay into any slave who didn't move fast enough for his liking, Dagr was a conceited fool who had driven them mercilessly across the hills and valleys to reach this inhospitable place and it seemed he was not yet done.

They were to have shelter, it would seem, since the structures in whose shadows the Celtic captives now crouched did at least appear sound and weatherproof, but that was all that might be claimed as far as comfort went. It was not sufficient. The Celts needed food, they needed to rest, to recover from the arduous journey. And now this idiotic Viking cur seemed intent upon heaping more misery on them.

"Let them rest." Taranc stepped forward, his chin held

high. "No one has the strength to stand any longer. We need to eat, and—"

The whip cracked and pain blistered across Taranc's chest, but still he did not back off. Dagr's pugnacious features darkened in fury. The man did not like to be gainsaid. "Now. All stand. All will work…"

"Tomorrow," replied Taranc, his tone deliberately calm. "We will work tomorrow, when we have rested."

The whip whistled through the air again, and this time Taranc did stagger back, though his resolve was undimmed. Dagr could posture and screech all he liked, the bare facts were clear enough. His people were on the point of dropping. There would be no work done today.

The standoff was interrupted by the arrival of a small, horse-drawn cart loaded with roughly hewn logs. The young karl who drove it spoke to Dagr in their coarse Nordic tongue and pointed to the seated slaves. Dagr shook his head but the lad was having none of it. He started to unload the cart, arguing all the while with the slave master.

Firewood.

Taranc could but hope. Acting on his hunch, he stepped around the slave master and started to assist the sweating karl. As the other thralls realised what their leader was about, one or two struggled back onto their feet to lend their efforts to the unloading. Dagr was quiet for once, and soon the pile of fuel was stacked in a neat pile beside the door of the barn. As soon as the task was completed, the karl clambered back into the cart and clucked at the stocky little pony between the shafts. The wagon trundled off, leaving the Celts to contemplate their firewood.

"Gather kindling and load the fire pits. Get on with it. Do you think your fire will light itself, perhaps?"

Taranc spun in surprise at the haughty female voice behind him, and almost swallowed his tongue. The tall, blonde woman who approached across the meadow beside a loaded barrow and flanked by two young thralls was nothing short of stunning. She fought to keep a crate of squawking poultry balanced on top of what appeared to be a pile of blankets, her waist-length plaited hair shining in the early afternoon sunlight. If he had ever beheld a vision more beautiful he could not recall it, and Taranc was a man normally possessed of an excellent memory.

He stepped forward to catch the crate before it tumbled to the ground. It would be a pity if those birds were to escape after all the trouble this trio had gone to in order to drag the clucking fowls all the way over here. He lowered it to the grass and peered through the slats at the irate chickens within. Could this be their supper, perhaps?

"Light fires." The Viking woman cast her gaze about the sorry crowd, clearly irritated by their inactivity. "You will need to cook, to keep warm. Here is firewood." The woman gestured at the pile of logs. "I shall send bread…"

"Thank you." Taranc offered the woman a polite bow. "We would appreciate that."

She fixed him with a cold stare. "And I would appreciate it if you would set your quarters to rights. Here are blankets, since it will be cold later. You will find kindling hereabouts if you seek it." She glowered at him, her jaw clenching. "Move. You have not been brought here in order that you may sit about taking your ease the entire day."

She might be lovely to look at, but the woman was sorely lacking in compassion, concluded Taranc. She had eyes in her head, a perfectly delightful shade of pale blue, he noted. Could she not see the state his people were in? She was seemingly as misguided as Dagr.

"Lady, we have walked for two days, had almost nothing to eat and no rest. We are tired and hungry, and can do no more this day. We thank you for the firewood and the food you have provided, and as soon as a few of us have our breath back we will do as you suggest. But once the fires are lit, I believe it is fair to say we *will* be taking our ease the rest of this fine afternoon."

Her expression was a delightful mix of outrage and incredulity. Her lovely mouth worked though she appeared

47

at a loss for words. Dagr, too, seemed near enough ready to explode and his whip was already curling in the air. Taranc had had enough and stepped forward to disarm the man, then tossed the weapon to the ground. He was at once surrounded by Viking warriors, their swords drawn.

The Viking woman stepped forward and slapped the man closest to her on the shoulder. "Stop, all of you. Are you quite mad? My brother did not have these slaves brought here only for you dolts to slaughter his workers before so much as one stone has been laid. Our granary requires live thralls to build it."

"Lady, this does not concern you," intoned the arrogant Dagr as he retrieved his whip. "I shall deal with the slaves, and—"

"All at Skarthveit concerns me," corrected the vision of loveliness. The venom in her tone did not escape Taranc, even if Dagr seemed oblivious. "And you," she turned her attention to Taranc, "you will do as I ask. Now."

Taranc bowed his head. He had no serious objection to carrying out this woman's instructions to render their new quarters habitable since that was of benefit to his people. He gestured to the Celts closest to him "You two, go and collect kindling. The rest of you can carry the blankets inside."

Most of the Celts dragged themselves back onto their feet and started about these latest duties.

"You women, you will accompany my servants back to the main village. You will be found places in the longhouses." The Viking female issued her further instructions and the four Celtic females eyed each other uncertainly. None of them moved as they looked to Taranc for guidance.

"What will happen to them?" Taranc stepped in front of the Viking woman, ignoring the furious chuntering of Dagr. He had already surmised where the real power lay in this little group, and whatever the slave master might like to think, it was not with him. "You will understand, they are afraid…"

The Norsewoman frowned at him. "They will not be harmed. The women will work in our longhouses, cooking, cleaning, weaving, caring for our livestock. They will have food and shelter."

"Will you give me your word on that, lady?"

"Of course." She sounded indignant. "Why would I tell you false?"

"Of course," he agreed pleasantly. "You may go with them," he added, for the benefit of the Celtic females.

The blankets were soon transferred into the newly constructed barn and Taranc watched as the women who had made the gruelling journey with them trudged slowly across the grassy meadow in the company of the two slaves. The little wench chattered ceaselessly in a dialect of Gaelic, which was more or less comprehensible. The young man was more taciturn, though he did appear friendly enough. Perhaps life here would prove bearable after all.

They would soon see.

He turned to face the woman again.

"There was another woman with our group when we were taken. Her name is Fiona, and she was in the company of your chief. Has she arrived safe?"

"What is this female to you?"

"She is—was—my betrothed. I would know that she is safe and well."

"The Celtic female is to be my brother's bed-slave."

Taranc drew in a shuddering breath. The prospect of another man fucking Fiona disturbed him less than it surely should, but he was concerned for her even so. They were to have been married, eventually and he bore some responsibility for her now. Fiona was a lovely woman. They had grown up together, first as playmates, then as a couple. There had existed an understanding between their families since he was but ten years old and she just five summers, but their betrothal had been formalised a couple of years ago now. They had been fond of one another from childhood, constant companions and firm friends but she had never struck him as being overly demonstrative. In a less generous moment he might even describe Fiona as cold, though he knew his own lack of enthusiasm had been as much at fault in their failure to find carnal pleasure in each other. He would not begrudge Fiona any happiness she might glean from her current predicament and Ulfric Freysson had not seemed unduly cruel. Nevertheless, the possibility that Fiona's virginity might be taken by force caused him real anguish.

"He had better not harm her…"

"She is my brother's property now. He will do as he sees fit."

"If he—"

"Silence. The wench is well enough, and will remain so as long as she remembers her place here. All slaves must learn that."

Had Fiona been beaten? The words of this she-Viking certainly implied as much. Taranc eyed the woman with suspicion. "I wish to see her."

"My brother will not permit that. Nor will I."

Taranc was unimpressed. He had already made up his mind that he would seek out Fiona at the earliest opportunity and satisfy himself as to her circumstances. To accomplish this, he needed the Vikings to relax their guard in order that he might slip between them when he chose to do so. He bowed his head in apparent acquiescence and briefly considered the other tidbit of information he had gleaned from this exchange.

The woman before him was sister to Ulfric Freysson. He told himself it was for Fiona's sake that he was relieved the beautiful Norsewoman was not Ulfric's wife.

"Did you mention a granary, lady?" He deliberately softened his tone.

She narrowed her eyes at him, clearly surprised at the change in subject. "I did. That is to be your task, the reason you were brought here. You are to construct the new granary, then you will commence work on our harbour."

"I see. And is there some reason that your menfolk do not build your own granary and harbour? I can hardly imagine the task to be beyond you."

She bristled and regarded him down the length of her straight and, to Taranc's mind, utterly perfect nose. "We require the granary to be erected and in use before the onset of winter in less than two months' time so extra labour is necessary in order to accomplish that. This is why you will commence work at once. We cannot delay."

Ah, we are back to that, are we? Taranc sighed. "Tomorrow, lady. Today, we rest. And we eat. I thank you for the generous gift of the chickens. Did you mention bread, also?"

"Food must be earned. You will begin work today."

"Lady, I give you my word that the granary will be completed before winter, in exchange for your assurance that food will be brought, and straw too in order that we may fashion beds. The blankets are most welcome, but will not be sufficient. We will rest, nurse our bruises, and start work on your granary tomorrow, after we are refreshed."

He could have simply refused to cooperate at all, but saw no point in that. The Vikings would force them to work, and it would be harder on all. Maybe by negotiating with their new masters he could secure a better existence for his people, glean some comforts for them in this hostile world. And he found he rather liked discussing the deal with this beautiful Viking. She had a way of flushing when riled, and the lush curves lurking beneath her bright yellow linen dress caused his cock to respond in a manner he had never experienced with Fiona.

How strange. And how utterly fucking delightful.

"You cannot know how long it will take to construct the granary. That is an empty promise, Celt. You lie, as do all of your sort. I do not bargain with cheats and frauds. You will obey, and you will do so now."

"Is that it?" Taranc chose to disregard her slurs on his

character though they did not pass unnoticed. He gestured to the foundations of a circular structure located some thirty paces from where they now stood. The stonework had reached a height of perhaps three or four courses. "Is that your granary? Or at least the start of it?"

"Aye. That is it," confirmed the Norsewoman.

"Where is the stone to be brought from?"

"The beach." She tilted her chin in the direction of the coast.

"Less than a mile away. It would take the ten of us no more than a month to carry sufficient stone up here, then a further two weeks to complete the building. Your granary will be ready in six weeks, lady. Less, if your Vikings help with the labour, or if you use timber for the higher structure, which could be cut from yonder forest."

Her brow furrowed. "How do you know all this?"

"You think we never build anything in our own land? This is no different. Six weeks. You have my word on it. Now, do I have yours?"

"What?" She peered at him in confusion.

"The food, and the straw. And a day to rest."

She opened her mouth to reply, and Taranc had little doubt what her response would be. This haughty Viking was unused to negotiating with those she considered beneath her and was about to reject his suggestions. He groaned inwardly. This would prove awkward...

The clatter of cart wheels on the rutted track caught the blonde Norsewoman's attention. "Ah, more firewood. You should have sufficient now. You will help Otto to unload the cart."

Taranc and three more Celts dealt with stacking the logs alongside the first lot, while Otto released the horse from between the shafts of the cart. This was a larger wagon than the first so the horse was accordingly bigger and somewhat frisky. The driver muttered something to the Norsewoman, who replied in the Nordic tongue. They both seemed intent upon examining the animal's rear hoof and spoke quietly together.

Taranc listened, frustrated that he could not understand their conversation. This placed him at a disadvantage, which he would not countenance. He resolved to make it his business to learn their language as quickly as he might accomplish that feat. He was a fast learner when it suited him.

The cart driver manoeuvred the horse back between the shafts and leaned in to secure the leather straps as the Norsewoman turned to leave. She cast one last glance at Taranc.

"I expect to see you start work within the hour."

He shook his head and watched, arms folded in front of his muscled chest, as she made her way back across the meadow. Despite her ridiculous intransigence, he could not help but admire the gentle sway of her hips as she walked.

A screech from the excitable horse brought him spinning about in time to see the animal rear up between the shafts then lurch forward. The leather strap attached to the halter snapped and at once the beast was free. It sprang forward, demolishing the flimsy cart shafts in a volley of flailing hooves as the driver leapt to grab in vain for the dangling reins.

"What the—?" Taranc also made a lunge for the trailing straps but was too far away. The horse reared up on its hind legs then dropped back onto all fours. He stamped, pawed the earth for a few moments, then took off across the meadow at a headlong gallop.

"Lady Brynhild, look out!" The driver yelled his useless warning as the Norsewoman stood transfixed. The crazed horse bore down on her, hooves thundering across the springy grasses as he tore up the distance that separated them.

Taranc did not pause to think. He had but a few yards' advantage over the bolting animal but he used them to best advantage. He sprinted as hard as he was able for the Viking woman and reached her perhaps half a beat before the frenzied horse. He lunged for her and bore her to the ground. The pair of them rolled together through the heather as the horse's murderous hooves missed them by fractions of an inch.

Only when he heard the pounding of the hoof beats disappearing into the distance did Taranc lift his head. The woman—Lady Brynhild—lay motionless beneath him. Her eyes were open but unfocused, staring at a point beyond his right shoulder. Her hair had become loosened from the neat plait and covered half her face. Unthinking, Taranc swept the pale locks aside with his fingertips.

"Are you injured, lady?"

She did not answer.

"Lady? Are you hurt? Did the horse catch you?" Taranc did not think so. He had been on top as they fell so would have taken any blow from the flying hooves. For reasons he could not quite fathom he believed himself miraculously intact.

Still no response. Taranc eased his weight from the slender yet curvy body beneath him and leaned up on one elbow. He cupped the delicately pointed chin in his palm and turned her face toward him, forcing her to meet his eyes. And he saw it.

Terror. Pure, mind-numbing, abject terror. The woman in his arms was rigid with fear.

"It is safe now, lady. Brynhild?" *That was the name yelled by the driver, was it not?* Taranc attempted a reassuring smile. "The horse will be back in his stable by now. I believe we may risk getting to our feet without fear of being trampled to death."

She lay still for several moments more, then something shifted in her deep blue gaze. Her eyes darkened, she drew in a ragged breath, and where moments before she had been motionless, she burst into a hysterical frenzy of writhing and clawing. She fought him like a woman possessed and it was then that Taranc realised she did not fear the horse.

Her terror was of him and she was fighting for her life.

He rolled from her at once and leapt to his feet. She scrambled away from him on her bottom, ignoring the hand he offered to help her up. "Let go of me. How dare you touch me. You have no right, no—"

"Lady, I meant no offence. The horse—"

"You are not to touch me. I shall have you flogged. I shall… I shall…" She staggered to her feet and turned her back on him, hugging her arms tight across her middle. She bent at the waist, and for a moment Taranc thought she might be about to be sick but she settled for several long, heaving breaths. At last, her senses gathered, she straightened and turned to face him again. "A thrall may not lay hands upon a woman of the Jarl. It is a crime punishable by death. You will do well to remember that, Celt."

He shook his head in exasperation. "Standing in front of a bolting horse tends to yield a similar result. I suggest *you* bear that in mind, lady."

This woman might be lovely to look upon, but she was every bit as deluded as the ridiculous little slave master who now approached, his whip at the ready. Taranc executed an exaggerated bow to Lady Brynhild, ignored the pompous karl, and turned to stride back to where his countrymen had watched the bizarre exchange with open mouths.

"Have we any kindling yet? We have a fire to start, chickens to slaughter." His voice was harsher than usual. "And we have a granary to build. We start at first light. Tomorrow."

Neither Brynhild nor Dagr contradicted him. Taranc stalked into the empty slave barn and snarled.

Bloody Vikings! They were mad as a pail full of frogs, the whole fucking lot of them.

CHAPTER FOUR

"Aunt Brynhild, are you ill?" Njal whispered the question, his high little voice shrill with concern.

Brynhild rolled over on her narrow cot to face him from within her nest of furs. "No, I am fine."

"Then why are you still abed? It is light, I have fed the chickens for you, and collected the eggs. I do not know how to milk the cow or I would do that also."

"I shall do it. I am just being a little lazy this morning. If you could give me a few minutes…"

"Father has already left." Her nephew delivered this news as though Brynhild were somehow to blame for this turn of events.

"Ulfric is gone?"

The little face nodded. "Yes. Hunting. He said I am to do as Fiona tells me, until you get up. Will you be very long, Aunt Brynhild?"

"Has she done something to upset you?" If that bloody Celt had harmed so much as a hair on this child's head, the wench would pay dearly for it, whatever Ulfric might have to say on the matter.

"No, Fiona is nice. But I cannot understand what she says and she cannot make porridge properly. Hilla is fetching water, and—"

"I shall come." Brynhild slid her legs from beneath the pile of furs and blankets and placed her feet on the straw that covered the floor of her sleeping alcove. "Would you pass me my tunic, if you please?"

Njal dutifully handed her the plain over-tunic of green and blue wool, the one she normally favoured on cooler days. He chattered merrily as she dressed. "I shall ask my father to teach me the language of the Celts then I shall be able to talk to all who are here. There are new thralls in the barn and—"

Brynhild leaned over to take his face between her hands. "You shall stay away from them. You have no need to go anywhere near the new slaves and 'tis not safe."

"Why?" As soon as his aunt released him to pull on her stout leather boots, the lad perched on the end of her low pallet and regarded her with lively curiosity. "Is it true that Celts have blue tongues and can see as clearly in the dark as in the daylight? Like wolves?"

"No, they do not have blue tongues. As for their eyesight, the thralls are always locked in the slave barns at night so even if they can see in the dark it would be of little use to them. But they are rough, and they do not know our ways, and…"

"They would not hurt me. They would not dare."

Brynhild did not share his confidence. As far as she was concerned these foreign slaves so favoured by her brother were little short of feral and best avoided at all costs. "I have told you to stay away from the thrall quarters, and you will do as I say."

"But—"

"Njal, I shall not argue with you over this. Promise me you will not go near."

His mouth flattened in a mutinous line, but she was adamant.

"Njal? I am waiting."

His lower lip jutted and the boy scowled at her, then his

stomach growled loudly.

"I shall start the porridge just as soon as you give me your word."

He shrugged, as though none of this was of any real consequence. Perhaps it was not when set against the prospect of a delayed *dagmal*, the early morning meal shared by the entire household once their first chores of the day were completed. "I promise."

"Thank you. Now, I wonder if we might have a little honey laid aside. If so, a spoonful of that would be just right to sweeten the porridge."

Njal shot past her and back into the main hall of the longhouse. "Hilla, Harald, we are to have honey with the porridge. Hilla…"

Once out of her bed, Brynhild set about her morning tasks with vigour. Work would help her to think about matters other than the fact that she found herself surrounded by the Celts she loathed. She welcomed the diversion. It seemed to her that the wench, Fiona, was always about. Every time she turned around she would encounter the woman in her hall, chatting with the other thralls, laughing with Njal, or if no one else was there the girl would go silently about her tasks. Fiona rarely approached Brynhild, and for this at least she could be thankful. She had nothing to say to the wench and simply wished her gone.

Ulfric was besotted. Brynhild had never considered her brother a man given to thinking with his dick, but he seemed oblivious to the difficulties created by his new plaything. Why did he have to insist that she share their home? He could fuck her just as well, surely, in the slave barn or the longhouse where the majority of unwed female thralls had their beds. Brynhild had suggested as much to him, several times now, and he had simply ignored her.

And as if this was not quite bad enough, her heart still pounded when, in an unguarded moment, the events of a few days prior popped back into her head. She vividly recalled that moment, suspended in time, when the loose and panicked horse bore down on her, then the rush of movement as the leader of the slaves burst into motion and dived upon her. He had borne her out of harm's way, tumbling the pair of them to the ground and risking his own safety in the process. At one level Brynhild knew all of this and was well aware that she ought to have thanked the man graciously for his quick thinking and for saving her from serious injury or worse. Instead, she had lain on the ground, winded at first, unable to move or speak. Then he had stroked her face, smoothed her hair from her eyes, and it was just like that other time. As clear, every bit as powerful as though everything was happening to her right here and right now. The sense of helplessness, of fear and vulnerability and utter worthlessness returned to swamp her. For a few moments she had thought she was drowning, unable to breathe, consumed by a desperation to be free and to be safe. So she had fought, as she should always have fought. She was a woman now, able to defend herself and she had done so at last. She had lashed out, overwhelmed by the need to escape.

The thrall had released her at once. He had even apologised and offered to help her to her feet, but she was too shaken by the experience, too confused to hear it or to accept his aid. She had lashed out again, with words and threats this time, and he had responded with cool disdain.

He considered her ridiculous. She knew it. His contempt had been there in his manner, in his icy, sardonic gaze as he responded to her empty threats then turned and simply walked away from her. He thought her a fool, unreasonable, a woman who could neither manage her household nor command her servants. What was more, the arrogant savage had taken it upon himself to determine who would work, and when. He had undermined her authority in the settlement just as the insufferable Celtic wench did here in her own home.

And there lay her other major cause for complaint. She

was not permitted to beat the new slave, despite the girl's insolence and insubordination. Brynhild was reduced to complaining to Ulfric and asking him to discipline the wench. He had done so on occasions, not averse to taking a switch to the girl's bottom. Brynhild would take more satisfaction in this were it not for the reproach and disapproval such episodes earned her from the rest of her household. And for the fact that any punishment invariably resulted in a bout of noisy and, by the sound of it, extremely satisfying bedsport.

Who was mistress here?

Brynhild felt a need to assert herself but was at a loss. She was not a woman normally given to cruelty, quite the reverse. She had been brought up to be a lady of the Jarl, and was expected to be a fair but firm mistress. She had a reputation for kindness, did she not, as well as efficiency? She treated all in her household well. She cared about them, was concerned for their welfare and saw it as her responsibility to ensure that the longhouse they shared was a happy home. Yet since this Fiona had invaded her domain she found herself ill-tempered all the time and ready to scold those about her for the most trivial matters. It was not like her.

Or it did not used to be.

She still brooded as she took a little of the *dagmal* with her nephew and thralls, but found her appetite to be sorely lacking. Making her excuses, she left the table and slipped through the outer door into the damp, fresh air. It was still summer, but had been raining in the night and the grass was wet. She sloshed through mud and small pools of water as she made for the weaving shed, then ducked through the low door. Within, the three large looms were all occupied, and she was pleased to note that the work was progressing well. She spoke briefly with Sigrunn, the woman who generally took charge of the looms and agreed to provide more washed and combed fleeces ready for spinning.

As their settlement grew in numbers so did the need to

produce good, warm fabrics for clothing and for bedding. As mistress here, sister to the Jarl, it fell to Brynhild to ensure that all were supplied, everyone's basic needs met. They would not shear their ewes at this time of year, that was a task for the spring, but she had several untreated fleeces stored that she could set Hilla and Fiona to work on. This resolved, she set off back to her longhouse, determined to attend to her duties and not allow the distraction of these bloody Celts to disrupt the smooth running of her home.

She might have succeeded were it not for the loud shouts that reached her from across the meadow. She paused, shaded her eyes to look, and was unable to miss the tall, solid form of the brown-haired Celt leader who had so shaken her on the day of their arrival. His name was Taranc, she had learnt, and he had been the chief of this particular group in their village in their own land. His leadership was undiminished by captivity since the rest clearly looked to him for direction. Brynhild had no doubt whatsoever that regardless of who held the swords and whips, the Celts would do Taranc's bidding before any other. That he and Fiona should have been married was a detail upon which Brynhild chose not to dwell.

Taranc was the one whose voice she heard. He marched up and down a long column of his men as they formed a chain and passed large lumps of stone along their ranks. The Celtic chief directed them, urging them on and every so often stepping into the line himself to take over when one of the thralls needed to drop out to rest or to seek the privacy of the soil pit that the Celts had dug at the rear of the barn.

She had no intention of wasting her day watching him. She was a busy woman, with far better things to do with her time than stand here gazing at some lowly thrall, however beguiling the view might be. But there was something about this Celt that drew her attention and held it fast. He was tall, she had discerned that much during their confrontation on that first day, but that was not unusual. Most males were at least a head taller than she was, and Brynhild was not short in stature. His eyes were a deep shade of green, which put her in mind of the mosses that adorned the north-facing side of the Nordic pine trunks on the hillside above Skarthveit, and his hair was a deep shade of brown. His locks were thick, curling slightly around his neck. He wore his hair hacked to shoulder length, as did most of the Celtic males, and she imagined it would feel soft under her fingers though that was not a theory she would ever put to the test. His shoulders were solid, his torso muscular, but she would not describe him as heavy set. He had strength, she had felt that power ripple through his limbs as he bore her to the ground, then the unyielding weight of him as he lay on top of her. Despite the speed and purpose of his movements he had not been rough with her, though as she fought him in those moments of blind panic he had been unmoving. She would not have escaped him had he chosen not to let her go.

In the brief interlude before she was seized by hysterical dread she had even been conscious of the steady thump of his heart beneath the soft leather jerkin, though she preferred to bury those memories. It did not do to think on such things. Male strength was dangerous, she knew this well enough, and these Celts with their base, uncontrolled urges were especially so. She must avoid them.

Despite the many tasks awaiting her attention, Brynhild permitted herself a few minutes more to observe the progress of the building. It was the project she needed to assess, of course, not the thralls working on it.

The new Celts, along with her brother's existing thralls who had been brought from places as far afield as England and Ireland, had already been at this task for several days now. The pile of building materials was growing at a rate that she knew pleased her brother and she could not help but be impressed herself. Previously, the practice had been to heave the materials up from the beach as they were needed. Each man would struggle up the steep incline carrying a chunk of the rock that he had collected, dump his burden at the build site, and stagger back down to the beach for more. The stonemasons would fit the pieces in where they might, and continue on.

Now, under Taranc's leadership, the construction itself was halted whilst all the materials were to be gathered and transported. Once all the stone required was assembled, they would commence the building again and from there the work would be completed quickly. By forming this line and passing the rocks from one to another, they avoided the need for each of them to struggle up the hillside carrying the heavy rocks. The work was not light, not by any means, but Brynhild could appreciate the merits of this approach.

So could her brother. Brynhild knew that he had overruled Dagr's ridiculous posturing when the slave master attempted to flog the thralls into more forced marching up and down the cliffs. Instead, Ulfric told the karl to heed to the advice offered by the Celt and to try it this way. The new method was clearly better, and the disgruntled Dagr had been sulking for days.

Idiot man. She flattened her lips in annoyance as the resentful karl wrapped the lash of his whip around the shoulders of one hapless Saxon who had not shifted fast enough for his liking. The unfortunate man staggered forward and dropped the huge lump of granite cradled in his arms. It took a moment or two for the scream to reach her across the distance, but Brynhild did not need to hear the shriek of agony. Even from where she stood she could see full well that the huge boulder had crushed the Saxon's toes.

"Oh, sweet Freya," she murmured and set off across the meadow at a run. By the time she arrived at the scene the angry thralls were advancing upon Dagr, a menacing mob of resentful, vengeful slaves intent upon wreaking their justice on the man who had pushed them too far. Dagr lashed at them with his whip while other Viking guards circled the rioting slaves, their swords and axes drawn.

It would be a bloodbath.

"Stop. Stop this, all of you." Brynhild rushed to stand between the two groups and faced the Vikings. "Put up your weapons, there will be no bloodshed here today." She pointed to Dagr. "Take him and secure him in the stocks until my brother returns. Ulfric shall decide what is to be done with him."

Dagr had other ideas and lunged for Brynhild. "Lady, stand aside. I will not have some meddlesome fool of a woman siding with thralls who need to be punished. I am master here and—"

"Seize him," repeated Brynhild, this time addressing her command directly to the warrior closest to her. "My brother is master here, and he will settle this matter."

The mention of Ulfric's ultimate authority seemed to convince the man who flung his arms about Dagr and lifted the smaller man from his feet. The slave master's already ruddy visage was puce as he kicked his feet and heaped obscenities upon Brynhild, upon the man who held him, and most particularly upon the thralls who he promised to skin alive then leave what was left out on the hills for the wolves to devour.

"The stocks," reminded Brynhild. "Let him cool his heels there for the rest of the day. And the rest of you can stand back. There will be no fighting here." *She hoped.*

Brynhild allowed herself a sigh of relief when the Viking who held Dagr set off across the meadow, his reluctant burden wriggling and kicking in his arms. The man was built like the side of a mountain and seemed oblivious to his squirming captive. Satisfied that at least one of her instructions had been carried out, Brynhild deliberately turned to face the angry thralls. Their features betrayed their anger, and their fear that any one of them might be the next to fall victim to the violence and sadistic cruelty of their Nordic overlords.

Brynhild could not really fault them for that. Dagr was a lackwit, pure and simple. Surely Ulfric would be rid of him after this.

Beyond the throng of furious men a small cluster had gathered around the one who was injured. Taranc was among those who tended him and having prevented further violence Brynhild was sorely tempted to leave them all to it. She had no desire to face the enigmatic Celt ever again if she could help it.

But Brynhild Freysson was no coward. The injured man required help and it was her responsibility to see to it. She squared her shoulders and skirted the band of slaves to reach the man on the ground.

"How bad is it?" She addressed her query to all of them, but it was Taranc who turned to glare up at her.

"Bad enough. His foot is broken. Your needless Viking cruelty will do nothing to speed the building of your precious granary, lady." His words were delivered in a cold, angry tone, his contempt for her and her people all but palpable.

She bristled, but did not back away.

"I saw what happened. Dagr was the one at fault and I shall ensure that Ulfric knows this."

"And how will this help a thrall who is unable to work? We have seen at first-hand how Viking murderers dispose of useless slaves."

Brynhild was at a loss, but would not lower herself to seek an explanation for his comment. The injured man at her feet was moaning, his face ashen with pain and she preferred to invest her energies there where they might make a difference.

"I shall need two or three of you to help carry him down to the village. We have a healer—"

Taranc stood up and rounded on her. "He cannot work. He cannot even walk. He may lose that foot. At the very least he is likely to never walk without a limp again."

Hands on her hips, Brynhild glared back at him. "I can see that, Celt, but find no useful purpose in drawing this man's attention to that possibility until we are sure. If you do not wish to help then you will stand aside and allow me to aid him as best I might."

The Celt narrowed his mossy green eyes and his mouth thinned to a narrow, angry slash across his face. Even in his anger he was handsome, she had to acknowledge. She dashed that unruly thought aside. He was a Celt, and they were all handsome bastards. That was part of the problem.

She bent to examine the mangled foot in greater detail. It did not improve upon closer inspection and she suspected the Celtic chief's prognosis would be correct. They must just hope that the injured limb did not become infected, for that was where the true danger lay. Without doubt this man would be of no further use in building the granary, though he might well possess other skills. They would find out, she supposed, once the limb was healed.

If it healed.

Ulfric would be furious at the waste of a good, able-bodied thrall but perhaps this would be sufficient to convince him to find other duties for Dagr. The man was not fit to have the care of valuable assets such as slaves.

"What is his name?" she demanded.

Taranc briefly consulted men from the Saxon contingent. "Selwyn."

Brynhild nodded and addressed her next words to the slave on the ground. "Selwyn, I am sorry this has happened. My brother will be sorry also, and he will wish me to care for you now. I am going to take you to the village where our healer will do what she may to alleviate your pain." She turned to Taranc again. "So, will you help or will you step aside?"

The Celt narrowed his eyes at her and she thought he intended to refuse. Instead, he shook his head in bewilderment. "I do not understand you, lady. Such cruelty and arrogance presented in a truly beautiful package, but I know you to be dark at the core. Yet you show concern and compassion for an injured Saxon slave. Perhaps your hostility is reserved just for us Celts. Am I right?"

"You are insolent, Celt, and you are in my way." Brynhild resisted the impulse to step back in the face of his unerringly accurate assessment and piercing gaze. Somehow this vile thrall possessed the ability to look at her and see right through her, to peel away her carefully constructed layers and observe what lay beneath. If she was not careful he would strip her bare and know all her secrets.

Brynhild was the first to lower her eyes.

The Celt glowered at her, but gestured to another man to come over and move to Selwyn's other side. Then the pair bent at the waist and looped their hands together behind the injured man's knees. Selwyn draped his arms around each of their necks and they stood up, lifting him between them.

"Where is the healer, lady?" Taranc regarded her, his hostility barely muted.

"Follow me." Brynhild turned on her heels and marched off, her chin tilted high.

CHAPTER FIVE

"Does your father know that you are here?"

Taranc leaned against the outer wall of the slave barn and managed not to laugh out loud at the guilty expression on the small boy's face as the lad emerged from the wholly inadequate cover of the undergrowth. He had watched the boy for the last few minutes. The Viking child, Njal, he had learnt, and son of Ulfric Freysson, was regularly given to creeping around the edges of the thrall quarters and observing the activities of the slaves. The child appeared fascinated and terrified all at once, and Taranc would not have minded betting that the latter response owed at least something to the aunt who had the day-to-day care of the boy. She had made her revulsion perfectly clear and would have no doubt conveyed it to the child.

Taranc repeated his question, but the boy just stared at him, uncomprehending. Taranc switched to a halting Norse and tried again. This time the lad frowned, obviously catching at least some of his meaning.

"You can speak my tongue?" The boy could not have looked more impressed had the god Thor materialised before him, silver hammer in hand.

"A little," conceded Taranc. "I have been practising."

"My father speaks the language of the Celts. So does my aunt, and now Fiona who lives in our longhouse. Will you teach it to me?"

"Your father could teach you."

"He is busy. And he is a Viking. I am, too and we speak the Norse tongue. My aunt says I have no need of other languages."

"Perhaps she is right."

"Will you teach me?" pleaded the small boy as he hopped from one foot to the other. "I will teach you a word, and you will give me one. We shall swap our words."

A reasonable enough bargain, conceded Taranc to himself. "Very well. My name is Taranc. Who are you?"

"I am Njal. Son of Ulfric Freysson. You know who I am. You asked about my father."

Sharp boy. "Yes. I did. Now, in my language..." Taranc repeated his introduction in Gaelic.

Njal beamed and attempted to repeat the words. Taranc coached him and soon the boy managed a decent enough rendition. It would have been pleasant to continue the lesson, but Taranc had a granary to build.

"I must get back to work. Thank you for your company, Njal."

"But I have not given you a word yet."

"Perhaps next time you are here."

"My aunt says I am not to come to the slave quarters. She says you are dangerous, but that you do not have blue tongues. She is not sure if you can see in the dark."

"Your aunt is correct."

"About your tongue?"

"About everything. And we see well enough in the dark, I daresay. Now..." Taranc rose from the tree stump he had been sitting on.

"You will not tell them I was here, will you? I promised, you see..."

"A promise is important. You should keep your word."

"I know. But I wanted to speak to you."

"We will speak again, that is my promise to you, Njal, son of Ulfric. For now, you should return to your longhouse so that your aunt need not worry over you."

• • • • • • •

Several weeks had passed since their arrival at Skarthveit and Taranc had adjusted to the life of a thrall as much as he was prepared to. For now. The work was hard, but not overly so since he had managed to convince the Viking Jarl that a better method of organising the task might be had. As a result, the granary was nearing completion ahead of schedule and they were already turning their attention to the harbour. Ulfric had declared himself well pleased since he had not intended to commence that project until the spring. Dagr had not been relieved of his duties but his violent tendencies were much curbed these days so Taranc had to assume his chief had warned him of the consequences if any more slaves were lost due to needless ill treatment.

Selwyn still shared the slave quarters but his labours were restricted to looking after the sheep on the neighbouring hillsides. It suited him well, apparently, since he had been a shepherd in his native Ireland. He had not lost his foot, but did hobble around with a pronounced limp using a crutch that Fiona had given him. Taranc recalled that she had injured her ankle on the forced march to reach Skarthveit so assumed the crutch had been provided for her use originally by her Viking protector.

Ulfric baffled him. The man was a thief, a murderer, a killer who lived by violence and thought nothing of slaying those who stood between him and what he wanted. Yet he had spared Fiona's life and from what Taranc had observed since, the Viking had treated her well. There had been no occasion to speak with Fiona herself, but the female thralls came and went freely between the village and the slave barns and he had ample opportunity to ask them how she fared. He learnt that Ulfric protected her, that she shared his bed and his home, and appeared happy with him.

This was borne out by his own observations on the rare occasions he went into the village. On one such visit he was at the forge when Fiona sauntered past outside. She did not see him. Her attention was focused on the Viking chief who she had spotted across the way. Taranc watched as she trotted up behind her Viking and poked him in the middle of the back then made to run away. Ulfric caught her within three paces and lifted her, squealing, in his arms. Still laughing, Fiona flung her arms about his neck and kissed him on the mouth as he lowered her back to the ground. The kiss deepened as Taranc watched, then Ulfric lifted his head and whispered something in her ear. She smiled and took his hand as he led her back to their longhouse.

Yes, matters looked to be fine between his once betrothed and her Viking captor, and Taranc was glad of it. He did need to speak with her, of course, to be certain, but he was coming around to the belief that he might safely leave her here when he made his escape.

It had been his intention from the outset that his captivity would be a short-lived affair. Had he chosen to do so he could have eluded the Viking guards and left Skarthveit at more or less any time. These arrogant Norsemen were complacent, believing that their superior might and brawn rendered them invincible, that their swords were all the surety they required. They were fools, but they were dangerous too and would seek to hunt him down were he to run. He would need to pick his moment with wisdom, and plan his return to his homeland. The matter of procuring a ship was the most challenging obstacle, but he would find a way.

Brynhild Freysson continued to perplex and baffle him. The woman was lovely, to be sure, and the mere sight of her as she moved with both grace and purpose about the settlement never failed to stir his rampant cock in a manner he found both disconcerting and utterly delicious. He allowed himself to savour the fantasy of sinking his hard length into her warm, welcoming cunt, though he knew better than to imagine that might become reality. She made her distaste for him, and for all Celts, painfully obvious. Taranc might lust after the Viking noblewoman, he was a male and drew breath so how could he not? But he did not like her, and he had never yet fucked a woman he disliked.

He spoke often with Njal as the boy sought him out on a regular basis. The lad was an avid pupil and constantly pestered Taranc to teach him more Gaelic words. Their conversations ranged from exchanging opinions on the relative merits of carrots or turnips to who was the most skilled at the game of kingy bats. Njal showed Taranc how to pass the ball made of tied rags from one round bat to another, and they spent much convivial time thus occupied. In return Taranc taught Njal to play skittles, a game he had much enjoyed as a small boy in Aikrig.

"My father plays a game called *hnefatafl*. It is complicated, with many pieces which must be moved about on a board." The boy crinkled his nose in disgust. "Running about is not allowed whilst playing, however, so I do not care for it."

Taranc shrugged. "Perhaps it is similar to chess, which is a fine game and one you must learn should you ever master the art of remaining still for long enough."

Njal was clearly not convinced. "Are you permitted to come to the river this evening? There are fine salmon to be had there, and trout. I will show you. It is best to fish at night…"

The day's labours were over so Taranc saw no serious objection, though Dagr always insisted upon locking the thralls in the slave barn as evening fell. Taranc and the other thralls were compliant enough since they found little difficulty in slipping the lock and letting themselves out as they pleased.

"I shall see you there later," he promised.

The night was cool. Summer had more or less given way to the onset of autumn, and Taranc shivered as he made his way to the river. He had yet to experience a Nordic winter and did not relish the prospect. His homeland offered a harsh enough climate, but these frozen lands to the north would be far less hospitable. He hoped to be gone soon.

Njal was already at the river bank, his short fishing pole secured at an angle so the line dangled in the water. He leapt to his feet when he saw Taranc's approach, no doubt scattering any trout curious enough to have seen fit to investigate the wriggling worm impaled on the sharp hook at the end.

"You came!"

"Did I not say that I would? How has the fishing been so far?"

The lad knelt to peer into the fast-flowing water. "Nothing so far. This is the best spot, though. I caught a huge pike here in the spring."

"We shall try our luck, then. First, I must fashion a fine pole like yours." Taranc had selected a decent length of willow on his way down to the river and now sat on the bank to whittle away the sharp twigs protruding from the edges. "Do you have spare line I might borrow, if you please?"

"Aye, I brought some. Here. And spare hooks." The boy tugged free a sack which he had suspended from the belt at his waist, the bag almost dangling to the ground. He shoved it at Taranc. "Take what you need. I shall find you some worms."

"Thank you." Taranc proceeded to attach the line and tied a hook to the end, then waited for the boy to return with bait. Soon the pair were gazing contentedly upon their bobbing lines though Taranc doubted the creatures of the deep would venture their way unless Njal could manage to restrain his high-pitched chatter. That seemed unlikely so he resigned himself to a pleasant if fish-free evening and settled onto his back to stare up into the inky blackness peppered by a thousand glittering stars.

Did the same brilliant display sparkle in the skies over Scotland? Had the season changed there also or did the summer still bathe their land in her warm glow?

"I have one. Look! Look, I have a fish!" Njal leapt up and hopped from one foot to the other pointing at his rod. The pole had almost jerked free of the ground where Njal had jammed one end, and Taranc grabbed for it before the entire paraphernalia disappeared into the river. He sat up and beckoned the boy to his side.

"We must reel it in. Take care, now. You do not wish to lose your supper."

Njal took the rod from Taranc and, face contorted in blissful concentration, he started to wind the line around the pole. Soon the splashing on the surface of the river showed them the location of the trapped fish. It looked to Taranc as though Njal had taken a sizable trout and he tilted his chin in acknowledgement of the feat.

"You do indeed appear to have the touch, my young friend. Let us hope I can do as well. We would welcome a nice fillet of plump trout to augment our rations in the slave barn this night."

"You may have this one," offered Njal as he landed the squirming fish and knelt to extract his hook from the upper lip of the gasping mouth. The trout gleamed silver in the moonlight, his bright scales catching the thin glimmers of light as the creature waggled and twitched on the bank, then lay still.

"No, that one is yours. The next is mine."

Njal merely grinned as he reloaded his hook with fresh bait and tossed the line back into the water.

The boy caught a smaller trout next, then a decent salmon. Taranc's admiration was not feigned. This lad would never want for a decent meal. He, on the other hand...

"What are you doing here?" The strident tone brought them both whirling to their feet. Brynhild stood a few feet away, her fine blue cloak billowing in the crisp breeze. She gathered it to her, clutching the soft wool to her chest. Her head was bare, her magnificent pale blonde hair lifting in the wind. She was furious, her eyes a deep and brilliant blue as she glowered first at Taranc then at her nephew.

Njal shuffled, awkward at first then opted to attempt to mitigate his transgression by gesturing to his impressive catch.

"We are fishing, aunt. Is it not a fine night for it? My father allows me to come here in the evening, as long as I do not stay too late. It is early still, and look, we have caught trout, salmon—"

"You will be fortunate not to catch the flat of my palm across your disobedient little backside, young man. Did I not expressly tell you to stay well away from the thralls?" She paused to eye Taranc with undisguised distaste. "In particular, Celts."

"Taranc is my friend."

The lad was nothing if not loyal, especially in the face of his aunt's mounting anger. Still, Taranc could not allow him to make matters worse for himself if that might be avoided.

"It is getting late, perhaps. And you have thoroughly humiliated me with your fishing prowess. I know when I am well beaten so let us call it a night for now."

"But—"

"Your aunt is right, you should be heading for your home now, and your bed. I shall do likewise, and I will see you soon."

"Oh, no, you shall not see my nephew soon. I forbid it. I—" Brynhild stepped forward to take the boy by the arm and started to tug him away from the river bank. "And you." She turned to glare at Taranc over her shoulder. "You shall be flogged for being outside after dark. I shall tell Dagr, and—"

Njal wriggled free and planted himself in front of her, his small body quivering with indignant yet impotent rage. "You shall not have him flogged. You shall not! He is my friend, I told you. My father will not allow it, and—"

"Go home. Now." Brynhild's tone was low and uncompromising. "I shall deal with you when I get there."

"But—"

Taranc interrupted his further protests. "It is all right, lad. Do not worry about me. Go straight home, now, as your aunt has told you. I shall see to your rod, your bag of tackle, and your fish. You may collect them from the slave barn whenever you like."

"I already told you, you and the other thralls may have the fish."

"That is most generous, Njal. I thank you on behalf of all. Now, I must bid you good night."

The lad hesitated a further few seconds, then ventured a glance into his aunt's stern features. Whatever he saw there was sufficient to convince him of the wisdom of leaving without further ado. He turned and sprinted away across the springy meadow grass.

Taranc watched him out of sight, then bowed politely to Brynhild. "Lady," he murmured as he bent to wind Njal's line around his pole.

He expected Brynhild to stalk off after her nephew, but she did not. Instead, she remained where she stood, her eyes narrowed in a malevolent glare that remained fixed upon him as he busied himself clearing up his own fishing rod. That task accomplished, he attached each of the three landed fish to hooks from Njal's bag in readiness to hang them from his own belt for the journey back to the slave barn. All set to leave himself, he made to pass the still fuming Norsewoman.

"You will excuse me," he murmured.

"Why?"

He glanced at her, surprised. "Because I am leaving."

"I mean, why are you spending time with my nephew? What do you plan to do?"

"Plan? Nothing." *Well, nothing that concerns the boy, at least.* "He is lonely, and curious. There is no harm in him. And I mean him no ill."

"I do not believe you."

Taranc's slender patience frayed. "And I do not care

what you believe. Good night."

She moved fast, he would allow her that much. He barely even saw the slender hand that snaked from within the confines of her cloak to land a resounding slap across his cheek, and certainly he had no opportunity to dodge that first blow. Not so the second. As she drew back her hand to strike him again, he grabbed her wrist and squeezed, only relaxing his grip marginally when she let out a startled squeal.

"I shall let the first slap go, since you are a woman and no doubt consider yourself provoked. But you shall not raise your hand to me again, lady, lest you wish to find yourself upended across my lap and spanked. Do I make myself clear on this?"

"How dare you? Let go of me! I shall—"

"Do I make myself clear?" His grip remained firm despite her frantic tugging to be free.

At last, with no other choice if she was to be released, Brynhild gave a sharp nod. "Very well, I shall not slap you."

"Excellent decision. And I shall not spank you. This time. Instead…"

He bent his head, lowered his face to hers. Taranc took in the startled expression, the widening of her kingfisher-blue eyes as his mouth descended to brush across hers. Despite his words of just moments ago he was without doubt inviting another slap and the Viking woman could hardly be blamed for delivering it.

Her mouth was soft under his, her breath warm in the cool evening. She parted her lips as though unable to prevent her artless response and his tongue found the seam of her mouth. She opened fractionally more, and it was enough. He slipped his tongue between her lips and caressed the inner surface of her teeth with the tip.

Her hands were on his shoulders, and she clung to him, her fingers curling into his rough tunic. The sane part of his mind expected a protest, expected her to shove him away, to screech her outrage, to summon her guards, but the madness that drove him now ignored all of that.

What am I doing? I don't even like this haughty, cruel woman.

His cock disagreed. His rampant erection liked her perfectly well and tented his pants in instant recognition of the Norsewoman's ample charms. He deepened the kiss, tunnelling his fingers through her blonde locks to hold her head still. Brynhild let out a soft moan, followed by a gasp. Now, at last and somewhat belatedly, she stiffened in his arms and sought to be free.

Fuck!

Taranc broke the kiss and released her, his own breath less than steady. Brynhild backed away, her stunned expression one he found he did not entirely care for.

"You... you should not have done that."

Probably not.

"Why...? I do not understand..."

Neither did he.

"Go! Go back to the slave barn. Now!"

A decent plan, at last.

Taranc stepped back to execute an exaggerated bow. "Sleep well, Lady Brynhild."

• • • • • • •

Taranc was not in the least surprised when, a half hour or so later, Dagr burst into the slave barn, Brynhild at his heels. The slave master had his whip at the ready and stomped across the bare earth floor to where Taranc crouched beside the fire pit. He had a juicy fillet of trout impaled upon a stick and was holding it above the blaze to cook. It appeared his meal was to be disturbed. The other slaves stared in stunned amazement but Taranc merely sighed as he turned to face the irate karl and the Viking female.

"You were out. By the river, and you threatened the Jarl's own son. You know the punishment for this." Spittle sprayed from Dagr's lips as he enunciated the charges.

"Twenty lashes. You, and you…" He gestured to several of the thralls who hovered closest. "Seize him and hold him fast."

No one moved to oblige the slave master in his quest. Taranc smiled. "It appears you must manage unaided, karl. I wish you joy of that." He had no idea what had possessed Dagr to charge up to the slave barn accompanied by no one but Brynhild, but it seemed the man had been stupid enough to do just that. Taranc had not the slightest intention of cooperating with the promised whipping, so he doubted it would happen. At least, not yet. Dagr was malicious, Brynhild seemingly even more so. They would not forget.

Dagr stepped forward, his pugnacious chin jutting at Taranc. He trailed the whip along the floor, then flicked it in the air with a loud crack. "You think that I will not, thrall? You think to defy me, to make a fool of me? You will learn, Celtic cur. You will learn who is master here."

"I was under the impression that *I* am master here."

Dagr spun to face Ulfric as the Jarl entered the barn, Njal panting at his rear. The Viking chief paused to take in the scene, then turned to his sister. "Perhaps you will be so good as to explain to me what this is about, Brynhild. A fishing expedition, I gather…"

"I caught this man, this *Celt*, with your son by the river. Anything might have happened…"

"And what *did* happen?" Ulfric's voice remained low and even, though his irritation was apparent.

Brynhild stamped her foot. "I do not know. I arrived, and—"

"Njal? What did happen?"

"We caught three fish, Father. Two trout and a salmon."

"Ah, yes. These would be the fish, I imagine. Or what remains of them." The thralls had made short work of filleting and cooking the welcome fare and nothing but the heads were left to bear witness to Njal's largesse. Those would find their way into the next day's broth. "I trust you all enjoyed your meal."

"Aye, Jarl," confirmed Taranc. "It was most flavoursome. We must thank you, Njal. Again."

Ulfric folded his arms across his chest and leaned against one of the upright beams that supported the roof of the barn. "And how, I wonder, did you come to be fishing at the river with my son when you should have been securely locked within these walls? Do you care to explain that to me, Celt?"

Taranc shrugged. "The locks are flimsy."

"Evidently." Ulfric shifted his regard to Dagr. "I find myself sorely disappointed in your management of my thralls, and not for the first time of late. Flimsy locks, indeed. You must do better than this, Dagr, or I shall find you alternative work to which you may be better suited. Perhaps you might prefer to herd sheep since they do not require much in the way of locks, or maybe you should work in the fields."

"I am no farmer, Jarl." Dagr drew himself to his full, yet still less than impressive height, his expression indignant. "I shall not scrabble in the soil or—"

Ulfric's tone hardened. "You will do as I deem fit, karl. Remember that. And you may start by replacing the lock on this barn with one which actually works. In future you will ensure that none of my slaves are free to wander the countryside at will, or you will answer to me for it."

"But, this man… he should be punished. He knew he was not permitted to leave, and—"

"It was your responsibility to ensure that he did not, and you failed. Do not fail again. You will spend the rest of the night on guard outside, and at first light you will seek out Ugo at the forge and have him fashion a stout lock. There will be no more nocturnal wanderings. Is that clear? To all?"

This time Ulfric's blue gaze fell upon Taranc, who kept his own visage impassive. A stronger lock would make things more difficult, but he had little doubt he would find a way out should he choose to. Ulfric might be blessed with more brains than Dagr, though that was not to say much, but even he was not infallible. Taranc was no fool and saw no reason to provoke the Jarl needlessly. He shrugged and arranged his features into an expression of resignation. Hopefully this would satisfy Ulfric, for now at least.

The Jarl stepped closer to him, his brow furrowed. "This was not the first time you have been outside the barn after dark." It was a statement, not a question.

"No, Jarl."

"Then why are you still here? Why have you not already made your escape when you could have easily done so?"

"I will leave here at a time of my choosing." Taranc met Ulfric's gaze and held it. He could not be entirely certain, but he believed he detected the flickering of respect in the Viking's cool blue eyes.

Ulfric flattened his lips in a mirthless smile. "We shall see, Celt. We shall see." He turned to leave, his hand resting on his son's narrow shoulder. "Thank you, Njal, for alerting me to the problem here." His azure gaze swept the nervous, silent thralls who surrounded him. "I trust there will be no further... disturbances this night?"

They responded with murmurings and head shakes, seemingly eager to return to the monotony of a night in their barn. Ulfric nodded and strode to the door. "Brynhild? I trust your business here is concluded also?"

"He should be whipped. He was... belligerent and, and..."

Ulfric was not impressed by her claims. "The fault lay with Dagr. There will be no whipping."

Bright spots of colour blazed across Brynhild's pale cheeks as she cast one final, fulminating glare at Taranc before following her brother from the barn.

He watched her go with mounting unease. This latest act of spite had little enough to do with illicit fishing and much to do with that kiss by the riverside. She had responded, briefly, but he was not mistaken, and she had then sought some manner of misplaced vengeance for what had occurred between them. Dagr had been her tool, her means of exacting retribution for Taranc having humiliated her, if indeed that was how she viewed their recent encounter. He could understand her anger, to a point. He had taken advantage of the Viking noblewoman in a weak moment, taken her by surprise and she was entitled to resent his familiarity. Indeed, her towering pride would demand it.

But her hatred went beyond what was rational or deserved. It was near enough palpable, and he could not even start to fathom what lay at the root of it.

CHAPTER SIX

The granary was complete and all the thralls were now working on the foundations for the harbour. The labour was harsh and cold, involving the hauling of huge boulders across the beach and depositing them in the icy waters of the fjord to eventually create a barrier that would offer protection for the Jarl's dragon ships, as well as a shallow place upon which to ground the vessels over the winter. Viking dragon ships were constructed with flat hulls, designed to be hauled up onto a beach and to be agile in shallow water. They were safer moored out of the water, and Ulfric had declared it his intention to construct boathouses for their even greater protection in future years.

Taranc had no intention whatsoever of contributing to that project. He would be long gone.

For now, though, he toiled alongside his comrades as they dragged the huge rocks into place. As usual, Njal strutted up and down the cliff path where they worked, offering his lively commentary to proceedings. The boy never stopped asking questions, and Taranc was not the only man who was happy enough to pause and answer.

"How deep is the water here?" demanded Njal. "Is it higher than I am?" He reached his arm high above his head to indicate his full height.

"Aye, and plenty besides," confirmed Taranc. He would estimate the depth to be at least seven feet of churning water, and they needed to reduce that by half to enable the dragon ships to land there.

Soon it would be too dangerous to continue the work, once the weather turned really cold and stormy and the shoreline was lashed day after day by frigid, numbing waves. They would be forced to abandon the project for the winter. He wondered what labour would be found for the thralls then, to pass the long, dark months until spring.

Taranc did not see the small body slither across the slippery rocks and into the swirling, foaming waves, but he heard the splash and the harsh shout of warning from someone behind him. He swirled, almost lost his own footing, but could not see who had fallen in.

"There! There…" A thrall named Macklyn pointed to a spot perhaps five or six feet from the rocks. "He is there, see?"

Taranc groaned when he recognised the bright red of the lad's tunic. He turned to the closest Viking. "Can he swim? Can he?"

The man shook his head. Another Norse guard was already dragging off his cloak and Taranc expected the man to dive in and haul the boy from the water. Instead the guard knelt on the rocks and cast the cloak out over the waves, yelling to the boy to grab hold.

Njal sank beneath the surface, disappearing from their view. He could no more grab the cloak than he could take to the air and fly back to the safety of the shore.

Taranc watched in disbelief. Why did no one act? There was but one way…

Fuck! Taranc pulled his heavy woollen tunic from his shoulders and flung it aside, then kicked off his shoes. A strong swimmer, he had no doubt he would be able to pluck the lad from his watery grave, provided he could reach him before he was swept out to sea. With no more ado he dived into the frothing waves.

Fuck, fuck, fuck—it was cold!

It took but two powerful strokes for Taranc to reach the spot where he had last sighted the lad, but Njal was nowhere to be seen. Treading water and his teeth chattering as his inner temperature plummeted, Taranc sought to peer down into the murky depths but could not discern anything more than a few inches below the surface. He emptied his lungs, then filled them again with fresh air, and tipped forward to dive beneath the waves. Still he could see almost nothing, and his senses were already dulling with the intense cold. He spun around beneath the surface, disoriented. Which way was the shore? Was the boy in front of him or behind? He might be right here, inches away, or already being dragged out into the open sea.

Taranc reached out, flailing about blindly with arms outstretched. And he made contact.

Something brushed the fingers of his left hand. He turned in that direction, propelled himself forward and grabbed wildly. His reward, a handful of wet, wool tunic. Taranc dragged the boy's small body against his own and kicked hard for the surface, which glittered just inches above his head. He was pleased that at least he had been correct in his estimate of the depth.

He broke the surface gasping for air. Njal was wriggling in his arms but went still as Taranc clutched him against his chest and stroked hard for the rocks where willing hands, Viking and thrall alike, reached down to drag the boy from the water. Others aided Taranc and he scrambled, gasping and shivering, onto the wet rock path where he lay still.

Several moments passed, during which Taranc offered up thanks to the dear, sweet Saviour that they had both survived the ducking. Or, he believed this to be so. He pushed himself into a sitting position and peered over to where the boy lay on his side, coughing and gasping in great lungfuls of air.

The pounding of footsteps heralded the arrival of Ulfric.

He dropped to his knees beside his son and hauled the boy into his arms.

"C-cold, Daddy," spluttered the boy, his features ashen now as shock began to take hold.

Ulfric rose to his feet, the lad cradled in his arms, and he started back up the cliff path, his stride long and purposeful. He paused to glance back as Taranc fumbled to retrieve his tunic. The garment had remained dry, though his leggings were soaked. Taranc looked up and met Ulfric's gaze.

"Thank you." If anything, Ulfric looked even more devastated by this day's events than did Njal. Such was the love of a father for his only child, surmised Taranc.

"You are welcome." He pulled his tunic over his head.

"Come." Ulfric beckoned Taranc to accompany him as he strode back up the hillside, his shivering son bundled in his arms. "You too require a warm bath and dry clothing."

Taranc was not about to argue with that assessment. He got to his feet and followed.

In the longhouse all was a flurry of activity. Word had preceded them and a tub of steaming water awaited Njal by the time they arrived. Brynhild, pale and shaken by the news of her nephew's brush with disaster, rushed to fuss over him. To Taranc's surprise the Viking woman paused to thank him for his actions in effecting a rescue, though he noted she did not call for hot water for him.

It was of no matter. Ulfric issued instructions and bade Fiona attend to the drenched thrall. The grateful Viking Jarl invited Taranc to sit close to the fire pit to remain warm as his own bath was prepared, and he charged Fiona with finding dry blankets for him.

It was a warmer, and infinitely more comfortable Taranc who hauled himself at last from the cooling water that lapped the brim of Ulfric's own bathtub and accepted the thick blanket handed to him by one of the Jarl's house thralls. The lad, Harald, had scurried back and forth with buckets of hot water and had even managed to procure a mug of fine mead for the thrall all now hailed as a hero.

Taranc was vaguely embarrassed. He had only done what anyone would have. Well, anyone able to swim.

It remained a complete mystery to him why such an adept seafaring race as these Vikings should neglect to master that simple skill.

His own clothing was still wet so Taranc accepted a pair of dry leggings that he suspected might have belonged to the Jarl himself since they were of a similar size and the fabric was finely woven. His own shoes and tunic were fit to wear, so Taranc donned those and set about his remaining task for this day. Here was an opportunity to speak with Fiona, and he was not about to miss it.

His once-betrothed was not in the longhouse when Taranc finished his bath so he asked Harald where she might be found.

The lad scratched his head. "Oh, I think she is feeding the chickens. In the pen, around the back."

Taranc thanked him and made his way around to the rear of the dwelling where Fiona stood among a bunch of squawking fowl. She had never looked more beautiful, in Taranc's opinion. Or more distant. He leaned his elbows on the top of the fence that penned the hens in and watched her for a short while before speaking.

"Fiona? Walk with me?"

She whirled around to face him. "I... I cannot. Ulfric..."

"Ulfric has not forbidden you to speak with me, has he?"

"No, but—"

"Then, walk with me. I need to talk to you."

She met his gaze, hesitated but a few moments more, then gave a brief nod. She set aside the basket of corn she had been feeding to the hens and exited the pen, closing the gate carefully behind her.

"Where shall we go?" She looked up at him, her dark grey eyes the colour of wet slate.

"The meadow, over there. It is but a short walk and you will hear if you are summoned."

They walked side by side, in silence, until by mutual and

unspoken consent they stopped in the shadow of a huge pine. Taranc sank to the ground and leaned back against the tree. Fiona lowered herself beside him. He glanced down at her and contemplated a life that could have been.

Would have been, had either of them truly wanted it. Taranc saw now what he had not properly recognised before. They had grown up together, friends from childhood, promised to one another more or less from the cradle. He loved this woman, loved her dearly, but as his sister not his bride. Had the Vikings not come, perhaps they would have married, eventually. They would have exhausted all their excuses and done their best to make a success of their union. They would have managed it, too, because they liked each other and they cared. But there would have been no passion, no fire or spark. Fiona would never have run across his village to poke him in the back, then shyly followed him back to their cottage to make love.

It was time to move on.

"Tell me of your Viking. Is he kind to you?"

His question seemed to startle her. "I suppose—"

Taranc chuckled. "Other than in his bed. Are you happy living in his household?"

Fiona nodded and wrapped her arms about her legs. She rested her chin on her knees as she answered. "Ulfric is kind but his sister hates me and I avoid her at all costs. She is not allowed to beat me, but she will do all in her power to convince Ulfric to do so."

He was not surprised to hear this. The tales of Brynhild's hostility had carried as far as the slave barn, and he had seen enough of it himself to know what the Viking woman was like. It bothered him that she could manage to harm Fiona, if only vicariously.

"And does he? Beat you?"

"Once or twice, with a switch. It was… not so bad and after, he… he…"

"You find pleasure with him, sweetheart? Is that what you are trying to tell me?"

"I could not help it. He is very... compelling."

Taranc laughed out loud at this. He was genuinely glad for her, and knowing that she found pleasure in her Viking's bed relieved the lingering guilt he might feel at contemplating leaving her here. As though she discerned the way his thoughts were turning, she leaned her head on his shoulder.

"When you escape from here, and I know you will, I want you to take me with you. I want to go home."

As did Taranc, but it was not so simple. "If we were to escape, we would be stranded here, in this frozen wilderness unless we could procure a ship of some sort. We must bide our time, Fiona. A chance will come, and we will take it."

"No, we should—"

"Things change, always. Events we do not control. You are safe here for now."

"I want to be free. Do you not long for the same thing?"

"I am free, though for now I choose to remain here. Your Viking brought us to this place against our will, so I see no reason not to enjoy his hospitality for a while longer. He feeds us well, clothes us, provides decent shelter."

"He is not my Viking."

"No? I believe he is, or could be, but that is for you to judge."

Fiona might have argued further, but at that moment Ulfric appeared from around the tree where they had sought refuge. Taranc knew without needing to ask that the Jarl had been listening to their conversation, to their talk of escape. He hoped Fiona would not bear the brunt of the Viking's anger, but he suspected not. Ulfric appeared more thoughtful than vexed, and fiercely possessive, which amused Taranc more than a little.

"I shall escort my thrall back to her place in my bed," announced the Norseman, his mouth set as though to brook no challenge.

Taranc rose to his feet and tugged Fiona up with him. "Treat her well," he said, his voice low.

Ulfric narrowed his eyes and muttered something about returning to the slave barn, but Taranc was already on his way, ambling casually away from the pair who remained under the tree. Ulfric called belated thanks, for his actions in saving Njal. Taranc raised his arm in silent acknowledgement and did not look back.

CHAPTER SEVEN

The next few days were uneventful. Brynhild was glad of the respite as it afforded her the welcome opportunity to seek refuge in her weaving, an activity she found both soothing and therapeutic. The repetitive labour gave her time to think, to plan, to calm her rattled nerves. She had been more distressed than she cared to admit over the near loss of her beloved nephew and even now, more than a sennight later, she shuddered at the recollection. Life could be so fleeting, so fragile. Her peace was shattered by the unexpected arrival of her brother, Gunnar, who descended upon them, his new family about him. The three Freysson siblings were close, but Gunnar preferred to maintain his own settlement a couple of days' ride to the north. He had grown up at Skarthveit and visited often, but not usually without warning.

"This is Mairead," her youngest brother announced with obvious pride when Ulfric and Brynhild strode out to greet him, to bid him welcome. "My bride of these past couple of months. And these are our children, Donald and Tyra." Brynhild was at a loss. Had both her brothers run completely mad? As if it was not enough that Ulfric had brought a Celtic bed-slave into their longhouse, the usually taciturn and serious Gunnar had actually gone a step further and taken a Celt as his wife!

What was more, the bride, Mairead, already had two children and Gunnar appeared determined upon treating them as his own.

"Welcome, sister." Ulfric barely missed a beat before leaning in to kiss the pale-featured Celt. "It is good to meet you. Please, come inside, take your rest. You must be tired after your journey."

At Ulfric's urging, Brynhild hurried to organise the feasting that would mark the family reunion. She would play her part, no one would find fault with her hospitality but she was not fooled by the effusive welcome. Ulfric had been as astonished as she was by the announcement of their brother's wedding, but had made the woman welcome, and of course that upstart Fiona had been falling over herself to befriend the jumped-up thrall.

Brynhild never would. Sister or no, this Mairead was a Celt, a slave, nothing more. Fiona, too, needed to learn her place. The sooner her idiot brothers came to their senses and stopped thinking with their dicks the better, and safer, their homes would be.

As well as news of his marriage, Gunnar brought worrying tidings from Hafrsfjord. For several years now their family had been embroiled in a blood feud with the Bjarkessons, their closest neighbours to the west. The two families had been close once. Ulfric's wife, Astrid, had been a Bjarkesson, and Brynhild had been betrothed to another. Her hopes of marriage had been dashed when Eirik Bjarkesson met an untimely end in a raiding expedition on Orkney, shortly after Astrid died of a sudden fever.

Brynhild missed Astrid dearly. She had always longed for a sister as she grew up, and when Astrid came to Skarthveit to wed her brother the pair became close. It was a natural enough development that Brynhild should accept the offer of marriage from Eirik, Astrid's cousin. Eirik was a year or so younger than Brynhild, and always put her in mind of a lively puppy. A large man, he was gentle and unassuming, eager to please and gave the impression of being utterly besotted with his bride to be though she knew the situation to be rather more complex than that. No matter, he would have made a fine, malleable husband, Brynhild had no doubt of it. Eirik had been exactly what she needed.

But it was not to be. Her failed hopes merely added to the bitter disappointment her life had become. Her brothers both urged her to consider other men and she was assured of an enviable bridal settlement were she to require it, but Brynhild refused to even discuss the matter. She was confident that in time she could have made something of Eirik, but another candidate might not be so obliging. She had no interest whatsoever in a man who would seek to take charge, to assert his authority, and to dominate his household as did her brothers. Brynhild had to be in charge, nothing less would suffice. Nothing less could be trusted to offer her the security and safety she craved.

The untimely and tragic deaths of both Astrid and Eirik had soured the relationship between the two families. Olaf Bjarkesson, their Jarl, blamed Ulfric for the death of Eirik since he had led the raid in which the younger man perished. And even more bizarrely, Olaf sought to suggest that Ulfric had actually poisoned his wife. It was ridiculous; Ulfric had loved Astrid and her death had caused him great anguish. Olaf was convinced, however, and nothing Ulfric did or said could dissuade him from his ill-conceived malice.

In the years since, Olaf Bjarkesson had made numerous attacks on the Freyssons. Their crops had been destroyed, sheep stolen, trade disrupted. And now their enemy appeared to be ready to escalate the feud yet further, according to Gunnar. Olaf had made no secret of his intentions as he blustered about Hafrsfjord telling all who would listen that he intended to bring Ulfric Freysson to his knees. He knew Gunnar heard his threats and would bring the news straight here to Skarthveit. A challenge had been issued.

Ulfric was no stranger to battle, but always preferred to choose his fights with care. From the outset he had sought to placate Olaf, to restore the peace with his neighbours, which had always served both sides well. They had prospered together, and this senseless fighting threatened to destroy them. Brynhild knew that Ulfric had more or less lost hope of finding a peaceful solution, but he was determined upon one final attempt. Gunnar had not long departed Skarthveit to return to his own settlement when Ulfric announced that he would go to Bjarkessholm one last time to offer reparation and seek to make peace with Olaf.

Bjarkessholm was a day's ride away so Ulfric would be gone for one night, possibly two. There had been a quarrel between her brother and his precious bed-thrall just before he left. Brynhild did not know what had caused it but had heard the unmistakable sounds of a hard spanking and Ulfric had left instructions that Fiona was not to leave the longhouse. Now the wench sat at her table, chopping vegetables, her features set and sullen, clearly fuming over some imagined slight.

How dare she? The girl was fortunate to have the favour of the Jarl. What had this Celt to complain of?

Brynhild observed from her loom, quietly fuming. She opened her mouth to issue a sharp rebuke but swallowed it at a pained squeal from Njal. The lad had been seated at the table sipping his mug of buttermilk but now he doubled over, clutching his stomach.

"My tummy hurts," he mewled, his small features scrunched in pain.

Brynhild abandoned her weaving and rushed to his side. She laid her palm on his forehead and winced. He was hot to the touch, clammy. A fever was the thing she most feared, having witnessed the speed with which Astrid lost her fight for life once the illness took hold.

Njal leaned forward and was violently sick, then lay on the bench shivering. Brynhild fought back her mounting panic and dismay as Hilla, the smallest of her house-thralls ran to fetch a mop.

"You, go get a pail in case he is sick again." The command was directed at Fiona who hurried to obey. Brynhild helped Njal from the table and carried him to his bed where she made him lie down. He did so without argument, his small body racked with huge shudders.

Brynhild wrung her hands in helpless terror. She had some knowledge of healing herbs, though her skills were scanty. She had heard somewhere that chamomile tea might help in such cases so for want of something better she set about preparing that.

Why did such a thing have to happen when Ulfric is away? Why do I always have to cope with things alone?

Hilla dealt with the mess on the floor and Fiona brought the bucket. Brynhild was oblivious to the rest of her household, her entire attention riveted on her sickly nephew. Not for the first time, she reflected on the fragility of life and how swiftly it could be snatched away. Children were the most vulnerable, so precious and so easily lost. Had Njal been rescued from the sea, only to succumb to disease just days later? Perhaps death refused to be cheated...

She did not know how long she sat beside the gasping, wheezing boy. He coughed from time to time, and continued to shiver despite the extra blankets that Brynhild piled upon him. He did not vomit again, and she wondered if perhaps that might be a good sign, but his face was pallid and his breathing shallow.

Brynhild had never been so scared in her life.

At last the demands of her own bladder forced her to abandon her place at Njal's side in order to use the privy. She hurried around the side of the longhouse and did what she must, then scurried back toward the door. The sight of Fiona standing out in the open and staring up into the night sky brought her up short.

The wench knows full well that she is confined to the longhouse. Can she not obey the simplest instructions, even now?

Brynhild's temper, always simmering as far as Fiona was

95

concerned, boiled over in that moment of perceived defiance.

"You, what are you doing out here? My brother instructed you to remain inside."

The wench started, caught off guard by the sharp tone. Fiona muttered something about just stopping for a moment to look at the stars. Brynhild bristled further. Would that they all had time to pause and contemplate the heavens but some of them had real concerns to attend to. She could well do without disobedient thralls demanding her attention this evening, on top of everything else.

"Do you require another thrashing this day?" demanded Brynhild, her tone sharper than she intended. She knew perfectly well that Ulfric had forbidden her to lay a hand on the girl.

Fiona knew it too and did not hesitate to remind Brynhild of that fact. "You may not beat me. In any case, I was just coming in..."

Brynhild had heard enough. She would teach the insolent wench a lesson, and could easily do so without breaking Ulfric's rules. "Since you seem to enjoy the outdoors so much, perhaps I should allow you to remain here. I think a spell in the stocks will teach you the benefits of obedience."

Fiona staggered back as though Brynhild had actually struck her. She started to protest, but Brynhild had no time to listen. She needed to get back to Njal. A movement to her right caught her attention and she summoned the hovering Harald to her.

"See her set in the stocks, at once. Secure her well." The thrall's reluctance was obvious, but Brynhild was mistress here and would be obeyed. If Harald saw fit to argue he might take his place alongside the wench, a fact which she was quick to point out to him. Brynhild moved to pass the pair, stopping to issue her instructions to Harald.

"A half hour or so will be sufficient to teach her some manners. You will take charge. You know what you have to do. See to it. I am needed inside to tend to Njal as his sickness has worsened, but be assured I shall be back to check that you have done exactly as I have instructed."

Brynhild watched as Harald caught the struggling, pleading wench by the wrist and dragged her across the settlement to where their stocks were located at the rear of the forge. She did not follow to supervise the punishment. Harald was well aware of how this would go and she could leave it to him to release the girl when she had learnt her lesson. Satisfied, Brynhild dismissed the troublesome thrall from her mind and hurried back indoors to take up her vigil beside her nephew.

The chamomile tea had made little difference. Perhaps if she were to sacrifice one of their finest goats her nephew might be spared. She was ready to try anything.

Njal's fever broke after an hour. Brynhild could have wept with relief. She remained at his side, stroking his damp hair and muttering her thanks to the goddess Freya who she was sure must have interceded for them in return for the promise of the goat. It was a good bargain, one she would be happy to keep.

Exhausted, Brynhild got to her feet and stretched. It was late, very late, and the longhouse was silent but for the soft breathing of Hilla asleep on her pallet by the fire pit and Njal's occasional snuffles.

An icy trickle of unease snaked down her spine. It was too quiet. What was wrong? Something—someone—was missing.

The girl! Had Harald brought her back indoors? He must have, though Brynhild could not recall hearing them enter. Her heart in her mouth, Brynhild rushed to peer behind the curtain that separated her brother's sleeping chamber from the rest of the longhouse. The bed was empty.

"Oh, sweet Freya..." murmured Brynhild as she grabbed her cloak and flung it about her shoulders. Surely Harald had released the wench by now. He knew he was supposed to leave her in the stocks for no longer than half an hour, she had told him that quite specifically.

How long had it been? An hour? Closer to two, she acknowledged as she flung open the door.

Brynhild was shoved roughly back into the dwelling as the large and clearly enraged form of her brother rushed past, his bed-slave in his arms. The wench was limp and pale. Brynhild's heart sank.

Harald! I will flay the skin from his back for this.

"Ulfric, you are here…"

He glared at her, his expression little short of murderous.

Brynhild stood, rooted to the spot. "Brother, I can explain. She was—"

"Not a word, Brynhild. Not a fucking word. I have heard enough from you."

Brynhild reached for his elbow, anxious to explain that the matter was not as it first appeared, but Ulfric shook her off.

"Leave us. I shall hear an account of this in the morning, and believe me, Brynhild, there *will* be a reckoning."

He left her there and disappeared into his chamber with the wench. Brynhild spun on her heel, paused to check once more on Njal who had somehow managed to sleep through the entire commotion, then she stalked from the longhouse in search of Harald. By Odin he would regret his part in this night's work.

Harald was nowhere to be found. Not that night, or the following morning. Brynhild discovered he had passed a good portion of the night with Adelburga, a Saxon slave with whom he was inclined to spend his rare moments of leisure. She had to assume that he had seen an opportunity when, for reasons only he might fathom, he had believed his absence would not be noted, and he had taken it. According to a tearful Adelburga, Harald had fled her cottage on hearing the enraged Jarl bellowing for assistance when Ulfric returned and discovered Fiona. She had no idea where he went.

Brynhild racked her brains. She went over and over the

conversation with Harald and was quite certain she had made her instructions clear to him. Even had she not, Harald knew as well as she did that no one should be left outside in the stocks overnight as Ulfric now seemed convinced had been her intention.

His mission to make peace with the Bjarkessons had met with implacable hostility from the moment he arrived at their settlement and Ulfric had quickly determined that the entire errand was futile. He had abandoned the attempt and left at once for home, arriving in the middle of the night. Despite Brynhild's assertion that he was wrong, he remained convinced that had he not changed his plans, Fiona would have died.

That was ludicrous, it would be tantamount to murder and Brynhild Freysson would not stoop to such an act of cowardice. She was confident that her brother would realise that, once he calmed down and saw matters more clearly.

Brynhild explained to him that Njal had been ill, and that she had been distracted by that or she would have noticed Harald's dereliction of his duty much earlier. The girl had been badly frightened, Brynhild would allow that, but no real harm was done. She would have released the girl herself. Indeed, she was on her way to do exactly that when her brother barged past her into the longhouse. Ulfric had simply arrived before she did, that was all. After his initial rage had calmed, Ulfric became oddly silent on the matter. He listened to her account, but asked few questions and Brynhild knew he did not believe her. No matter, he would come around. She was telling the truth. Why would she lie?

Fiona was not the only one deeply shocked. Brynhild was no fool, and she knew that the incident might have ended differently. Had Njal's fever not broken, had Ulfric not returned, it was by now clear that Harald would not have done as he should and the wench might well have perished. That had not happened, but Brynhild was ready to admit, at least to herself, that it had been a near thing.

This could not continue. Brynhild was a grown woman,

mistress of this settlement. She had duties, responsibilities, and she could not continue to allow her dislike of this wench to control her actions. Her fear and loathing of the Celts was real enough, but at some level Brynhild knew it to be irrational and based upon childish concerns. She could not let her adult life be ruled by events that took place when she was but fourteen years of age.

She was a Viking, a woman of the Jarl and she was better than this.

CHAPTER EIGHT

"My apologies, Viking, for I fear I misheard you." Taranc turned his head to regard the Jarl at his side. Ulfric's profile was stark against the inky blackness of the night, illuminated only by thin slivers of moonlight that penetrated the lowering cloud.

The Viking did not move, simply continued to stare ahead into the darkness. When he spoke, his tone was harsh. "You did not mishear, but I shall repeat it anyway. I will help you to regain your freedom, on condition that when you leave here, you take Brynhild with you."

Taranc could only gape at the other man. He had not known what to expect when the Viking had come to the slave barn in the dead of night, woken Taranc, and bade him come outside to talk, but it was not this. Nothing remotely like this.

"You are asking me to abduct your sister? Why? Why would you even dream of such a horrendous act?" The whole thing was beyond Taranc's comprehension. Even for a Viking such an act was unthinkable, surely.

Ulfric drew his hand across his brow and for the first time Taranc noted how weary the other man appeared, and how careworn. He turned to regard Taranc. "Fiona told you of the enmity between them?"

"Between your sister and Fiona? Yes, but—"

"Tonight, Brynhild tried to murder Fiona. It was only by sheer good fortune that I arrived home in time to prevent it. She survived, but next time, we may not be so lucky."

Taranc was stunned. "Sweet Lord. What happened?"

"I was away from Skarthveit, not expected back for two nights. Brynhild had Fiona locked into the stocks and would have left her outside the entire night had I not returned earlier than I had intended. Fiona would have frozen to death, very nearly did."

"Are you quite certain? Perhaps there was some mistake, some misunderstanding…?" Even as he uttered the words Taranc harboured no real doubt that Ulfric had the right of it. The Viking was not given to hasty conclusions.

Ulfric shook his head. "I know what I saw, and I have heard Fiona's telling of it. Of course Brynhild denies intending any real harm, but I no longer trust her word. I have to do something, and this seems like the right solution. I can trust you to take care of my sister."

Could he? Taranc was not so sure. Rage boiled within him at the injury almost done to the woman he cared about. And if Ulfric had the right of it, this cast an entirely different light on his decision to leave Fiona here with her Nordic captor when he made his own escape. He could not abandon her to the ruthless mercy of Brynhild Freysson.

His tone was bitter as he responded. "After what I have heard, I do not believe I even like your sister let alone wish to spend any time in her company."

Ulfric was not to be deterred. "Brynhild cannot continue as she is. She is tearing herself apart." The Viking turned his haggard gaze upon Taranc. "Despite her vicious words and deeds, I know that at heart my sister is deeply unhappy, and very lonely. She blames the Celts for all that is amiss in her life, and has lost any sense of perspective she might have once possessed. She needs to be forced to think again, and I need to act before this ends in tragedy. One of them must leave, and I will not let it be Fiona. So, will you do this? For Fiona, if not for me?"

Taranc leaned forward to study the grass beneath his feet. He could not see how this might end well. It was all too… complicated.

"Your sister will despise you for betraying her. She will hate me."

Ulfric nodded. "At first, perhaps. But you must understand that I do not wish her harm and I will require you to offer her your protection, whatever happens."

"She will not come quietly. I would have to subdue her." Even as he uttered the words Taranc could not quite believe that he was contemplating this. Was he actually going to agree to this mad scheme?

"You will do what is necessary to ensure her compliance, but you will not injure her. I must have your word on this."

"You would trust my word? The promise of a Celt? A slave?"

"I once offered you my word and told you that you may rely upon it. I did not let you down, and I know that you will not let me down. So, do we have an agreement?"

Taranc met Ulfric's gaze, considering the options that faced him. He made up his mind. "Very well, Viking. For the sake of Fiona's safety, I will do this thing." He offered his hand and Ulfric took it.

The Viking got to his feet. "I shall do all in my power to aid you. You will require a horse, and provisions. Warm clothing, and a ship to take you back to Scotland. I assume that is where you will go?"

Taranc shrugged, though in truth there was nowhere else he might consider. Aikrig was his home, and now he had the means, probably, to return there. However, if he was to do this, it would be on his terms.

"Where I go once I leave here is my concern."

"But—"

Taranc put up a hand. "*My* concern, Viking. I will take your sister with me, but I will decide when, and where we go."

Slowly Ulfric bowed his head, and Taranc had the grace to pity the man. This was tearing the Viking apart. "Very well, and thank you. Now, let us return to our beds before either of us is missed. I shall tell you on the way back just how I plan to aid you in this endeavour."

· · · · · · ·

Two nights later Taranc lay on his straw pallet staring into the dark. The soft snores of the other thralls surrounded him like a warm, familiar blanket. This was the last time he would lie here, listening to the sounds of a Nordic night in the thrall barn. He had eaten his final supper cooked over the slaves' fire pit, hauled his last rock across the beach at Skarthveit. It was to be tonight, he had determined.

He had not spoken again with Ulfric, but had no doubt that the Jarl would make good on all his promises. Supplies would be stowed in the place they had agreed upon, a mount would be waiting, hooves suitably muffled to reduce the risk of discovery. They had agreed that he would make his way with all haste to Hafrsfjord where a fishing vessel, the master well paid by Ulfric, awaited to convey him and his Viking captive over the sea. The plan was not without risk, but it could work.

It *would* work. It had to. Only Lady Brynhild stood between him and his freedom. She would need to be managed with care and ruthless efficiency. Taranc could lay claim to both. He would not fail.

He rose from his pallet in silence and made his way to the door. A deft flick of the hinge lifted the heavy wood from the door surround and Taranc was able to slip through the gap between the door and the wall. He paused to replace the hinge in its socket. There was no point in advertising to Dagr how his departure had been effected. Then he crouched low to sprint across the meadow in the direction of the village.

• • • • • • •

"You should go to bed now, Hilla. It is late."

"Aye, lady, but I have not yet secured the poultry. There is a fox about, and—"

Brynhild smiled at the lass. "You have been working since first light. Go get some sleep and I shall see to the chickens when I check on the rest of our livestock."

Locking up their animals at night had been Harald's job but it now fell to Brynhild, one of her many duties in her brother's longhouse. She did not mind; it was best to be busy, to be needed.

Her glance strayed to Njal, already fast asleep in his little bed by the fire pit. The small boy kept her busier than the rest of her responsibilities combined but she had no complaints. She was just relieved that he was well again, and showed no lingering ill effects from his indisposition of a few days previously.

A low chuckle reached her from behind the curtain that separated Ulfric's chamber. It was followed by a breathy sigh, then a little squeal. She gritted her teeth. She had resolved not to rise to the bait, but it was not easy. She might manage to curtail her dislike of her brother's bed-thrall, indeed, she was determined to do so since she had no option but to accept that the Celt was here to stay, but she would never warm to the wench.

Brynhild set aside the hank of wool she had been combing and reached for her cloak. The night was chilly; the sooner she could ensure that all was secure and their animals settled for the night, the better. She hugged the thick woollen garment to her chest and stepped outside.

The chickens were as stupidly uncooperative as usual but Brynhild managed to usher them into the small crate that offered them protection during the hours of darkness and dropped the lid. That accomplished, she made her way to the pen where their three goats and two kids bleated softly at her approach. Until yesterday there had been four fine goats, but one was owed to Freya and Brynhild knew better than to renege on such a deal. She checked that the gate was fastened securely and paused to lean on the low fencing to admire the young animals. She was proud of her goats, and the fine milk they provided, not to mention the good eating her family would enjoy in a few months' time.

Now for the heifer—

She never heard the approach of her assailant. Brynhild was stunned momentarily when a hand snaked across her mouth and she was seized from behind. The man was strong, lifted her easily from her feet to swing her away from the longhouse. Brynhild was not a slight woman, and after the initial shock she fought like one possessed. Her attacker was powerful, and within moments he had rammed a rag into her mouth and secured it with another tied around her face. Then he dragged a sack of some description over her head and Brynhild really started to panic. She could not breathe, was sure he meant to suffocate her.

Please, please… Ulfric… help me…

She pleaded silently as she fought to keep the waves of terror at bay. If she was to survive it would be because she remained calm, awaited her chance.

It was Bjarkesson. It had to be, no one else would dare. The mad, deluded fool had taken it upon himself to abduct the sister of his enemy and he would pay dearly for it. Ulfric would never let this insult pass unavenged.

Her attacker spun her around and tied her wrists in front of her. He did not speak, just grabbed the binding that secured her hands and dragged her forward. Brynhild followed, stumbling blindly, trying to discern her location in the settlement by the feel of the ground underfoot.

Soon the hard-packed earth gave way to the crack and crinkle of undergrowth and she knew they had left the security of the cluster of longhouses. They were entering the woods that surrounded the village and still her abductor tugged her onward, forcing her to break into a run to keep up with him. More than once she tripped on a root or branch, but he just hauled her upright again and forced her on.

Her side burned. She was gasping, struggling to breathe behind the gag and the sacking that covered her head. As their pace slowed she began to succumb to the mind-numbing panic that now threatened to overwhelm her. It was as though the years fell away and she was fourteen again, young, helpless, hopelessly out of her depth and at the mercy of a man who meant her harm.

Her captor came to a halt and Brynhild stopped too. She sank to her knees, shaking. She would not beg, she would not plead.

Or would she? She was a survivor, she would do what she must.

His hands were on her shoulders now and he gripped the bag that covered her head. The sacking was drawn up and over her hair and at last she felt the welcome chill of the night air on her skin. She tilted her head back and opened her eyes.

The forest-green gaze that met her was the last she expected to encounter. The thrall, Taranc, grinned at her, his teeth flashing white in the moonlight. "Good evening, lady. I must apologise for the unseemly rush. I trust you are not too uncomfortable."

She recoiled, stunned.

How dare he? What was this dolt thinking, laying his filthy hands upon the person of a lady of the Jarl? Ulfric would have him hanged for such an offence.

His smile did not waver. "I will not harm you, but I must insist on your silence, at least for the time being, until we are well away from this place. Do not move from there." He had been balancing on his haunches looking directly into her face but now he stood and walked slowly around the clearing in which they had arrived. Brynhild scanned from left to right and recognised the spot, perhaps a couple of hundred yards from the closest dwelling. If she might just get to her feet she could run hard and maybe get back to the village before he caught her. If she could just get this gag from between her lips she would be able to scream loud enough to rouse Valhalla and by Odin she would do so. She pursued the Celt with her eyes as he paced the perimeter of the clearing, and watched in amazement when he crouched to reach under a spiky holly bush.

The thrall withdrew a large leather bag that he had obviously secreted there earlier. When had he had such an opportunity? She knew for a fact that all the slaves had been occupied down at the harbour the entire day. No matter, she would ponder such mysteries later, in less urgent circumstances.

Slowly, with care, Brynhild rose to her feet and started to back away from the Celt. He was busy checking the contents of his bag so his attention was not on her. This was her chance, and might well be the one opportunity she would have.

Brynhild turned and she ran.

Less than six paces later she was hauled from her feet and slung unceremoniously over the slave's shoulder. She kicked and wriggled, which efforts earned her a hard slap direct to her upturned rump.

"I told you to stay put. Try that again, and I shall take a switch to your pretty arse, lady."

Brynhild emitted a silent screech of outrage into the gag. How dare he manhandle and threaten her? She would see him dangling from a rope for this. She would see him whipped, and, and…

The wind was knocked out of her when Taranc deposited her back on the ground in exactly the same spot he had left her. Now he towered over her, his hands on his hips.

"Allow me to be plain since I wish there to be no misunderstanding between us. You are coming with me. You will be silent, and you will be cooperative. If you cause me no problems we shall get along quite well, but I will tolerate no disobedience from you. You have been warned. Further attempts to thwart me will result in you being punished, and a decent switching will be just the start of it. Do not test me on this, Brynhild. You *will* regret it."

Gagged as she was Brynhild could not reply, though she hoped her eyes would convey her outrage and give this ruffian pause. If he let her go, now, she promised herself, she might yet allow him to live.

He merely shook his head in amusement. "Ah, such temper. Still, I suppose I cannot blame you. Do you understand what I have said to you?"

She narrowed her eyes and glared at him.

"A nod will suffice. Do you understand the consequences should you cross me again, or disobey my instructions?"

Still she refused to grant him the satisfaction.

He cupped her chin in his hand and lifted her face up to meet his gaze. "If you require a demonstration of my power over you, I shall be delighted to oblige you. A few strokes of my belt should do the job."

He could not be serious. Even as she told herself this, he was unfastening the leather band about his waist. Horrified, Brynhild wriggled back and away from him. The thrall paused in his actions.

"A nod will suffice," he repeated.

Brynhild slowly bowed her head.

Taranc picked up the leather bag and peered inside again. He pulled out a cloak, which he slung across his shoulders. Brynhild blinked. Surely that was her brother's garment. Yes, she was certain of it for she had woven the fabric herself. How had this thrall managed to steal it from Ulfric?

Taranc hung the bag over his right arm and with his left he reached to aid Brynhild to her feet again. "Come."

His hand on her elbow was sufficient to propel her through the trees at his side. The night was cold and she was glad of the thick cloak she had thought to pull on before leaving the sanctuary of her brother's longhouse. How much further would they go? She may have a warm cloak, but her shoes were not the stout boots she would normally choose to hike through the forest.

After just a few minutes the thrall paused again. This time he stood, his head tilted to one side, listening. Suddenly his features broke in a wide grin and he released her elbow to stride into the trees. Despite his threats of a few minutes ago Brynhild contemplated making a run for it again, but had not the time to do so before the man returned, this time leading a horse.

Not just any horse. This was one of Ulfric's, a fine little mare, swift and dainty. The animal was saddled, and her hooves were wrapped in thick sacking to muffle the sound they made.

"Lady, we have a long ride ahead of us. You will mount quickly, if you please…" He beckoned her to approach him.

Brynhild retreated, all talk of switching and punishment flying from her head. If she got on that horse he would have her. They would soon be miles away, she might never see her home again. She could not, would not…

As though seeing the dismay in her features, the thrall's expression softened. "I have promised you will not be harmed, as long as you obey. Come, we have a long journey ahead."

Brynhild had no desire to embark upon any journey with him, long or short. She shook her head and backed away, ready to run again.

Taranc was swift. He tossed the reins of the horse over a branch and lunged for her. In moments Brynhild found herself upended over his knee as he planted himself down on a fallen tree truck. Her wool skirts were about her waist, the chilly air caressing her naked bottom.

"I promised you a switching. I had hoped to delay the need, at least for a while since you will now be extremely uncomfortable when you do mount the horse. Still, it cannot he helped, I daresay. You may consider yourself fortunate that I foresaw this eventuality and prepared a switch or two in readiness. I am sure you would not have relished being forced to lie here, your lovely bottom bared, whilst I waste half the night searching out a suitably supple branch."

Brynhild squirmed in his grip, wriggling and writhing, spluttering her fury into the infernal gag. None of it did any good since the thrall simply tightened his grip by wrapping his arm about her waist and pinning her flailing legs under one of his. There was a whistle as the switch rent the frigid air, then pain exploded across Brynhild's right buttock.

For a moment she forgot to breathe. Her bottom was aflame, surely. She went rigid, flexing, clenching in readiness for the next stroke.

Taranc did not keep her waiting. Three more slivers of fire snaked across her bottom, each worse than the one before. She gasped and whimpered in shocked disbelief. She had never been punished thus before, not even as a child. Her father had been indulgent with his only daughter, her mother stern but never resorting to use of the switch or even a mild spanking.

Almost as quickly as the spanking had started, it ceased. Taranc did not let her up, but he did lay the switch down on the ground. His palm caressed her quivering buttocks as though to smooth away the hurt as Brynhild lay motionless under his hand. As he stroked her bottom she was seized with a sudden urge to part her thighs. She resisted it, of course.

She would never willingly spread her legs for a man.

"Are you ready to ride with me now, Brynhild?"

His voice was low and soft, seductive even. Despite her terror, Brynhild found herself nodding again.

He helped her to her feet and over to the horse. The rough wool of her skirts rubbed against her freshly punished bottom as she stumbled beside him, her eyes blurred with tears of rage, fear, and pain. He cupped his hands to assist her up into the saddle and she winced as her buttocks made contact with the unrelenting leather. The bastard actually smirked as she shifted and tried to find a comfortable position. He leapt up onto the mare behind her and reached around for the reins.

"So, let us be on our way," he announced pleasantly. "You may get some sleep if you are able and I do advise it. You have a difficult time ahead, my lovely she-Viking."

CHAPTER NINE

Taranc sought the correct word to describe the woman in his arms. He settled upon brittle. Lady Brynhild, the proud Viking lady, sister to the Jarl of Skarthveit sat the horse with a stiffness he could not entirely attribute to the switching he had dealt her, though without doubt that played its part. She held her body straight, her spine rigid and unyielding as she refused to lean back against him. It was as though she could not bring herself to be in contact with his body, to touch him at all.

He flattened his lips in irritation. She would learn the hard way that comfort should be had where it might be found. In her situation, he was the only source and she would do well to remember that.

They rode in tense silence for perhaps an hour. It was Taranc's intention to travel through the night and, with luck, reach Hafrsfjord shortly before first light. The fishing vessel promised by Ulfric should be waiting for them in the small harbour there and he saw no cause to doubt it. The Jarl had been as good as his word up to now. Taranc hoped to enter the port under cover of darkness and put to sea before the inhabitants of Hafrsfjord were up and about. The fewer who saw them, the better.

This evening had gone more or less to plan thus far. He had bargained on spirited resistance by Brynhild and she had not disappointed him. It was to be hoped that the sore bottom that must pain her with every jolt and roll of the mount beneath her would be sufficient reminder of the perils of crossing him again. They would see. He was not averse to issuing a further demonstration of his mastery of her fate should that prove necessary.

He might have been able to dredge up a little more in the way of sympathy for the Viking's plight were it not for the many tales he had heard of Brynhild's ill treatment of Fiona. Though he knew her to be mean of spirit and malicious, Taranc could not help believing that the taciturn woman who now shared his mount might shatter into a thousand pieces at the slightest jolt. She had a quick temper and would think nothing of venting it upon those who could not defend themselves. She was not deserving of his compassion.

Still, this night's work was not her punishment. It was not for him to seek retribution for the hurts done to Fiona. Her banishment from her home was the forfeit she had paid and he had no cause to compound Brynhild's misery.

"You should sleep, lady. I will make sure you do not fall." A decent enough offer, in Taranc's view, given the circumstances.

Brynhild did not favour him with so much as a reply. She continued to stare straight ahead, her shoulders stiff and unmoving, her silence unrelenting even though he had removed the gag once they were mounted and on their way again and she was free to speak should she so desire.

Taranc shrugged. She might please herself.

Another hour passed. Hafrsfjord still lay a good four hours' ride away, but they were making brisk progress and Taranc saw no reason not to pause for a bite to eat and a mouthful of the fine ale supplied by Ulfric. He reined in the horse and offered his hand to Brynhild. "We shall halt here for a few minutes."

She ignored his offer of assistance and grabbed the front of the saddle with her bound hands before slithering down to the ground. Her legs seemed to crumple beneath her and she landed heavily upon her knees.

Foolish woman. Taranc kept his opinion to himself as he dismounted and took her elbow to help her up. She would have shaken off his hand but he did not permit that, holding onto her until he was certain she was steady. Then he slung the reins over a tree branch and walked around the mare to access the bag he had slung from the saddle. A hunk of cheese and a lump of bread was not the finest fare he might have hoped for, but it would do. He withdrew the food and returned to offer it to Brynhild.

Or he would have, were she still where he had left her.

For fuck's sake! He spun around, scanning the darkness. The woman could barely stand, how had she managed to make a break for it, and in silence? She had had but a few scant seconds, and—

There! The snap of a twig betrayed her direction. Taranc had the moonlight to thank for the brief glimpse of a slender shape slipping between the trees some fifty or so paces from where he stood, but it was enough. He stuffed the bread and cheese back into the bag and set off after her at a dead sprint.

He had to acknowledge that she was determined in her attempt to elude him. Brynhild abandoned all semblance of stealth once she heard his pursuit and ran as though her life depended upon it. He did not really blame her, it probably seemed so to her. Still, he had warned his captive what would be the result if she tried such foolishness again. She would live to bitterly regret this ridiculous impulse, but first he had to get his hands upon the recalcitrant wench.

Had her wrists not been bound he had no doubt she would have been harder to catch. Not impossible, but harder. The Viking's long legs ate up the ground and she leapt over fallen trees and roots with an agility he envied. Still, Taranc was gaining upon her and it was but a matter of time. His lungs burned as he closed the distance, but he managed to come within an arm's length.

"Stop, lady. Give it up and I shall not hurt you. Much."

"May you rot in your own filth, Celt," came the panting response.

So be it. Taranc found one final burst of speed and hurled himself at the woman in front of him. He caught a handful of her cloak. It was enough to tip her off balance and she lost her footing. The pair tumbled to the ground, rolling over and over in the undergrowth as Taranc sought to subdue the wriggling, screaming demon he had grabbed. She landed a decent kick to his shin. Taranc grunted, muttered a curse she could not possibly understand despite her passable Gaelic. Brynhild's struggles became more furious, more desperate. She clawed at his face with her bound hands, screaming at the top of her lungs.

How did she still have the breath to screech like that? It was all he could do to gasp out a half-decent obscenity.

Taranc had had enough. He grasped the leather strap he had used to bind her wrists and dragged her hands above her head, pinning them there. His weight was on top of her, one leg slung across her hips to pin her to the ground. He used his free hand to cover her mouth. The bloody screaming had to stop.

Brynhild went still. No, not still, he amended. She froze. Where one moment he was wrestling with a woman crazed, the next he could have been lying on top of a corpse. Brynhild was stiff, absolutely rigid, not even breathing as far as he could tell. He instantly removed his hand from her mouth and was relieved to detect the light feathering of her breath on his fingers.

Taranc leaned his weight on his elbow but did not relinquish his hold on her hands. He leaned over her and gazed into her face, and was stunned by what he saw there.

Terror. Blind, abject terror. Her eyes were dark, the irises almost completely obliterated by her pupils, but he believed she no longer saw him. Her nostrils flared, her lips were parted, and he could swear her teeth were chattering. Gone was the angry, resentful, spitting and fighting she-cat of just moments ago to be replaced by a frightened, beaten girl.

It was exactly as before, on the day he had saved her from being trampled by the horse.

Taranc released his grip on her wrists and rolled off her. Still Brynhild did not move. She appeared paralysed by her fear of him, unable to defend herself or even plead for her life.

Taranc knelt at her side. "I am sorry... I did not mean..."

She flinched as though he struck her.

"Brynhild, you are safe. I shall not harm you."

Her breath came in shallow gasps now, and the blue of her eyes slowly returned as panic receded. Still she stared straight up, at some point beyond Taranc. She started to shake so he dragged off his cloak and wrapped it around her although she already wore her own. She had reason to fear him, to fear the spanking she must know to expect, but this reaction went far beyond that and he did not believe it to be feigned. Brynhild was in a place of her own imagining, a place he did not comprehend where she had found danger and terror and helplessness. He had caused this, and he did not care for it at all.

"Brynhild? Little Viking? Speak to me. Please." He lowered his tone, his words gentle as he sought to coax her back into the here and now. The merest hitch of her breath betrayed that she heard him. "Brynhild, I shall help you to sit up. Is that all right?"

He did not know why, but it seemed important to seek her permission before he touched her again.

"May I?"

She closed her eyes, and she nodded. Just once, but it was clear enough. He slid his hand under her shoulders and eased her from the ground. "Take deep breaths. We shall wait here until you are ready to move."

He was in a hurry. Hafrsfjord beckoned. Why had he

promised her all the time she might need?

Her eyes remained closed and she lifted her hands to cover her face. Brynhild leaned forward, her head bowed now, and her shoulders started to shake. She was weeping.

At a loss, Taranc acted on instinct again. He wrapped her in his arms and turned her to face his chest. He half-expected her to struggle, to try to escape his hold but her resistance was entirely spent. Instead, she scrambled toward him as though she sought to crawl right inside his rough tunic. Her sobs became louder, more despairing, wrenching from her as the pent-up grief poured forth. Taranc just held her, stroking her hair and muttering words of comfort that he doubted she would comprehend as he rocked her back and forth.

At last the anguished weeping subsided. Brynhild sniffled and gulped, her body shuddering as she fought to regain control. Taranc willed himself to be patient and was rewarded when, eventually, she turned her tear-ravaged face toward him.

"I am sorry. I do not know what happened. I... I..."

"Hush," he murmured into her hair. "It is all right."

"But—"

"We shall talk, if you wish it. And soon. But now, we go to Hafrsfjord."

Her eyes widened in surprise. "H-Hafrsfjord? But, why?"

"Is it not obvious, little Viking? We need a boat. We are going to the land of the Celts."

She shook her head. "I cannot. No, it is impossible. My brother will come, he will stop you, and—"

Taranc laid one finger over her lips, the merest of pressure, just enough to halt the flow of words. "We go to Hafrsfjord. Come."

He got to his feet and extended his hand to her. This time Brynhild accepted his assistance and fell into step at his side as he led the way back through the woodland to where the mare waited patiently. Given the episode in the forest

Taranc was tempted to forgo the promised spanking. The last thing he needed was another emotional outpouring. His mind was made up when Brynhild regarded him from beneath her still-damp lashes.

"You will beat me again. Because I tried to escape."

It was a statement. She fully expected him to carry out his threat. Not to do so, whatever the reason, would be unwise.

Taranc inclined his head. "I shall, yes." He glanced about them. "You will lean against that tree, over there, and raise your skirts."

"The switch?"

He nodded. "Six strokes this time. I shall increase your punishment by two strokes every time I have cause to discipline you so you might do well to bear that in mind."

"You do not frighten me, Celt."

No? Taranc thought otherwise but made no comment. He found her defiance in the face of a switching somewhat reassuring. She would accept this well enough.

He gestured with his thumb. "The tree, lady. Let us be done with this and on our way."

Obedient as a lamb now, she moved to position herself before the tree he indicated then turned to regard him over her shoulder. "You will require your cloak back. Or should I say, my brother's cloak."

Taranc offered her a tight smile as he extracted a prepared switch from the half dozen or so he had stashed in his saddlebag. "A fine garment, lady. Your work?"

"Of course." She removed it from her shoulders and offered it to him.

Taranc took it and set it to one side, then accepted Brynhild's own cloak which she duly unfastened and slid from her body. He folded that and laid it on top of his own. "Can you manage?" He had not untied her hands.

"I believe so. You will require me to lift my skirt?"

"Naturally. A switching is always on the bare buttocks. I find it more effective that way and I would not wish you to

119

harbour any illusions regarding your future obedience."

"You are a barbarian."

"Aye, if you say so." He swung the switch through the air and noted the widening of her eyes at the high-pitched whistle it made as it rent the air. "And I am a barbarian in a hurry, so if you would be so kind…?"

Brynhild offered him a hostile glare, then she turned to face the tree. She bent to grasp the hem of her skirt and wasted no time in dragging the fabric up and around her waist. Her apparent lack of modesty surprised Taranc, not least given her state of near collapse earlier when she found herself lying beneath him on the ground, but he chose not to analyse this conundrum quite yet.

Brynhild managed to secure the fabric of her skirt by tucking it under the band of woven wool that served as a belt, though a fold of it did dangle down, partly obscuring her right buttock. This would not do.

"Allow me." Taranc stepped forward and lent his aid, securing the skirt at the back as well as in the front as Brynhild had done. Satisfied, he stepped back. "Six strokes. Are you ready?"

"I do not understand this. What good does this do? Why do you waste time here, punishing me for doing what you must have known I would, when you could press on to Hafrsfjord?"

Taranc paused. "You Vikings are not averse to meting out a spanking when it is deserved. I know your brother to be of that persuasion and I hardly think you have escaped such chastisement your entire life, Brynhild."

"No, not even when I was a child, though perhaps, on occasion my mother considered it. Now, as a woman grown, it makes no sense."

"It makes perfect sense. You and I find ourselves thrown together by circumstances. I do not know how long we shall be in one another's company, but I expect it to be a while. Your obedience and submission are vital to my safety, and did you but know it, to yours also. This way, if you cross me, I shall punish you, and then the matter will be closed. I have no wish to constantly drag up past hurts, and a spanking puts an end to the matter. We need never speak of your wrongdoing again. You will be forgiven."

"Why would I desire your forgiveness?" She glared at him over her shoulder as she snarled the words. "You are a Celt, a thrall, a runaway slave. You will be recaptured soon enough, and—"

Taranc's patience was at an end, and the infernal woman did have a point. He had precious little time to waste. "You may not want my forgiveness, but you shall have it anyway. Once you have taken your spanking. Are you ready?"

"Just do it, Celt." She managed to inject a note of real venom into her tone. His rebellious Viking was back.

She hissed when the first stroke landed across her right buttock. Taranc paused to allow her to regain her composure, admiring the faint stripe that bloomed across her pale flesh. The four wheals from earlier already decorated her pretty arse and he would take care to avoid the exact same spots. He selected his next target.

Brynhild let out a squeal when he laid the switch on her left cheek, but she did not move.

She managed not to actually scream until he reached number five. Taranc was impressed. The sixth stroke landed across the backs of both thighs and he knew it hurt. She screamed again and danced on the spot.

"Stand still. I have finished, but you will remain as you are while I ready the horse."

She leaned forward to rest her forehead against the bark of the tree but offered no protest. Taranc allowed himself a few moments to admire the glorious sight of her punished bottom, the stripes he had placed there crisscrossing each other, a deep, sensual pink in contrast with her milky skin.

This Viking might consider herself his enemy, and he supposed she was right. Still, he could appreciate a beautiful woman when her bottom was bared to him.

It did not take him long to ready the mare. He returned

to where Brynhild waited, her shoulders bent as she gripped the tree. Was she crying?

Taranc resisted the temptation to explore the stripes, to feel the raised ribbons beneath his fingers and to listen to her gasps of pleasure or pain as he did so. He would not touch her unless she gave her permission. Instead he made short work of releasing her skirt from its confines, front and back and dropped the fabric to cover her lower body once more.

"Ready?"

"No," she snapped.

So, not crying, then. "I thought as much. Surely we do not need to repeat this exercise so soon?"

"I hate you." She turned and marched toward the little mare.

Did she? She had every reason to, and as little as an hour ago Taranc would not have cared one way or the other. He followed her back to the horse and was both surprised and pleased when she allowed him to assist her into the saddle. He handed her back her cloak, then swung up behind her.

"You might find it more comfortable to rest on my thighs."

She said nothing, but adjusted her position as he suggested.

"So, my Viking. Onward to Hafrsfjord." Taranc nudged the horse with his heels and they were in motion again.

· · · · · · ·

The mare was a sturdy little beast and maintained a steady canter despite the double weight upon her back. Taranc was not called upon to remind the animal of the need for haste and soon he considered the time he had lost in the forest recovered. Thus reassured, his thoughts turned to the incident that puzzled him. He turned over the sequence of events in his mind, though why he should entertain any real interest in the cause of his captive's extreme distress was somewhat beyond him. The Viking woman possessed no such finer feelings nor compassion, and it was these failings that had led to her kidnapping. She was not deserving of his sympathy or concern. He should just leave it and concentrate his efforts on making certain they both left these Godforsaken frigid shores with all the speed he could muster.

But he could not. She had been fine, or what passed for fine with Brynhild Freysson, right up until he had lunged for her and brought her to the ground. That was when everything had changed.

"What happened, back there?" He opted for the direct approach.

"I do not know what you mean." Her spine stiffened and she continued to stare straight ahead.

"Liar. What happened, back there in the forest? You were terrified. Of me?"

"I have told you, I am not afraid of you, Celt."

"Yet you were. It was there, in your face, your body. You were paralysed by fear. Then you sobbed as though your heart was broken."

"Do I not have the right? I have been abducted from my home, beaten, threatened. I am entitled to be upset."

"It was more than that. I caused your terror, or so it seemed, but did it really have anything to do with me at all?"

"No!" She turned to peer up at him over her shoulder. "It had nothing whatsoever to do with you. Not then, not now."

He tried another tack. "I would wish to avoid causing you such distress again. Perhaps if I knew—"

"It is not your concern, Celt." Her tone hardened and she became even more rigid in his arms. Brynhild was again the haughty Nordic lady and she drew that imaginary cloak of superiority about her as she lifted her chin to gaze at the route ahead. "If you wish not to distress me, then release me. Allow me to return to my home, my family. Continue on to your homeland if you are determined upon it, and if you are able to secure a boat, which I doubt will prove as simple as you imagine. But leave me here."

Taranc sighed. He was getting nowhere on this but he did not consider the matter closed. Far from it.

They passed a large outcrop of flat rocks, then a tree that had been struck by lightning. Taranc recalled the landmarks described by Ulfric and knew that they were nearing Hafrsfjord. The sky had not yet started to lighten, but it would in the next hour or so. He preferred to arrive at the port just before dawn if he could manage it, before the townspeople started to rise, but with the full day's sailing ahead of them.

Taranc nudged the mount to a full gallop and covered the remaining five miles until the rooftops of the small port came into sight at the foot of the next hill they crested. He reined in the horse and strained his eyes in the thinning gloom to pick out what he sought.

Yes. There. A small fishing boat was moored at a jetty just outside the main town. The craft bobbed on the water, sails rigged and ready to go. Taranc turned the horse in the direction of the boat and urged the mare forward again.

CHAPTER TEN

Brynhild perched in the saddle before her captor, shifting her weight as best she might to protect her punished bottom. The Celt helped by drawing her up onto his lap and allowing her to wedge her foot under his leg to provide the anchorage she needed. His arm was about her waist and he held her secure. She would not fall, however hard the mare galloped. After the delay in the forest he seemed intent upon making up the lost time, and for her part Brynhild had abandoned any attempt to thwart him in that.

This was not to say that she was at ease, however. Quite the reverse. Her head whirled. She was confused, baffled, and she did not care for the sensation at all.

Worse, she was scared. Not of the arrogant, slack-witted oaf who thought to carry her off and believed he might subdue her by taking a switch to her bottom. She had not the slightest doubt she would find a way to elude Taranc before much longer, definitely once they arrived in Hafrsfjord. Did he think no one there would recognise the sister of the Jarl of Skarthveit? That none would rush to her aid should she scream for help? The Celt was a fool, and he would likely die for his stupidity.

No, Brynhild did not fear the Celt. She feared herself.

What had happened to her, back there in the forest? One moment she was running for her life, ready to fight if she must and die in the attempt. The next she found herself prone on the forest floor, the stars swirling above her in the inky blackness, the weight of a strong, determined male pressing her into the ground. In those moments, she had been a girl again, helpless, vulnerable, desperate to escape the man who pinned her to the ground but unable to lift so much as a finger in her own defence. His voice grated in her ears, harsh and guttural, demanding, accusing. Her nostrils were filled with his odour, so strong she could almost taste it. He was real. He was here…back, after all these years and she was in his power all over again.

Brynhild gave herself a mental shake. It had been a hallucination, a nightmare … there was no other explanation. She did not confuse the spectre from her childish imaginings with the thrall who now held her captive. But this Taranc had been there. He had been beside her when she emerged from the horror, his voice soft, reassuring her, coaxing her back into the present where the earth did not shake, her wits did not betray her, and her courage was intact. He had held her while she wept, saying nothing, demanding nothing, simply waiting for her to return to her senses. And now he asked if he was the cause of her breakdown.

As if he held that level of power over her. No man did, or ever would again.

The Celt sought an explanation. He was not the only one, and he, too, would be disappointed. Even if she did properly understand what had happened, and if she had wished to confide in this escaped slave, Brynhild did not believe she could have found the words to tell him. And she did not choose to. It was private, her secret, buried even deeper this time and she would never allow that vision from her past to emerge again.

Thus fortified, Brynhild turned her thoughts to the rest. An idiot he may be, but this Taranc had planned his escape well and she had no notion how he might have accomplished that. She knew for a fact that he, along with all the thralls, had spent the entirety of the previous day toiling on the beach. The harbour was coming along slowly but her brother was determined to make as much progress as they might before the winter halted the work. At no stage, as far as she could work out, had this man had any opportunity to creep into their settlement and steal a horse, even less lead the beast away and conceal it in the surrounding woods. He had somehow managed to steal Ulfric's finest cloak, and that did not leave her brother's chamber except for when he wore it. Had Taranc entered their longhouse?

He had food too, and probably other supplies in that leather sack he slung from the saddle. Did he have blankets in there, purloined from Brynhild's own stores? Weapons? Had he stolen other valuables from Skarthveit? Coin that he might use to bribe a boatman?

It was not possible that he had achieved all of this unaided so he must have had an accomplice. Fiona. It had to be. Who else? So much for Ulfric's unshakable trust in his little bed-slave.

The other part of the puzzle concerned her own presence here. Why had the escaping slave taken her? It would have been far simpler, and safer, to make his bid for freedom alone. It was not as though she had done anything to aid him, quite the reverse. She had complicated everything, surely. He must intend to offer her for ransom, or in exchange for his betrothed. Or perhaps she was a hostage, offering him some semblance of security if he should be challenged. It had to be that, nothing else made sense.

Satisfied that she had arrived at the truth of the matter, Brynhild turned her thoughts to planning her escape. She would demand that the fishermen of Hafrsfjord come to her aid and she had no doubt that they would. This Taranc would soon enough find himself back in her brother's slave barn. If he was lucky.

The Celt tugged on the reins and brought their mount to a halt. The harbour of Hafrsfjord lay at the foot of the hill, the surface of the sea glittering as the backdrop. It was a fine night, chilly but not overly cold and the next day promised to be fair enough. Within the next hour or so the people of the port would begin to stir and go about their business. That would see an end to this Celt's tyranny over her.

She tilted her chin up and drew the shreds of her dignity about her as they descended into the coastal town.

· · · · · · ·

The Celt headed for the small fishing vessel, which was moored at a distance from the rest. Brynhild recognised the craft at once. It was owned by Eileifr, one of Ulfric's own karls and unless she was very much mistaken that was he, seated on the deck as though he was expecting them. The fisherman got to his feet at their approach and leapt onto the quay.

"Eiliefr?" Taranc murmured the name, keeping his voice low so as not to alert others. Their mare's hooves were still muffled and although Brynhild cast her gaze wildly from left to right she saw no one else. No matter, Eileifr was her brother's man and he would have to do.

"You know me?" she demanded.

"Aye, lady," confirmed the fisherman, though his eyes were on Taranc.

"All is in readiness? We may leave at once?" Taranc addressed Eiliefr, and both ignored Brynhild.

"Aye, within minutes. You have the money?"

"I do." Taranc reached into the saddlebag and withdrew a purse. Coins jangled within.

"Ten pieces of silver, the Jarl said."

"It is all there. You may count it." Taranc tossed the purse to the man who tipped the contents into his hand.

Seemingly satisfied, he nodded once to the Celt. "Bring

her aboard. We shall be away before first light."

Taranc dismounted from the horse and reached up to help Brynhild down. Stunned, she slid down into his arms, then staggered on the rough cobbles of the quayside.

What was happening? The man said he knew her, yet was still prepared to see her taken aboard his fishing vessel by an escaping slave and carried away from these shores. Worse, he had been *paid* to take them, and the Jarl was aware of the bargain.

Ten pieces of silver, the Jarl said. At last it all fell into place.

Ulfric had made this deal. He had provided the payment, and no doubt the rest—supplies, horse, his own cloak! There had been no other accomplice. In all likelihood, there had been no escape, really, since Ulfric had known all along what was intended and Taranc had his permission to be here in Hafrsfjord, embarking on the voyage home.

But the Celt had no right to abduct her. That was impossible and she would die before she would go meekly with him. Whatever deal had been struck between her brother and this man, Ulfric would never have countenanced such disloyalty, such wickedness. They had quarrelled lately, that was true, but he was her brother and he loved her. Surely Eileifr must realise that this was all wrong.

She turned to the fisherman. "You must help me. My brother will reward you, he—"

Eileifr had the grace to shuffle before her and found it necessary to inspect his shoes most carefully, but he made no move to come to her aid. The karl dropped the coins back into the purse and tied it to his belt, then vaulted back over the rail to land on the deck of his boat. "If you can manage the lady, I shall get us under way. The tide is good, and the wind fair. We will make good time."

"But—"

Brynhild's protest was cut off as Taranc stepped forward. *Was that compassion she detected in his green-eyed gaze? Why? Why should he feel sorry for her?*

Taranc took her elbow and urged her toward the boat. "I shall lift you aboard, lady. Do not worry, I shall not drop you."

"No!" She shook off his hand and backed away. "My brother will kill you for this. Both of you. Are you quite mad?"

"Best you keep her quiet. The Jarl wants no fuss. He was most definite on that. Get her away under cover of darkness, he said, and no one else is to know." Eileifr busied himself loosening ropes in readiness for setting sail. "Let's not be wasting time now."

Brynhild gaped, open-mouthed as the full, horrific reality of her situation finally dawned. Ulfric *had* planned this, all of it. Her brother had arranged everything. No wonder their departure from Skarthveit had all seemed so easy for this Celt, so well-prepared. Her disappearance had probably not even been discovered yet, and she could be certain that Ulfric would not be sending men galloping in the direction of Hafrsfjord to rescue her. He would direct the search elsewhere whilst she was spirited away with his full knowledge and consent.

She would never see her home again. Her family, her nephew... Would they even know what had happened to her? Could she ever get word to those she loved and who would grieve for her?

She backed away from Taranc, but he pursued her. She turned to run, but he was faster. He slung her over his shoulder and stepped over the rail onto the roiling deck, then set her on the bench in the stern of the boat. "It is a shock, I know. We shall talk later. For now, you are to sit here and keep still." He did not even wait for her response before he strode the length of the vessel to lend his assistance to Eiliefr's efforts. In moments the craft would be away, and with it her last hope of seeing those she loved again would be gone.

Brynhild glanced over her shoulder. The quay was already three or four feet away, but surely she could leap that distance. Taranc was keen to be out of the port before the town awoke, he would not come back for her, especially if she was standing in the middle of the harbour screaming fit to rouse the dead. She wasted no further time contemplating the matter; every second increased the distance she would have to jump to reach safety. Taranc's back was turned, she could do this.

Brynhild got to her feet and stood on the bench. From there it took a large stride to bring her teetering onto the rail at the bow. She balanced precariously for a moment as the craft dipped and rocked under her feet. Could she?

A shout behind her decided the matter. She bent her knees and launched herself for the receding shore.

She might have made it. Brynhild was convinced she would have made it but for the sudden lurch of the boat that meant she not only had to jump a distance of several feet, but she had to gain something in height also. It was too much, and she hit the water with a resounding splash.

The murky blackness closed over her head. It was cold, colder than she had ever been. Instinct demanded that she fight, that she struggle for her life and she did so now. Just once, she broke the surface and gulped in a lungful of salty air. She caught sight of the two men peering down at her from the stern of the boat, then she sank again. This time she could not find a way back to the surface however hard she fought. She kicked her booted feet, thrust her still bound hands upward, but could grasp nothing but empty water. Her lungs burned, her eyes stung. It was deep, much deeper than she had imagined, and so cold. So very, very cold...

A hand grasped hers. Then another. A face was before her, green eyes bore into hers.

Taranc. He had come into the water after her. Why? Brynhild closed her own eyes and allowed her body to go limp.

When next she prised her eyelids apart she was back on the deck of Eileifr's small boat. The sail was full, billowing

131

above her and the wind whipped across her shivering body. They were out at sea.

It was too late.

With a groan she rolled onto her side and without further ado cast up the contents of her stomach. At once Taranc was beside her.

"Welcome back aboard, lady. I trust your wetting has taught you the folly of attempting to fly."

"And I trust that Freya will grant me the strength to slay you in your bed one night, Celt."

"I shall bear that in mind, lady. Meanwhile, if you wish to survive your recent experience, I suggest you get out of those wet clothes before you take a fever. We can dry your skirt and tunic on the rail, and I have blankets here."

She glared at the yellow and blue weave and recognised it, naturally. More of her brother's largesse to this thrall, no doubt. Brynhild had never been so angry, so bitter. Never had she felt so utterly and thoroughly betrayed.

And so cold. Her teeth started to chatter as Taranc hauled her into a sitting position and released the leather strap that bound her wrists. She noted that he was himself bare chested, and his leggings were dripping wet, then she screeched in protest as he started to pull her tunic over her head.

"Leave me. What are you doing?"

"I am helping you, since you appear reluctant to help yourself. You will freeze in those wet clothes. Come now, be quick and you will soon be warm and dry."

Was he quite deluded? Perhaps the seawater had pickled such brains as he might possess. She would never be warm and dry again. In fact, she was perfectly convinced that nothing would ever be right again. Still, she did not resist when he released the buckle on her belt to loosen her tunic then tugged the garment over her head. The soaked clothing fell slapping to the deck beside her. He made similarly short work of her skirt, loosening the ties then rolling it down her legs. Her light woollen shift was all that remained. Brynhild glanced toward Eileifr but the man appeared much more interested in his sails than in her almost nude form. Still, she appreciated Taranc's consideration when he held up the blanket to shield her from the other man's view if not his own. Resigned to the inevitable, and tempted more than she was ready to admit by the prospect of the dry blanket, she dragged the remaining garment over her head and threw it at Taranc. It caught him on the shoulder than flopped onto the deck.

He chuckled and wrapped the blanket about her. "I shall allow you that display of temper, lady, but have a care in the future."

The Celt took his time. He arranged the blanket with care, ensuring that it enveloped her completely before he stood and turned his back to her. Before her startled gaze he peeled off his own leggings to reveal taut buttocks and finely sculpted thighs. Brynhild's mouth went dry as the Celt, gloriously and unashamedly naked, strolled the length of the boat to pick up another blanket. Brynhild recognised that one, also, and could not tear her gaze away as he wrapped it around his lower body. He spoke briefly with Eileifr then returned to crouch beside her.

"It is time to talk, lady. You have questions, I do not doubt. I shall do my best to explain."

Brynhild turned her gaze on him and uttered the one word that she could dredge up.

"Why?"

Taranc sighed and repositioned himself on the bench where he had initially placed Brynhild. He patted the seat beside him. "Come, lady. You might as well be comfortable."

Was he mad? Comfort was the least of her concerns. She shook her head and clutched the precious blanket closer to her chest.

"Are you warm enough? We have more blankets." He glanced up at the rapidly lightening horizon. "The sun will soon be fully risen and you will feel better then."

Brynhild seriously doubted that but allowed him his little fantasy. She repeated her question. "Why? Why did Ulfric do this? Do you know?"

Taranc nodded. "It was because of Fiona. You and she are not friends, I gather."

"Of course we are not," retorted Brynhild. "She is a thrall, my brother's bed-slave. Why would we be friends?"

"Allow me to rephrase that. You have treated Fiona as your enemy, since first she arrived in your longhouse. Is this not so?"

"The wench is insolent, and disobedient, and—"

"She and I were betrothed. Perhaps you have forgotten that."

"I—" Brynhild pressed her lips together. Of course she had known of this, he had said as much when they first met. Naturally, the Celt would take Fiona's side, even though the slave now warmed a Viking's bed.

"Yes, well, I thought you might prefer to bear that in mind, before you say much more about Fiona. Shall I continue?"

Brynhild nodded.

"There have been… incidents. A cold bath, I understand, if the chatter among your house thralls is to be believed, as well as numerous other insults and acts of meanness. You are not a kind mistress, Brynhild." His expression was grave, his deep green eyes chiding.

Brynhild bristled. What gave him the right to judge her? "I am stern, it is true. And I expect hard work from my house servants. Fiona was always difficult, always ready to make excuses, to… to…" She paused, tilted her chin back and met his gaze. "I run my brother's household, it is for me to decide how the house slave should be treated."

Taranc shrugged. "You tried to kill her."

Brynhild was dumbstruck. "Why would you say such a thing? I did not!"

"It is not I who say it. I was not there. Ulfric says it, and this is why he decided that it was no longer possible for you and Fiona to share a home. He fears for her. He believes you mean her real harm."

She shuffled away from him on her bottom, as far as she could go. Her back pressed against the planking that made up the hull of the vessel, her mouth opened and shut as Brynhild sought for words to rebut this nonsense. She was convinced that Ulfric had said no such thing, and certainly not to a slave.

"You lie."

He leaned forward, his forearms resting on his thighs. "There was an incident with the stocks, three nights ago, I gather. You had Fiona secured there and meant to leave her outside the entire night. She would have died of cold had your brother not returned and freed her."

Brynhild was incredulous. Of course she had heard that preposterous suggestion made, her brother had accused her but she had denied it at the time. Why was this Celt spouting the same ridiculous notion days later? "That is untrue. I did no such thing."

He appeared perfectly calm as he regarded her carefully before answering. "Ulfric says you did. He is convinced of it."

"Then Ulfric is mistaken. He would have come to realise that, eventually."

"He will not. Not now."

"But... this is ridiculous. Why would my brother believe such rubbish of me? He knows me, knows I would never stoop to such an act. I told him I was on my way back to her. He saw me, I was actually leaving the longhouse, I had my cloak on..."

"You decided to feign a rescue when you heard his horse."

"I did not hear his horse. I had no idea he was even at Skarthveit." Brynhild sat bolt upright now, her eyes locked on Taranc's cool, green gaze. For reasons she could not entirely fathom it was important to her that he, at least, believe her version of that night's events. "It is true I forgot to check on the wench. Njal was ill and I was worried for him. I sat beside his bed and for a while—a short while—I was distracted from my other responsibilities. I admit to that fault, but none of it was intentional. I left another thrall with her, Harald. It was his task to release Fiona after half an hour or so. I gave him instructions, he knew what was expected and I assumed he would obey me. I should have checked, I accept that, but I believed her to be safe. Certainly, I meant her no lasting harm."

The Celt furrowed his brow. "And this Harald confirms your story?"

Brynhild shook her head, her frustration almost choking her. "He was gone. I searched for him the next day but found no sign."

"That is... convenient."

"Is it? I hardly think so."

"And Njal? He could have told his father that you sat with him. Did he not do so?"

"He was asleep the entire time so he knew nothing of it. When he awoke the next morning his temperature was normal. I... I offered a goat to Freya and she interceded."

"So, no one but you knows about Harald. Or Njal?"

"Fiona knew. She knew that Njal was sick and she heard my instructions to Harald. She has lied to my brother, accused me falsely. And he has chosen to believe her rather than me."

"Fiona would not lie."

"Hah!" She waved a dismissive hand at him. "You would say that. You were to marry."

"Fiona would not lie, not about something so momentous. She told Ulfric that you tried to kill her."

"Then why is she not dead?" Brynhild spat the words at him. "Do I seem so inefficient to you, Celt? Do you not believe that, had I set my mind to do away with one insignificant slave, that I would have so spectacularly failed to carry out my intentions? That I would have relied on such a haphazard method, such a public method? How much more unreliable could it have been? Anyone might have passed by and set her free. And had I truly been intent upon murder would I have enlisted the help of another thrall, a potential witness to the act?" She paused again, her body shaking though it was with anger now, not the cold. "My brother should have known this. Ulfric should have known it was an accident, because if I had meant it I would *not* have failed."

CHAPTER ELEVEN

Taranc said nothing. He scrutinised the vehement features of the woman at his feet, could all but feel the heat of the crackling rage that coursed through her stiff frame. There was a familiarity to the set of her jaw, the determined glint in her deep blue eyes though he could not entirely place it. Of one thing he had no doubt, however. In that moment, he knew Brynhild Freysson spoke the truth.

He could not account for the misapprehension, but he did not doubt that it had been a mistake. Ulfric had got it wrong, Fiona too. Brynhild had her faults. No one could deny that and they were many, but attempted murder was not among them.

He stood and paced the length of the fishing boat, adjusted the blanket he had wrapped around his waist, then turned to view the fast disappearing shoreline of the Norse lands. What to do now? He could order Eiliefr to turn the vessel about and take her home, but he was not entirely certain the man would obey. Ten pieces of silver could be very persuasive. Even if the fisherman could be cajoled, Taranc was not prepared to return to Hafrsfjord as that would mean his own recapture and he had no intention of delivering himself back into slavery. He might set Brynhild

138

ashore elsewhere and leave her, but he could not be certain she would be able to make her way safely back to Skarthveit alone.

What reception might she expect when she got there? *If* she got there. Ulfric would be far from happy to see her. To all intents and purposes, Brynhild Freysson had no home to go back to.

And if, by some unlikely chance, she was able to convince her brother to allow her to remain, what would that mean for Fiona? Brynhild believed the Celtic slave to have lied to Ulfric, and that lie had cost Brynhild dear. She would not forgive it, and he had only to recall the glint of ruthless determination in the Norsewoman's eyes as she delivered the most powerful of reasons for accepting her word, to know that Fiona would never be safe from her now.

If Brynhild wanted to kill an enemy, she would. She would not fail. Fiona was now her enemy, of that there could be no doubt.

He drew in a long sigh and tilted his head back to peruse the heavens as though inspiration might be found there. Perhaps it might. Taranc made up his mind.

He returned to drop down on his haunches beside Brynhild.

"Very well, I accept your explanation. You are telling the truth. It was a misunderstanding. A dangerous one, and one which might have ended in tragedy, but I do believe you that it was not done on purpose."

"You do?" She eyed him with suspicion. "Why? Why would you believe me if my own brother would not?"

"Did you say to him what you just said to me? About not failing if you had truly set out to murder Fiona?"

"Of course I did not."

"Then you have your answer, lady. It is not a pleasant thought, I grant you, but I do believe you to be ruthless enough, and clever enough, not to fail at such an endeavour. Fiona lives, as you have pointed out, so..."

"You will take me home. I shall explain to Ulfric, again. He will believe me this time."

Taranc offered her a tight smile. "I am sorry, lady, for it is not quite so simple."

She narrowed her azure eyes. "Of course it is exactly so simple. Turn the boat around. Now."

He shook his head. "We cannot return. I would be recaptured and back to hauling rocks for Ulfric or some other Viking. This is not a prospect I am prepared to contemplate."

"I would tell them—"

"No, lady. We are not going back. You might convince Ulfric, or you might not. If you were to fail, he would not allow you to remain at Skarthveit. That much is obvious."

"I could go to my other brother, Gunnar. His settlement is to the north."

"You know the way? The location?" Taranc would be happy enough to consider a slight diversion. Perhaps this might offer a solution after all.

She shook her head. "I have never been there, but—"

"Lady, I am not about to spend a Nordic winter tramping across your land in search of your brother's village."

"You need not come."

"Do not even think of such madness. Alone, you would perish in the attempt."

"I would not. I—"

"Enough. You have been unjustly served, perhaps, though the dear Lord knows you contributed to the ill which has befallen you. That is of no matter now. You will come with me to Scotland, and—"

"I will not! I shall not. I refuse."

Taranc gestured about him, at the small vessel, the expanse of sea that surrounded them. "I hardly think you are in any position to refuse. You are aboard this boat, and we are bound for Scotland, so…" He shrugged. It was a pity, he supposed, and she had a right to resent the

140

circumstances in which she found herself. But it was done now, and they must make the best they might of the situation. "You should eat, and we have some fresh water on board. Then you might sleep for a while."

He rose to his feet, intending to seek out sustenance for his reluctant passenger. His own leggings were dangling from the rail, his leather belt in front of him on the bench. He picked up the belt and reached for the dagger he kept tucked in a small scabbard there. He would use it to slice off a few chunks of cheese for his captive.

She moved fast, faster than he expected, certainly. Brynhild's hand shot out from within the folds of the blanket. She grabbed the knife before he could get his hands on it, then she scrambled to her feet.

"Turn us about. Now. We return to Hafrsfjord or... or I shall kill the pair of you and sail the boat back myself."

Taranc and Eiliefr exchanged a look. They both knew she would fail. One woman, even with a knife, could not fell two grown men, one of them an escaped slave intent upon hanging on to his freedom and the other a Viking karl with every intention of living to enjoy the benefits of his newfound wealth. Even if she could subdue them, she had no more chance of successfully steering back into the port than she might sprout wings and take to the air.

"Brynhild, think." Taranc edged around in front of her outstretched arm, his eyes on the glinting blade. He always kept his weapon sharp. "This is madness. You cannot possibly—"

"Be quiet," she interrupted him. "Turn the boat about."

"No. We are going on to Scotland." He kept his tone low, so as not to alarm her further. Best if she were to see the folly of her actions and relinquish the weapon.

Brynhild scrambled to her feet, her actions awkward as she required her spare hand to anchor the edges of the blanket at her front. She glared at Taranc and jabbed the knife at him. Her actions were more desperate than threatening since several feet separated them still and she had no hope of drawing blood.

"Give me the knife." He held out his hand. "This will get you nowhere, and if I have to take that knife from you it will earn you a whipping you will never forget."

"You have no right to touch me, to threaten me. I am the Viking here, you are but a thrall, and—"

"My apologies, lady. I did not intend to threaten you." He ventured a pace forward, bringing him almost within range of the blade.

"Then you will return me to my home? Now?"

"That is not possible, as I have explained. And I did not threaten you. That was a promise."

"A promise? I—"

Taranc took advantage of her momentary surge of frustrated outrage to make his move. He lunged low and to her right, grasping the hem of the blanket and tugging it down, hard. Brynhild lost her slender grip on the fabric and it slithered to the deck to leave her standing naked before him. As she instinctively reached to cover herself, he leapt forward again to grab the wrist of the hand holding the knife and squeezed. Her fingers sprang apart and the knife rattled to the deck. Taranc kicked it toward Eileifr who calmly reached down and picked it up. The fisherman offered Taranc a casual nod as he returned to his sails.

Meanwhile Taranc had his work cut out as Brynhild fought him with all she had. She shrieked and wriggled and clawed at him, seeking, he was quite convinced, to put out both his eyes before she was done. She even sank her teeth into his forearm when an opportunity presented itself.

Despite Brynhild's determined efforts, the eventual outcome was never in doubt. Taranc wrestled her to the deck and pinned her wrists above her head with one hand. He was angry, his arm throbbed like a fucking demon and he had managed to lose his own blanket in the skirmish though that did not bother him overmuch. She might feel differently. He did not forget her extreme reaction when he had tackled her to the ground the previous night. He searched her hostile, contorted features for evidence of similar terrors but found none. Thus reassured, he allowed his far from disinterested gaze to roam the length of her, taking in the fullness of her perfectly upturned breasts topped with pretty pink nipples that tightened in the chill air. He considered taking one between his lips to taste the plump sweetness of it, but that would have to wait. He ventured further, admiring the softly curling blonde hair between her thighs, the long, shapely legs that were crossed tight at the thigh as though she might bar his entrance.

As well she might. He was no abuser of women. If she said 'no,' then…

With his free hand he swept the length of her pale blonde hair back from her face and offered her a tight smile.

"Let me go. Do not touch me…" Her voice hitched, panic starting to bubble forth.

He had expected as much. Taranc softened his features. "You are safe, lady, apart from the whipping you have earned, naturally."

Her eyes widened. "Wh-whipping. What do you intend to do?"

"We are at eight strokes, I believe, by my reckoning." He glanced over his shoulder. "We shall use the mast, I think…"

"The mast? What? You cannot—"

It was time to be firm, to assert his authority if they were to have any peace on this voyage. "Lady, you do not command here. I do, and I have already warned you of the consequences if you disobey or otherwise vex me. Eight strokes. Now, get up."

He released her wrists and rose to his feet. He did not miss the startled widening of her eyes when she found herself staring at his semi-erect cock, the darkening of her pupils as the implications of his arousal sank in. He could not help his response to her and was not about to apologise for it, but he did not need her to succumb to panic now. Taranc grinned at her as he retrieved the blanket and tied it around his waist again then offered her his hand to assist her up. She was not reassured. Brynhild shrank away from him, shaking her head. "No, please do not do this. I am sorry, I—"

"Up. Now." The sudden evaporation of her previous belligerence was not lost on him. Neither was her shock at the sight of his erection but Taranc was not entirely convinced. He would not put it past her to dissemble, to seek to manipulate him even now. He deliberately hardened his tone. "You may submit willingly, or not, but the end will be the same." He leaned down to offer his hand again.

Brynhild groped behind her for the blanket and managed to snag a corner of the fabric. She clasped it around her once more as she scrambled to her feet, ignoring his offer of assistance. Her chin tilted at a defiant angle as she glared at him, then eyed the mast with distaste. So much for her nervous apprehension and apparent contrition.

Taranc gestured to her to precede him to the mast where Eileifr waited with a length of narrow rope. Her steps slow, Brynhild did as he instructed, coming to a halt below the billowing sail. She looked up, then back over her shoulder at Taranc. "Shall I lean against it, then?"

"You will hug the mast, lady, and Eileifr, if you would be so good as to secure her wrists? Not too tight, but we must be sure she will not shift at an inopportune moment."

"That will not be necessary, I—"

"Eileifr." At Taranc's curt command the karl stepped forward and reached for Brynhild's wrists. She stepped away from him, her eyes blazing.

"Keep your hands off me. I will not permit this." She tucked her hands further within the folds of the blanket.

Taranc had heard enough. He leaned forward to murmur in her ear. "Ten, lady. And the count will increase with every act of defiance, every refusal to obey. Are you really so set on adding to your punishment? You will spend a great deal more time than you might care to imagine lashed to that mast if you do not have a care."

She spun to glower at him, and he could not miss the glisten of unshed tears. Whether it was her pride that suffered or genuine fear of the pain to come he did not know, but at last he believed the true Brynhild Freysson was starting to reveal herself. Now was the time to press his advantage. He nodded toward the mast. "Hug it, lady. And you will have no need of the blanket for the next little while."

She considered his words for several moments, then positioned herself before the mast and extended her arms about its girth. She did not yet relinquish the blanket. The colourful weave draped her slender shoulders as she leaned forward to rest her cheek on the smooth curve of the wood. She lowered her eyelids and gnawed on her lower lip with her teeth as Eileifr quickly tied her wrists together on the other side of the beam.

Yes, she was scared, and Taranc believed this was real. Her submission might be forced, but she recognised his power over her however much she might deplore it and had abandoned her attempts to resist, to refuse to cooperate. She might yet learn a valuable lesson this day.

Taranc took the blanket and tugged it away from her body. Brynhild flinched as the cool morning air caressed her naked back. She opened her eyes to meet his gaze, her expression fearful. "Please..." she mouthed.

Taranc moved in close and lifted the heavy length of her unbound hair that cascaded down her back. He draped it over her shoulder and on impulse bent to kiss the top of her head. "This will be quick, Brynhild. I promise. And you will come to no harm."

She closed her beautiful azure eyes again, and nodded.

Taranc wasted no time in retrieving his belt, which had been flung to the deck in the scramble for the knife. He removed the empty sheath and folded its length so he could grasp the metal buckle within his fist. He walked back to where his captive leaned against the solid wooden pole, her body shivering. The marks of her previous punishment still

145

streaked her pale buttocks, and Taranc believed he had never seen a sight more beautiful. Brynhild Freysson might be the most difficult, complicated, and frankly demanding woman he had ever encountered, but she was without doubt the most lovely. If their circumstances were different…

He gave himself a mental shake. The circumstances were not different. They were what they were—awkward, dangerous, and bloody inconvenient. He would do what must be done, and she would bear what she could not avoid. What came next he had not the faintest notion, but he would feel his way through this… somehow.

"Are you ready?"

Her lips tightened into a grimace. She made no further response.

"Ten strokes. I shall count. You may make all the din you like since we are far out of port and none but the gulls will hear you."

A single tear escaped the corner of her eye and snaked its way across her pale cheek. Despite her reluctance to embrace the mast a few minutes ago he noted that she gripped it like a devoted lover now.

The belt whistled through the air. Brynhild let out a startled yelp even before the leather connected with her quivering rump then danced on the spot as the stripe bloomed on her skin.

"One." Taranc shifted his stance to lay the next stroke a little lower and swung again.

"Two," he announced as Brynhild gasped and whimpered against the mast. She clung to the beam as though drawing comfort from its solid warmth.

"Three." He paused to allow her to take several much-needed breaths as she hopped from one foot to the other. Her bottom glowed red and he could almost feel the heat from where he stood.

"Are you all right?" He was impressed at her fortitude thus far, but felt compelled to ask even so.

Her answer was a tight nod and a flattening of her lips.

Her body was rigid, her punished buttocks clenching hard as she anticipated the next stroke.

"It is less painful if you soften your bottom," he advised.

"How do you know? Is this something you learnt from your betrothed? How often did you tie Fiona up and whip her naked bottom?"

A fair enough question, he surmised, though he considered it ill-judged of her to ask it right now. He was tempted to increase the punishment by a further two strokes but decided that might be unduly harsh. "No, I never had occasion to do so. I always found Fiona to be sweet-natured and compliant. You, lady, are an entirely different matter."

And privately, he thanked the sweet Lord for that.

"Four," he counted. "Five. Six. Seven."

On the eighth stroke Brynhild let out a high-pitched scream. Her bottom sported a dizzying array of bright red stripes, the lines raised and livid in the brightening morning light. She moaned softly between the strokes and he was glad he had not added more. She was close to her limit now.

"Two more, then we are done here. You can do this, my fierce little Viking."

She managed a quick nod, as though his confidence inspired her. Perhaps it did, and if so he would not let her down. The final two strokes would be delivered to her thighs, and would hurt more than the rest. This was where her lesson would be learnt, where the difference would be made. He intended her to remember this day's work.

"Nine."

Brynhild screeched at the top of her lungs as the leather wrapped itself around both her thighs. "You bastard, that hurts so much. I cannot... No more... Stop. *Stop!*"

Taranc did not stop. Neither did he draw out the agony. He swung one last time and dropped the final stroke in exactly the same place. Brynhild screamed again, clawing and grabbing at the mast as though she might climb up it to escape him. Her shoulders shook, her sobs were noisy and gulping and her breath came in ragged, tortured gasps.

Taranc tossed the belt to the deck and moved in close to wrap his arms about the shivering form.

Brynhild went motionless, though she still wept. He lifted her hair to kiss her neck, the delicate spot just below her ear. She did not resist the intimacy, nor did she draw away when he pressed his lower body against hers.

"We are done. You are forgiven and you have survived."

She shook her head, her eyes still closed. Tears streamed across her ravaged cheeks. "It will never be done, never be over. It is not enough to survive."

Taranc paused, puzzled. Did she mean the whipping, or had her thoughts fled elsewhere? "Brynhild…?"

"It hurts. It hurts so much…"

He flattened his palm against the scorching flesh of her bottom. The heat permeated his hand and he rubbed gently. Brynhild sighed and he fancied that her tight body relaxed, though he may have been mistaken. He caressed her again as though he might smooth the hurt away and she writhed under his hand.

"Is that better?"

"Yes. A little…"

"Good." He repeated the motion, his palm tracing a circular path across her buttocks.

"Why are you doing this? You meant to hurt me."

"I did, and it is finished now. Now, I want you to feel safe and to know that you may trust me."

"I do trust you."

Did she? Certainly, in this moment, she gave every appearance that she might be coming to do so. Taranc decided to push his advantage. "Spread your legs for me, little Viking."

"Why?" Instantly she was on the alert, anxious and wary. She clamped her thighs together.

"You know that I am not immune to you. You saw as much. Now, I wish to discover if you are aroused by me. By this…" He drew his palm across her bottom again, pausing at the furrow between her buttocks but exploring no further.

"I… of course I am not. Why should I be?"

"May I, Brynhild?" He pressed his palm against her flaming flesh.

She shook her head. "Please, no…"

"You do trust me," he reminded her softly. "You said as much."

She rested her forehead against the unyielding wood and rolled her face from side to side. "This is different. I cannot."

"Why? What is it that you cannot do?"

"I cannot open my legs for a man. Not you, not any man. Never. Never again."

"Brynhild, tell me." There was more, much more, he knew it.

"You do not wish to know. You cannot. No one would."

"Tell me," he repeated. "Why can you not spread your legs for me?"

"I am worthless. Unlovable. I am cold, and… and…"

Taranc tightened his embrace about her. "You are many things, my Viking, but not cold. Never cold."

"You do not like me. You said as much."

Had he said that? He could not recall. Certainly he had not intended to create that impression. He might dislike many of the things she did, and in particular her cruelty to Fiona, but he could not take serious issue with the woman who now trembled in his arms.

"I do like you. How could I not? You are beautiful, and resilient, brave, and sensual. And we have already agreed that you are both capable and determined. You are a fine woman, Brynhild Freysson, who any man would be honoured to take as his wife, were you to have him."

"But not you."

"Me?" He paused to consider her unexpected remark. "I would wed you in a heartbeat, my lovely Viking, but I fear we would spend the rest of our lives tearing each other apart."

CHAPTER TWELVE

Brynhild sank to her knees, her arms still extended around the mast. She watched through a blur of tears as Taranc crouched beside her and untied her hands then rubbed her wrists to ease the numbness from her fingers. Then he wrapped the blanket about her shoulders again and tucked it tight in front of her. She frowned when he reached for her right ankle and started to tie the end of the rope around it.

"What are you doing?" She could no longer summon the energy required to struggle to escape his grasp.

"You are to remain bound, but I do not wish you to be uncomfortable. You will have sufficient rope to move about a little, though not to reach the rail, and your hands will be free."

"Why? I cannot escape." She surveyed the vast expanse of the sea. The coastline of her homeland had long since receded from view.

Taranc grinned at her, an expression she found both engaging and oddly annoying. "Let us not tempt fate, eh? You have proved yourself to be unpredictable, Brynhild. I believe Eileifr would be happier were you to be restrained."

The karl appeared quite unconcerned one way or the

other in Brynhild's view. He busied himself winding a narrow line around a reel, which he secured to the side of the boat before releasing the end to trail in the waves. The fisherman was obviously not about to waste the opportunity of returning home with a decent catch if he could, as well as Ulfric's coins.

"Your clothes are almost dry. You may get dressed soon."

"You are most kind, Celt." She could not prevent the waspish tone that crept in, but immediately regretted it. The dreaded belt still lay on the deck, just a couple of feet away.

His smile was sardonic. "Guard your tongue, lady. Let us have a truce, shall we? I believe you will find that arrangement more to your liking than if I were to find cause to discipline you yet again. I expect you will toughen up. You will have to if you insist upon crossing me. But just now I fear your bottom is too tender to take much more punishment so do not push your good fortune with me."

Chastened, Brynhild dropped her gaze. She could not fault him for giving fair warning.

"How long will it take? To reach Scotland?"

"We will be at sea for another two nights, possibly three though the wind is fair and we are making good time."

"I am to remain tied to the mast the entire voyage?"

"I believe that to be best."

"And, when we arrive? Am I to be a slave?"

"We Celts rarely take slaves, though I daresay the life of a serf may well seem not so dissimilar. They are tied to the land they work, and therefore to the landowner, though serfs do have a choice of sorts."

"Of sorts?"

"Aye. The choice between a labourer's cottage to call home and food on the table, or the freedom to go cold and hungry."

"You are a serf?" She thought he must be, by the hint of bitterness in his tone.

Taranc shook his head. "No, I am chief in my village so

the serfs there answer to me for their livelihood, though I owe obeisance to the lord of Pennglas. He is Fiona's father."

"Is he a fair lord?"

"Aye, fair enough, and I try to be. I believe our people live well enough. It is better than being a Viking thrall, certainly."

"Ulfric was not a cruel Jarl."

"Slavery is cruel, Brynhild, however benevolent the master. You should consider yourself fortunate not to sample it yourself."

It may pain her to accept the truth of his words, but she could not find it within her to argue. And she did consider herself lucky. "Then what do you intend? If I am not to be your slave, and you will not wed me?"

"I am returning to my village. You may come with me and you are welcome to make your home there. I daresay your skills as a weaver will be sufficient to guarantee you a living. You will be a free woman in Aikrig, not a prisoner. If you choose to leave, to go elsewhere, I shall not prevent it."

"Where would I go? I know no one in your land. I have nothing…"

"I appreciate that. So you are welcome to remain with me."

She shook her head, despondent. "I am a Viking. My people have made war upon yours. Your people will hate me."

"Only if you invite them to do so."

"But—"

"Only you and I know what transpired in your land, between you and Fiona. No one here will hold you responsible for the actions of your brother or others from your land. No one has reason to hate you and I will not give them any such cause. You may start afresh, make friends, build a life."

"I had a life."

"And now you have another. Think about what I have said and make what you may of it." He completed the task of securing her ankle to the mast, leaving perhaps four feet of rope free to allow her to stand and move about a little. "Now, I believe Eileifr might appreciate some help in acquiring a fine supper for us. You will excuse me, lady."

The two men spent the next several hours at routine tasks about the small vessel. Taranc seemed to know how to arrange the sails, to read the wind and make adjustments to ensure that they remained on course. Eiliefr attended to his lines and also flung a net from the stern of the boat. He seemed well content with the outcome of his labours as he and Taranc hauled the catch aboard. Both men ignored Brynhild, so she was left to her own thoughts that whirled around in her head.

Where did it come from, her near confession? She had almost told Taranc. She had come perilously close to blurting out her secret. No one knew. No one must ever know, yet she had very nearly yelled it to the heavens. She must have a care, especially since his words about a new life seemed so tempting now that she properly considered them. Could it be true? Could she really leave her past behind and start afresh in this untried and alien land? She would be among strangers. Worse, she would be living among the Celts she had hated for years, but even so, the promise in Taranc's words called to her.

She wanted this. She wanted to choose this, for herself.

Taranc had passed her clothes to her, now dried in the sun so she was properly dressed once more. She chewed thoughtfully on the salted fish provided by Eileifr and washed it down with fresh water, then completed several circuits of the mast before gingerly settling down to kneel on the deck again. Her bottom throbbed without mercy, her thighs even more so when she allowed her weight to rest upon them. She could not sit in comfort and she wondered if she ever would again. She wriggled and fidgeted as she sought some ease but her efforts were in vain. Once or twice she caught sight of Taranc's knowing look as he regarded her from across the deck. She wondered if he might again offer to rub away the discomfort. If he did, she might be tempted to accept.

By late afternoon she was becoming seriously cold through inactivity, bored to the point of screaming, and she was hungry again. Taranc strode past her to attend to the rudder and she reached out to catch his tunic. "May I have another blanket, please? If there is one?"

"Of course. You may have mine." He passed it to her.

She frowned. "You will require it yourself. Later."

"We shall share. That makes better sense."

"Share?" She hoped he had not heard the startled squeak in her voice though thus far he had missed little enough.

"Aye. Share." He did not wait to discuss the matter. Seemingly their course required further adjustment and this demanded all his attention. Brynhild shifted her weight again and groaned as another sizzle of fire assailed her punished thighs.

They ate an evening meal of more salted fish with bread and a handful of nuts each. The men sat beside Brynhild to take their meal and the conversation was convivial enough, though in a manner Brynhild found quite bizarre. Eileifr asked after Njal and informed her that his own sister had recently been delivered of a fine boy. Brynhild smiled as though there was nothing in the slightest way odd about their current circumstances and wished the new family well, then turned to speak to Taranc.

"Do you have a family? People with whom you share your home?" She had not intended to ask, but the question had popped into her head, and then it was out.

He nodded. "My mother, Murdina, and her widowed sister, Morag reside in a cottage in my village though they do not share the chief's house. That was to be my home with Fiona but I daresay you will find it comfortable. My cousin, Annag, lives with Murdina and Morag and takes care of my house too. I hope she has continued to do so whilst I have been absent. It is a hectic family but I believe you will fit in well enough."

"I am to live in your house? On what basis?"

He shrugged. "On the basis that I see no other obvious solution."

"It is not decent. There will be talk."

"Aye, maybe. It will not last."

"I cannot live with you," insisted Brynhild.

"Very well. You may make such other arrangements as you please."

Brynhild fell silent. What 'other arrangements' might she even consider? She chewed on her fish and said no more on the subject.

As darkness fell, the men hauled in the nets and lines though they continued to tack onward, making a brisk speed across the rippling waves. It had been agreed between the men that Eileifr was to remain awake for the first watch, and Taranc would relieve him after a few hours. Brynhild peered out from within her cocoon of blankets as the Celt approached and crouched beside her little nest.

"You may have your blanket back," she murmured. "I do not require it."

"Do not be a fool, Brynhild. Roll over and I shall help you to remain warm."

"I am quite warm enough, thank you."

"Sadly, I am not. Roll over."

"But—"

"Remember our truce, lady? Now, do as I ask." He picked up the corner of her blanket and lifted one eyebrow as he waited.

"Just, do not touch me, that is all. I… I shall defend myself if you do."

He grinned at her. "And how do you intend to do that, my fierce Viking?"

"I… I shall—"

"Fear not. You may sleep safely in your bed this night."

Brynhild huffed at him, but recognised that she had no choice but to trust him. She rolled over onto her other side, taking care to favour her still sore buttocks as she did so.

Taranc slid into the space she had vacated, and she was surprised at the sudden warmth that permeated their bed. Still, she would take care not to actually rub up against him in the night. Brynhild curled up in a small ball at the furthest extent permitted by the rope still attached to her ankle and closed her eyes. If this Celt insisted upon sharing her bed, she would do the next best thing she could. She would ignore him.

• • • • • • •

She stretched. She was delightfully warm and comfortable. Her joints ached, as though she had seen many hours labouring in the fields about their settlement, and a tinge of soreness permeated her lower body. It was not unpleasant. The sensation might be better described as satisfying. Brynhild sighed and rubbed her cheek upon the blanket beneath her.

"Tell me, my Viking, who was it?"

What? Brynhild opened her eyes, dragged unceremoniously from her languorous state of relaxation by the soft masculine tone close to her ear. She wriggled backward with a startled squeak.

Taranc chuckled. "Do not pretend that you were asleep, my sweet Viking."

"I was. I—"

"Who was it?"

She shoved a heavy hank of blonde curls from her face and peered up at him, realising to her chagrin that her good intentions of the previous evening had come to absolutely naught. Far from avoiding touching him as she had planned when she submitted to this ill-judged sleeping arrangement, she had snuggled right up to the Celt in the night, absorbing his warmth and the unlikely comfort he offered. She had even used his chest as her pillow.

By Odin's teeth, I must learn to control such foolishness.

"What are you babbling about, Celt?"

"I want to know who the fool was who convinced you that you are cold."

"Who…? How…?" Brynhild was at a loss, but alert enough to know she was drifting into deep water.

Taranc continued as though she had not spoken, his tone deceptively conversational. "For he was surely an idiot, an addle-brained simpleton with the sensitivity of a dead slug. Why would you allow such a creature to influence you? You are an intelligent woman, Brynhild, and a lovely one, and without doubt as warm as any I have met. So why accept such a falsehood from one so deluded?"

"I… I do not know what you are talking about."

"I believe you do, but let me refresh your memory. Yesterday, you informed me that you are cold, unlovable, worthless. Did I miss anything?" He paused. "No, I believe that was the gist of it. Well, I feel compelled to point out to you that you are wrong, and that whoever planted those notions in your lovely head was an insensitive numbskull. So, who was it? Your betrothed?"

"My betrothed? I have no betrothed." She was drowning, every bit as surely as when she plunged into the icy waters yesterday.

"But you did. I heard mention of it in the slave barn. You were to wed a man from a neighbouring settlement."

She nodded. "Eirik Bjarkesson. But he died."

"I know that also. Did you love him?"

"Love him? No, of course I did not."

"Why so vehement? It is not unheard of for a bride to love her betrothed. Was it he who filled your head with this nonsense?"

"Of course he did not. Eirik was most kind to me. He was gentle, and… and… he would have made a fine husband. I miss him very much."

"Yet this is the first time his name has arisen between us."

"Why would I talk to you of my betrothed?"

"Did you spread your legs for him?"

Brynhild sat up, wincing as her weight settled on her punished buttocks. She glared at Taranc, outraged at the question. "How dare you ask me such a thing? What gives you the right?"

"Did you? Was it he who convinced you that you would not do such a thing again?"

Does he forget nothing? Am I to be challenged on every unguarded remark? Is every last one of my secrets to be scrutinised, examined, analysed, and explained? This is insufferable!

Her temper simmered. "May I suggest you mind your own business, Celt? I shall not press you on the intimate details of your relationship with my brother's bed-slave, and you shall not pry into my life."

"You may not suggest that, and you will have a care how you speak to me unless you are prepared to present your pretty bottom for another spanking. You will answer."

"Why? Why should I? What is it to you?"

"You are in my care."

"I… I am not. I am your prisoner, for now, that is all."

He sighed and reached for her, then drew her close to his chest. Brynhild lay stiff in his arms, the threat—or promise—of a spanking not lost on her. He nuzzled the top of her head with his lips.

"I would not wish you to consider me unduly harsh. How would you feel about an honest exchange? I shall tell you of my relationship with Fiona, and you shall tell me of your Eirik."

"I have no desire to hear about Fiona. She is nothing to me."

"Liar. You asked how often I tied her up and spanked her bare bottom."

"And you told me you never treated her in such a way, yet you will ill-treat me as you please."

"A man does not spank a woman for whom he cares nothing."

"You are speaking in riddles. Did you not care for your betrothed?" She could not believe this. He had seemed so concerned, so outraged on Fiona's behalf when he believed the little Celtic slave to be in danger.

"I did care for her, but as I would a sister. We spent much time together as children…"

"How long were you betrothed?"

"There was an understanding of sorts between her father and mine from when we were both quite young, but the arrangement was only formalised two years ago, just before my father died. He wanted matters settled, I suppose."

"But you did not wed."

"No, we did not."

"She was a virgin, when my brother first had her."

"Yes."

"You and she, you never…"

"Obviously."

"Why not?"

"We were friends, but there was nothing more between us. We would have done our duty, I daresay, eventually. Your brother's intervention changed all of that."

"Were you faithful to her? I mean, since you and she were not lovers?"

"I was, at least during the time of our formal betrothal. I would not have treated her with disrespect. Prior to that, no, I did not consider myself obligated, nor did I expect fidelity from Fiona."

"You must have been very angry with my brother."

"Oh, yes. It was a brutal attack on our villages. Fiona's brother died in the raid, as did several others. I think it is fair to say I was fucking angry, and I was desperately scared for Fiona. For all of my people who were taken."

"Yet you arrived at this deal with Ulfric. You agreed to abduct me."

"It is true that we came to understand each other after a while. Your brother has his faults but he is a man I can respect and I trust him to take care of Fiona. She will be happy with him, and that is what I want for her."

"You are not jealous?"

"Do I seem so to you?"

"No, and I do not understand why you would relinquish your bride so readily."

"We were not suited. It is better this way. Now, I would hear of your Eirik."

"There is nothing to tell. He was a warrior from a settlement about a half day's ride to the west of Skarthveit. My father arranged the match, with the Jarl of the Bjarkessons. It was a good alliance."

"Did you spread your legs for him?"

Brynhild hesitated, then shook her head slowly. "No. He did not ask that of me. He was… polite."

"Polite? I cannot believe he did not wish to fuck you. Certainly, I would wish to, were I in his position."

"He… he did not."

"Why not? And please do not trouble to mention your alleged coldness for it will not do. Why did Eirik Bjarkesson not wish to sample the delights of his very lovely bride to be?"

"I do not know."

"Brynhild, you are perilously close to a spanking right now. Are you sure you wish to continue to lie to me?"

"It… it is private."

"I imagine so. Tell me."

"I cannot. It is too… too… personal."

"I would say we have reached the point where nothing is too personal. Tell me, Brynhild. Now."

She drew in a long breath, then let it out. Her cheeks flamed and she squirmed under the weight of her embarrassment as she whispered the words she had never uttered to a soul before, words she had sworn she would never repeat.

"He preferred men."

"Ah. I see. You knew of this?"

Brynhild nodded. "I… I discovered him and another warrior. I was not intended to know, but I saw, and… I promised I would never tell anyone."

"Even knowing this, you were willing to wed him?"

"I was willing to wed him *because* of it. He would not expect me to… to… We had an agreement. He would have been perfect for me."

"Why would you settle for a man who would never desire you? What about children? Would you have settled for such a life?"

"I *have* settled for such a life and it has served me well. Until you and Ulfric turned everything upon its head."

"So, if not Eirik, who told you that you were worthless and unlovable? Who convinced you that you were cold?"

Brynhild flattened her lips in grim determination. He might spank her, but she had told him all she was prepared to. The rest, well, that was buried and would remain so whatever this meddlesome Celt might do to her.

"Please, no more. Please do not ask me any more."

"Brynhild…?"

"Whip me if you must, if you consider that necessary, but I will not tell you."

"I shall not whip you, little Viking, for I know it would do no good. However, I have one final question for you and I require an honest answer."

"What question?"

"You did not spread your thighs for your betrothed, and now I understand why. He had no wish to fuck you. But I do. So, Brynhild, will you spread them for me?"

CHAPTER THIRTEEN

What his question lacked in finesse it certainly made up for in the element of surprise. Naturally Brynhild did not answer and he had not really expected her to. She could only gape at him, wide-eyed. Most telling, though, she did not recoil in horror. Well, not entirely. She had backed away, shaking her head. He did not miss the sudden shimmer of tears, nor did he mistake the flash of curious vulnerability instantly quashed. Taranc took that as her wordless response and allowed the matter to drop for the time being. It was not as though he intended to take her right there on the fishing vessel, with Eileifr looking on. There would be time enough when they reached Aikrig.

He would need to revisit his view on marriage. Although his natural instinct had not changed, he still believed a marriage between himself and Brynhild Freysson would be a prickly affair at best, he had to admit the prospect was not without its compensations. Sweet Jesus, but the woman had his cock gripped in a more or less permanent state of hardness. It was beginning to actually hurt. For her part, she was wary of him, badly frightened by something she refused to name, but he was now convinced she was not immune to him and for that he thanked his Maker. For certain, the sort of marriage which Eirik Bjarkesson would have found acceptable would not suit Taranc. He intended to bed her, and he would do it well and thoroughly and very, very often.

His little Viking had but to come around to the idea.

She spent much of their second day at sea asleep, or pretending to be. He allowed that and busied himself assisting Eiliefr. Just before sunset they sighted land.

"Shetland," announced Eiliefr. "By first light we shall be at Orkney, and soon after we shall reach the coast of Scotland. Your village is perhaps a half day's sailing down the eastern coast."

Taranc nodded. He had a fair idea of the course they were on and fully expected to take his next noontime meal at his own table in Aikrig.

A couple of hours after dawn broke he crouched beside Brynhild and shook her by the shoulder. She peeped out of the blankets at him, her deep blue eyes apprehensive. Taranc produced a finely carved bone comb, yet another of the useful items so helpfully supplied by her brother.

"We are nearing our destination. I thought you might wish to make use of this before meeting anyone."

She blinked at him, but took the comb. "Thank you."

He smiled and reached for the rope that still bound her ankle. "We will be going ashore in an hour or so." He set her loose. "I trust you will not find it necessary to fling yourself overboard, but I should warn you, if you do I shall not be best pleased at being forced to dive in after you a second time. By now you will appreciate the likely consequences of such foolishness. You are no longer a prisoner, Brynhild. You are now a free woman... of Scotland."

He might have wished she appeared less daunted at that prospect.

Taranc stood at the bow and watched as his former home swelled in the distance, eventually filling his vision. Little had altered in the months he had been away, and he was glad of it. Brynhild came to stand at his side, her pale hair combed and freshly plaited, and her crumpled tunic smoothed out as best she might manage it.

"It is smaller than I imagined."

He nodded at her observation. "Aye, Aikrig is but a fishing village, a hamlet really. Pennglas, the main village, lies about a mile inland and is larger."

"Which house is yours?"

"Ours," he corrected. "That one, there, at the brow of the incline, just before the trees." He pointed to the largest of the dwellings, a single-storey structure made of stone and timber, with a turfed roof.

He supposed it was not unlike a Viking longhouse in external appearance, though no smoke billowed through the roof. In a Viking dwelling the fire would never be allowed to go out. He had to assume that in his absence his family had not found it necessary to keep the blaze going. That would have to change and he had no doubt that Brynhild would be equal to the task. He turned to regard her solemn features.

"You will keep our home and I know that you will do so with your usual efficiency. However, I will expect you to treat our servants well. Annag, my cousin, will help you and I expect to hear no tales of whippings, stocks, or cold baths. Do I make myself clear?"

She glared at him, her spine stiffening. "You hardly know me, yet you think to dictate on such matters. I am a fine manager of servants. I expect people to work hard, but I am fair and our house thralls loved me."

"Brynhild, let us not have any illusions on this matter. No one here is a thrall, or a slave. You will treat them accordingly or face the consequences. Do I need to elaborate?"

She glared at him, bristling with resentment. "No, you do not. You will spank me."

"Indeed. So, are you ready to greet your new family? I believe my mother is already on the beach. She has seen us." He raised his arm to wave at the diminutive figure dancing and skipping about on the dark gold expanse of damp sand. "She will be relieved to see me, I do not doubt. And surprised."

"I expect she will be even more surprised to see me," observed Brynhild.

Taranc did not disagree. He helped his reluctant companion ashore, lifting her in his arms to ensure she was not called upon to wade through the thigh-deep waves in order to reach dry land. He set her down then turned to accept the enthusiastic hug from his mother. Tears streamed across the older woman's cheeks as she greeted the son she had believed lost for good.

"I thought you perished, you and all the others. Oh, thank the dear, sweet Lord that you are returned to us. And the rest? Have they also escaped? What of Fiona?" She peered over his shoulder at the fishing boat, Eileifr was already setting out to sea again, eager to be away from this hostile foreign shore. "Are there no others with you?"

"Alas, no. Though I do have a companion I would wish you to meet. This is Brynhild Freysson. She is to make her home here, with us." He steadfastly avoided catching Brynhild's eye, but her tense intake of breath was not to be missed. He thought it best to press on. "Are Morag and Annag here also?"

"Aye. Though Annag has gone on ahead to prepare your house."

"Good." Now he did chance a look in Brynhild's direction. "I told you she would help." He extended his hand and took her cold one, then began to lead her up the beach. On all sides they were greeted by excited, joyful shouts as the villagers rushed to welcome him, to shout their questions about the fate of loved ones still missing, to pat him on the back and thank the Lord and all the saints for his safe delivery back among them. Taranc accepted their good wishes with easy charm, shouldering his way forward until he reached the threshold of his own dwelling. He gestured Brynhild to step inside, followed by his still beaming mother. He bestowed one final, grateful smile on the villagers who had flanked him all the way here, thanked them for their warm welcome, then he went inside and closed the door.

The room was windowless and the interior was dark when the door was shut. Four pairs of female eyes regarded him in the dim lamplight. The youngest among them, his cousin Annag, darted forward to throw her arms about him. "I knew you would return, I knew it. You could not be dead."

"Annag, it is good to see you. I trust you have been well."

"Aye, but I missed you."

"I missed you too, little cousin." He set her from him and smiled down into her excited features. "I have brought someone I want you to meet. This is Brynhild Freysson. She is to live here too from now on so I hope you will make her welcome and help her to settle in with us."

"Live here? With you? But... Fiona?"

"Fiona has stayed in the Norseland. She is to wed the Viking who came here." He was not entirely certain of this, though he believed it would eventually be the way of it so saw no reason not to embellish what would likely become the truth.

The girl paled. "But, he will be cruel to her. I saw him, he was fearsome and wild, a savage."

Taranc shook his head. "He will not, or I would never had left her there. She is happy with him, and safe. The Viking is Brynhild's brother."

"Her... brother? Then, she is one of them?" Annag eyed Brynhild with undisguised fear and suspicion.

"One of us now. And our journey has been a long one. Is there food, perhaps? A place where Brynhild might rest? Fresh clothing?"

As he had expected, his requests brought forth a flurry of eager activity as the women of his family rushed to provide for his needs. He guided Brynhild into the one decent chair and perched on the carved arm to watch as platters were brought to the table, fires relit, dust swept aside in a rush to make his home fit to live in. He laid his hand on her shoulder to prevent her from taking charge. "Soon," he murmured. "For today, you will watch, learn, allow them to know you."

"You told them I am to live here, with you," she hissed. "Why?"

"Because you will. It will be simpler."

"But you do not wish to marry me."

"I believe we would both live to regret such a move but I have decided I may be prepared to consider it even so."

"You need not trouble yourself, Celt. I shall make my own way."

Murdina glanced their way, her attention attracted by the sharpness in Brynhild's tone. Taranc smiled at his mother. "Brynhild is quite overwhelmed. It has been a stressful journey and she is very tired. I wonder, would you allow us an hour or so of privacy, perhaps?"

Murdina nodded and ushered her sister and niece from the dwelling. As soon as the door closed behind them Brynhild rose to her feet and stood before him.

"You will no doubt wish to use your belt again. I believe the current tally to be twelve."

"And I believe you to be far too eager to invite punishment." He slipped into the seat she had vacated and pulled her onto his lap. "Be still and quiet. And eat."

She would have wriggled out of his arms but he held her firm until she relaxed. When she sat still, Taranc selected a piece of cold mutton from one of the platters laid out by his aunt and cousin and offered it to her. Brynhild frowned at the meat, but took it between her fingers and tasted it, then shoved the entire piece into her mouth and chewed.

So far so good. He chose another slice of meat for her, then one for himself. He poured her a mug of ale made from the local heather and apologised for the lack of the mead, which he knew to be the usual preference at a Viking table. Brynhild shrugged and took a sip of the ale, grimaced, then took another.

They ate the rest of their meal in silence. Brynhild tried everything set before her—roast pigeon, the rich cheese made of goat's milk, oatcakes, and a soft pear pudding sweetened with honey. Taranc, too, was ravenous and delighted to sample again the familiar flavours of his home. Eventually Brynhild shook her head when he offered her another mouthful of the pudding.

"I have had enough. Thank you. It was—nice."

He smiled. She was trying, at least.

"I have much to attend to so I must leave you for a while. You should sleep."

"I am not tired."

"Rest, then. The bed is in the far corner."

"The bed? Just one bed?"

"Aye, just the one. Make yourself comfortable. I shall ask Annag to find fresh clothes for you since your own still have the salt of the sea upon them." He planted her on her feet and gave her a shove in the direction of the large raised cot in the corner. "I shall see you in a couple of hours or so. And remember, do try to be nice to everyone."

• • • • • • •

His tour of the village took longer than he had anticipated since he was called upon to pause at every dwelling to share news of those still in the Norseland. For the most part he was able to reassure his people that their loved ones were safe but still there was sadness, anger, resentment, and puzzlement at the presence among them of one of the hated enemy. It would pass, he knew, and much would depend on his own attitude toward Brynhild. If he accepted her, welcomed her, then his people would too.

He wanted her to be happy here. It mattered to him, more than he might have imagined. On every occasion he declared Brynhild to be a fine woman, honest and hard-working, skilled at weaving and homemaking, a woman who had lost her own home and family through no fault of her own, so had opted to accompany him to Scotland when the opportunity arose. Not entirely the true state of affairs but he felt it judicious to smooth the way for her. The rest was up to Brynhild herself.

Taranc returned to his house as the sun was setting. He entered, and was pulled up short by the sight of Brynhild seated in the small tub he used for his bath. She was submerged up to her shoulders in the steaming water, which rippled about her breasts and bent knees. Her eyes were closed and her head tilted back. Behind her, Annag sat on a low stool and rubbed a soap made of mutton fat and scented with lavender into her hair. Both women turned to him as he stood in the doorway.

"I can assist Brynhild from here. You may go, Annag."

"But—" His young cousin clearly found this suggestion less than wholly appropriate.

Taranc smiled and reached back to open the door, then gestured his kinswoman through it. Brynhild remained where she was, though she watched him with suspicion from the safety of her bath.

"You appear more refreshed than when I left. I trust Annag has taken good care of you."

"She has been very kind. She brought me fresh clothes, and she offered to prepare the bath. I did not ask it of her."

Taranc nodded, though he would not have considered it unreasonable had Brynhild made such a request. He should have suggested it himself. He moved to take up the position recently occupied by Annag and drew a pail of fresh, clean water close to his knee. "Allow me to assist you in rinsing your hair."

"I can manage..." She started to sit up, then seemingly realised this would reveal her naked breasts to him. She sank back into the water, her arms crossed over her chest.

Taranc made no comment, just proceeded to pour jugfuls of clean water over her now perfectly cleansed locks. The brightness of her flaxen curls, even when wet, near dazzled him as he drew his fingers slowly through her hair to tease out the tangles.

"Your hair is beautiful. It was the first thing I noticed about you."

She snorted. "The first thing I noticed about you was that you are quite ridiculously tall. And that you lacked the proper respect due to a Viking woman of the Jarl. You were far too ready with your demands."

"Aye, I daresay. And now you appear to be struggling to exhibit the required degree of deference due the chief of your village. Perhaps I should make more demands of you."

"What... what do you mean?" She stiffened, her slender shoulders tightening as she tensed.

Taranc released his grip on her hair and laid his palms on the soft skin that covered her clavicles. He drew his hands in toward her neck, thumbs outstretched, then began to trace lazy circles with the pads, right at her hairline. She flinched, and he increased the pressure, seeking out the spot where tension lurked.

"What are you doing?" Her voice was a breathless whisper.

"Making demands. Relax, be still. Enjoy."

"I cannot. I do not like you to touch me..."

"Liar. I shall not hurt you, and you know it." He kept up the relentless, sensual pressure, leaning in to kiss the outer shell of her ear as he did so. Brynhild let out a soft gasp, but offered no further objection.

Her taut and rigid body softened under his ministrations. He was not certain she even realised she had done so when she released her tightly folded arms to lay them along the rim of the tub and leaned back into his gentle embrace. He allowed his hands to move, reaching forward, then lower to cup the soft swell of both her breasts. She gasped, her posture tensing again, betraying her disquiet. But she allowed it.

Taranc caressed the lower curves, his thumbs now rubbing across her stiff, pebbling nipples. He longed to take one of the deep pink buds between his teeth but decided to save that pleasure for another occasion. For now, he had her where he wanted her. She accepted his touch, at least this far, his intimate exploration of her body. She was learning to trust him.

He continued to toy with her nipple as he drew his fingertips down the length of her sternum, pausing to explore the hollow of her navel before continuing on to tease the pale blonde curls at the apex of her thighs. He did not suggest she spread her legs for him as he knew what her answer would be. Instead he kissed her neck as he slid his fingers through her soft folds, seeking out the pleasure nub he knew he would find there.

Brynhild almost leapt from the tub when he reached his quarry. He tightened his grip across her chest to hold her in place.

"Relax. Be still. Enjoy." He repeated his sensual demands.

"What are you doing to me? That feels... wrong. It is not usual to feel so."

"No, perhaps not until now. It will become usual, I promise." He continued to draw the tip of his finger across the sensitive nubbin, noting the way it swelled under his touch. Brynhild trembled in his arms, her tension mounting. Undeterred, he continued his assault on her confused, untried senses. He was merciless, his goal clear. As her body spasmed he took the quivering bud between his finger and thumb and squeezed lightly as she shattered in his arms.

Brynhild lay still, her breath coming in quick pants. Her eyes were closed, her head against his shoulder. The water was cooling now but she appeared oblivious to it. Taranc was not and he did not wish her to become chilled. He stood, reached into the tub to take her in his arms, and lifted her dripping wet form. He carried her to the cot and laid her on the blankets there, then quickly pulled the top one around her. Brynhild did not resist when he rubbed her all over to dry her, then discarded the moist blanket and wrapped her in another before tucking the rest around her.

She was deeply asleep by the time he straightened to survey her still body, her relaxed features softened by satiated lust. Her pleasure had been a long time coming, but she had needed it and it would not be her last, he swore. Taranc turned to regard the cooling water in the tub and let out a long sigh. He quickly removed his damp clothing and sank into the bath.

CHAPTER FOURTEEN

The pace of life was slow in her new home. Brynhild was not unhappy, exactly, but neither could she truly settle in to her new life. Something seemed amiss to her, awry somehow. She did not belong, could not allow herself to be drawn into the intimacies of village life despite the friendliness and acceptance she encountered. Initially wary, and suspicious of her presence here, the villagers quickly seemed to accept her among them. Annag was friendly, Murdina and Morag too. Taranc was kind enough, and considerate. He insisted that Brynhild make such changes as she considered needful to the house they shared, that she make it her home too.

But it was all based upon a lie. The people of Aikrig did not know the truth. They were unaware of the cruelties and injustice Brynhild had heaped upon one of their number. If they but knew of her treatment of Fiona, they would reject her. They would hate her, and she would deserve their antipathy.

Although the dialect was unfamiliar, Brynhild spoke enough of their Gaelic to be able to converse easily. She learned the names of the serfs who shared their village, and quickly came to understand the respect commanded by

Taranc. He had always been a dominant presence, even as a thrall in her own land. He was a natural leader, she was ready to acknowledge, but here in his own environment he was truly formidable. People obeyed him without question. They sought his counsel, listened to his opinions, and no one gainsaid him.

Even Dughall, lord of Pennglas, respected Taranc's judgment.

The old man had summoned the pair of them to his manor house in Pennglas the day after their arrival. Brynhild had awoken that morning to the memory of Taranc's most unusual and evocative caresses the previous evening. She had no recollection of having been put to bed though she could recall most vividly the explosion of intense pleasure he had created as she lay helpless in the bathtub. She had been stunned, drawn to the erotic sensation, unable to resist and repulsed by her own vulnerability.

Now, in the cold light of a grey Scottish morning, she did not dare to make reference to what had happened between them, afraid he might insist upon repeating the experience.

It was not so much that Brynhild did not wish to recapture that sensual, heady delight, more that she feared she might fail if she attempted to do so. The disappointment would crush her.

"We go to Pennglas," Taranc announced as they broke their fast on oatcakes and the thick porridge prepared by Annag. "Dughall wishes to meet you. He will have questions, concerning his daughter."

"What will you tell him?"

"The truth. That she has found happiness with her Viking."

"I mean, what will you tell him about me. And Fiona."

"There is nothing to tell. What is past is past."

"But, he is her father…"

"Fiona is happy, content in her new life. That is what he needs to know."

174

And so the falsehood continued. Taranc appeared to be correct in his assessment. Dughall, lord of Pennglas greeted them cordially enough on the steps of his manor house.

"It is a delight to see you safely returned to us, Taranc, and I am pleased to meet your lovely companion also." He seized Taranc's hand and shook warmly, then hugged the Celt to him. Next he kissed Brynhild on each cheek. "Welcome to your new home, my dear. I hope you will feel able to visit an old man, if you have time to spare. I do miss the company of my own daughter and this house lacks the warmth of a beautiful young woman to fill my chilled hall."

"I would be pleased to call upon you, if that would please you, my lord," she murmured.

Brynhild did not miss the slight smile of approval that flitted across Taranc's handsome features.

"He is lonely," Taranc observed as they made their way back down to the coast after their visit. "Both his children are lost to him. He had expected grandchildren when Fiona and I were married, but now…"

"I shall go to see him," announced Brynhild. "I shall go often." It seemed the least she could do.

Her guilt grew with every day that passed. She recalled with bitter, unrelenting clarity each and every act of malice she had visited upon the Celtic slave whilst Fiona had been under her power. She had missed no opportunity to add to the girl's misery, and had done so for no better reason than ugly jealousy. It was true that Brynhild had worked hard to build the life she enjoyed under her brother's roof, and Fiona represented a threat to all of that, but none of it was of the thrall's choosing. It had started the first moment she laid eyes on the newcomer and recognised at once that Ulfric was smitten. The freezing bath, the whippings she convinced Ulfric to mete out, the constant haranguing and finding fault with all that the girl attempted to do. It had been beneath her, all of it. A woman of the Jarl should behave better, should be an example to those who looked up to her. She could see that now, and Brynhild bitterly regretted her actions. She was deeply ashamed, and her sense of guilt now threatened to mar her new life.

Remorse ate at her but it was too late to make amends. She had wronged Fiona, and would gladly seek forgiveness for those crimes if that were possible but she never expected to see her victim again. Fiona remained in Skarthveit, and Brynhild would never be able to return there. She would have no opportunity to offer her apology, to seek Fiona's forgiveness.

Instead, to all intents and purposes, she had taken over Fiona's old life here in Scotland. The villagers of Aikrig and Pennglas treated her with a respect she did not deserve, they accepted and welcomed her among them as though she were one of their own.

She and Taranc shared a bed, and as they lay beneath the furs and blankets in the darkness, Taranc would insist upon reigniting the sensual fires he had started to stoke. He did not, after all, disappoint her. Indeed, his touch seemed both effortless and faultless, and Brynhild came to trust her body's helpless response to him. He was gentle with her, but insistent and she no longer refused to spread her legs for his erotic exploration. He offered her pleasure that she did not deserve but found impossible to resist.

"You are wet for me, my greedy little Viking. So hot and wet and tight. I knew that you would be." She quivered as he slid his fingers inside her, stunned by the slick juices that pooled between her legs and eased his way. How had he known it would be so? She had never dreamed, never even imagined...

Her release came quickly now, easily. She never failed to marvel at the twist and curl of arousal as it burgeoned within her core, rising up, gripping her, then suddenly taking control of her scrambled senses to send her spinning into some weightless, swirling place where lights sparkled and the sound of rushing water echoed within her ears. Afterwards she would lie in his arms, warm and spent and utterly sated. And riddled with unassuaged guilt.

Taranc preferred to sleep naked. Brynhild found his casual approach to nudity disconcerting at first. She tried hard to avert her eyes, to not study his erect cock, to ignore the nudge of his swollen, solid erection against her hip as he wrapped her in his arms at night. She found herself both fascinated and fearful of his unashamed maleness, but fear won out. She was curious, wondered what it would feel like to take that hard erection between her hands and rub her fingers along the length of it, perhaps even taste the droplets of clear fluid that she noticed would leak from the end occasionally. But she did not dare. She knew what such foolishness would lead to, and however sweet the sensual web her handsome Celt might spin about her, she could not, would not go that far.

She knew better, knew the dangers. Taranc may seem gentle now. He may appear solicitous, knowing her body's needs and teasing out her response, giving her pleasure yet seeking nothing for himself. But men were at heart unpredictable and once lust took hold they could not control their urges. He would hurt her, she knew it. Always, it came back to that.

There would be pain, humiliation. The pleasure he employed with such skill to tempt her was merely an illusion, a trick of the gods—male gods, of course—designed to lure in the naive and the recklessly bold. She would not be fooled, not again.

A month passed before he spoke to her of marriage once more. Brynhild was at the loom he had acquired for her and installed within their home. She loved the new apparatus and took enormous pleasure in arranging the warp and weft, threading the yarn and blending the muted colours to create the soft designs she preferred. Annag stood at her side, watching in rapt fascination as the fabric evolved before her eyes. Brynhild had promised to teach her to weave, and the girl was proving to be an eager pupil.

At first she thought she misheard him.

"I am sorry, what did you say?"

"We are to wed at Michaelmas, a fortnight from now. My mother will help you with the arrangements, though there is not much to do since the feast is to take place anyway, and—"

"Wed? We are not to be wed. You said so. You said we would not be suited."

"I did, and I still think ours will be a turbulent union, but I have come around to the notion. So, two weeks from today. I shall send word to the abbey at Balseach to summon one of the brothers from there. He can perform the ceremony at the manor house in Pennglas. I am sure Dughall will not object."

The shuttle fell from her nerveless fingers with a clatter. "But I shall. I shall object. I do not wish to marry. Never. I cannot."

"Why can you not? It makes sense that we should. It is expected."

"It does not. It makes no sense at all."

"Enough. We are to wed and that is an end to it." He strode to where she stood, bent to retrieve her dropped shuttle, and placed it back in her hands. "You will soon become used to the idea." He dropped a careless kiss on the top of her head and turned to leave her.

The shuttle left her hand before Brynhild could so much as consider the recklessness of her actions. It hit him square between his shoulders. She stood, transfixed, as he turned to face her again.

"Oh, Brynhild, I had so hoped we were beyond all this." His tone was low, deathly quiet. Again, he picked up the tool from the floor, but this time he set it upon the table to his side. He turned his attention to Annag, who had witnessed the entire exchange with wide-eyed dismay.

"Cousin, you will accompany Brynhild to the coppice and show her where the finest switches are to be found. Help her to select a decent bundle, perhaps five or six, and none of them thicker than the width of my finger. Trim them well, I wish to see no sharp edges or thorns. Then you,

Annag, may go about your business and you, Brynhild, will return here with the switches."

"I shall not. This is unfair. You cannot—"

"Twelve strokes. Do you wish for more?"

"But…"

"Fourteen. Do not make matters worse."

Brynhild opened her mouth and would have surely deepened her plight but Annag seized her sleeve and tugged her from the dwelling. Once outside she rounded on the girl. "He is a brute. An idiot. Does he think me some foolish wench to be dazzled by his offer? I shall not marry him."

Annag narrowed her eyes, unimpressed by Brynhild's outburst. "But you will. Everyone knows that you will. You must, for you live here with our chief as his wife already. He is doing the right thing in summoning the priest."

"I do not live as his wife. We… I…"

"You should not have thrown the shuttle at him."

On that point, at least, Brynhild could agree. She clenched her buttocks in fearful anticipation. Why had she not stopped to think?

"The coppice?"

"It is this way." Annag set off along a narrow track between the tall heather which bordered their home. Brynhild saw no alternative but to follow.

• • • • • • •

An hour later, and five switches to the good, Brynhild made her way back to their house. Annag parted from her at the edge of the village and offered a reassuring pat on the arm. "'Twill soon be done, and switching is not so bad. Not really."

It had seemed perfectly unpleasant enough to Brynhild the first time she experienced it, in the forest as they left Skarthveit. She saw no compelling reason to amend her view now. Her footsteps slowed as she approached the door.

"Do not keep me waiting, girl." The stern voice from within brought her scurrying back inside.

Taranc sat at the table, a mug of ale by his hand. He glanced over the bundle of switches and nodded his approval when she laid them on the bench by his side. Then he reached for the pitcher and poured a mug for Brynhild and shoved it toward her.

"Drink. You will need it. Then you will undress and lie across the table."

Resigned to her fate, Brynhild obeyed, though her expression was sullen as she swallowed the pungent liquid. Would she ever become accustomed to this strong, brackish brew? She set the mug down and removed her leather sandals then started to unfasten the brooch that held her loose smock in place. Soon the garment was folded on the bench next to the switches. She regarded Taranc, hopeful that he might relent and allow her to retain her cotton leine. His impatient frown soon dispelled such foolishness and she pulled the undergarment over her head.

He pointed to the table as he rose to his feet. With a sob of frustration and bitter resentment at this treatment, Brynhild turned to drape herself over the smooth wood.

"I see the marks from your previous punishments have completely disappeared."

"You knew that already. You have seen often enough since I share your bed."

"Ah, yes. I believe I prefer your bottom adorned with my marks. It reminds me who is master here."

"I do not believe you need to be reminded," she spluttered.

"And yet, I find myself needing to evade your unprovoked attacks within my very house. The home I have welcomed you into, offered to share with you. And from behind, at that. It was not well done of you, Brynhild."

"You were high-handed. Haughty."

"I am sorry you found it to be so, but it is of no consequence. You will not raise your hand to me, whatever

180

grievance you may claim."

"Yet you may do this to me?"

"As I have said, I am master here. You will submit. And you will obey. Fourteen strokes, we agreed, did we not?"

"*You* decreed it. I have agreed to nothing."

"You will take the fourteen strokes, then you will apologise for your belligerence and your regrettable behaviour. Are we quite clear on that, Viking?"

She dragged in a shuddering breath. "Yes, Celt. We are clear."

He selected two switches and gripped them in his fist, then laid the ends on her upturned buttocks. He tapped her skin with them, causing her to flinch, then he lifted the pair and brought them down hard on her pale cheek. Fire sizzled, the pain flared then seeped deep into her tissues as he drew the ends of the branches slowly across her tender backside. He teased her, played with her, tickling her clenching bottom with the switches until she lay still.

"You may grip the opposite side of the table with your fingers, and be sure to remain exactly where you are. No wriggling, and certainly no reaching back to protect your bottom with your hands. And please, try not to make too much noise since it unsettles everyone within earshot."

She barely had time to nod her understanding of his instructions before he raised the switches again and this time brought them down on her other buttock. The stroke was harder, hotter. Brynhild let out a yelp as the hurt sank into her flesh. Only two so far, twelve still to go.

Sweet Odin, why could she not hold her tongue and keep her temper in check?

He wasted little time in delivering the strokes he had promised, each one harsher, fierier than the last. Brynhild tried to be quiet but by the seventh stroke she could contain her screams no longer. After the ninth she relinquished her grip on the edge of the table and reached for her smarting bottom, convinced her entire backside was aflame. Taranc took her wrist in his hand and laid it in the small of her back, then brought the other to join it. He held them there as he laid the final five strokes across the backs of her thighs, one below the other in rapid succession. Brynhild danced and shrieked and pleaded for him to stop, but he ignored her desperate screams. Only after the final stroke had been laid did he set the switches aside and release her wrists.

"You may apologise, and make it as pretty as you can for I shall expect a decent show of contrition." His tone was stern, uncompromising.

Arrogant Celtic bastard!

She would have loved to defy him, to refuse to allow him the satisfaction of her surrender, but she was hurting. She was humiliated, intimidated, defenceless, and entirely vulnerable, and convinced he would not hesitate to repeat the punishment if she did not do as he wanted now.

"I am sorry," she muttered, the words muffled by the wooden table top.

"Louder, if you please, for I fear I did not hear you."

"I am sorry. I apologise for throwing the shuttle at you."

"Ah, thank you. I am glad we have arrived at an understanding on this and I hope it will not prove necessary to revisit this discussion. As for the other matter we were considering, on further reflection I do believe the prospect of marriage between us would be perilous enough without the added complication of a reluctant bride. Since you have made it clear that you truly do not wish to be my wife, then please consider my offer withdrawn."

"What? You would allow this?"

"I will have no forced bride, Brynhild. But there is one further point I wish to make, and for this I will require you to spread your legs for me. Now."

It was the first time he had actually asked this of her, though she had parted her thighs for him many times by now in the relative safety and privacy of their bed. Never, though, as she lay face down over the table, in the light of day, her punished bottom throbbing and glowing before his very eyes.

"Please, do not hurt me." Pride fled. She was pleading in earnest, terrified of what he might decide to do to demonstrate his power over her.

He leaned forward to bring his mouth close to her ear. His words were soft now, his tone hushed and soothing. "I have hurt you all I intend to this day, and I would never do so in this way. You know that, do you not?"

"I… I do not know anything. Please…"

"Trust me." He placed his booted foot between her bare ones and nudged her ankles apart. "Open your eyes, Viking. Look at me."

Brynhild turned her head, then forced her eyelids apart and met his mossy gaze, the irises the rich, deep hue of the pine trees that surrounded her home in the Norseland. She longed for the safety and security of her old home, the certainty that nothing, no one would touch her there.

He edged her feet further apart and Brynhild forgot to fight. She forgot to breathe as he spread her beneath him, then laid his palm on her heated skin. He caressed her bottom, first one whipped buttock then the other as she squirmed under his touch.

"Be still," he admonished, though there was no roughness in his tone now.

She obeyed, unable to break his gaze as he slipped his fingers into the deep furrow between her buttocks and slid them down to her core.

He reached her tight rear hole and paused to linger there as Brynhild groaned in utter mortification. Then he continued on, rubbing between her soft folds and inserting two fingers into her slick channel. She tensed as the shaft of pure pleasure arrowed through her. The walls of her quim contracted about his fingers as he inserted a third. He was stretching her, his touch not so gentle now, more demanding, but it felt good. She wanted more. And less. She wanted it all, and she wanted none of it.

"Stop. Please, do not—"

He withdrew his fingers, only to plunge them deep again,

thrusting hard. Her climax was upon her in moments, deep and all-consuming, the most potent yet. She let out a harsh cry, more of a sob than an expression of pleasure, then shook as her body convulsed.

Taranc continued to stroke his fingers in and out of her, dragging every last shiver and shudder of her release from her reluctant body. Only when she lay spent and motionless beneath him did he cease his driving thrusts and withdraw his digits from her still spasming cunny.

He straightened and went to grab a blanket from the bed then returned to wrap it about her. He aided her to her feet, then lifted her in his arms and sat down in the chair with her limp form cradled on his lap. Brynhild clung to him, heedless now of the tenderness in her buttocks, the still burning flesh of her thighs.

"Why did you do that?" she whimpered.

He did not respond at once, just rubbed his face in her tangled hair. At last he raised his head, then tipped up her chin with his fingers so she had no choice but to meet his eyes again.

"You know all about pain and fear. You hide, as though it were in your power to protect yourself. But the pain never goes away, and it never will. However, pleasure is close, so close you can actually touch it if you will just allow it to flourish. You must see that now. Cowards hide, but it takes courage to trust. You are no coward, my Viking. I know that. Neither am I. When you are ready to tell me, I shall be ready to listen."

CHAPTER FIFTEEN

She awoke. The house was silent and Brynhild was
certain that she was alone.

Taranc had been there when she fell asleep. He had
remained with her as she lay on the bed, held her in his arms
as she drifted away.

Brynhild shoved herself up onto her elbow and knew
from the thin strands of light that penetrated the slight gap
around the door that it was not yet sunset. She felt as though
she had been asleep for hours, but seemingly not. Her body
hurt, both from the residual pain of the switching and the
inner torment of emotional upheaval that threatened to
drown her. She churned with it, unable to settle, unable to
gain any measure of comfort or relief.

He had said they need not marry. Indeed, he had
withdrawn his offer, only to then assail her senses yet again
with a taste of all that she stood to lose by shunning the
opportunity to become his wife. To be wife to anyone, since
if not Taranc then who? There would never be another who
would come close to handling her demons, who might come
face to face with her tormented soul and not turn away in
disgust.

She had resigned herself to this, had believed herself

content. Now, she was far from ready to accept the lot she had assigned herself.

He had ruined it, ruined *her*. Nothing would ever be right again.

Brynhild rose gingerly from the bed and made her way back across the room to where her clothing still lay folded on the bench beside the table. She dressed as quickly as she could and pulled on her sandals. She was not sure where she would go when she opened the door to peep outside, but knew she needed to be away from this place. She needed air. She needed to think. She needed to grieve for the girl she left behind in that meadow ten years ago.

Of course, she ended up at the manor house. Dughall, her friend, mentor and, she supposed, surrogate father now, found her in his solar, curled within the window seat there.

"I had not expected to see you today." He eased himself into the space beside her. "I heard you and Taranc had words."

She let out a mirthless chuckle. "I expect everyone heard. It was not quiet."

"Are you injured? A switching is not pleasant."

"I am not injured."

"I see. Taranc was here earlier. He tells me you are not after all to wed."

"No. He withdrew his offer."

"He explained to me that it was your wish that you not marry. You are content with this outcome?"

"It is best. He is right, we are not suited."

"Taranc is a fine man. I would have welcomed him as my son, had things played out differently."

"I know." Brynhild covered her face with her hands. "He *is* a fine man. I trust him, I like him. I believe that I could come to love him. I... I wish I could wed him."

"Indeed?" Dughall raised an eyebrow. "I believe we might all be forgiven for having failed to grasp that. I daresay that you could have him as your husband, even now, but you must tell him if that is your wish. He will not force you."

"He does not want me, not really."

"I suspect he does, though he has his pride and will not ask you again. You have made your wishes in the matter clear enough."

"My wishes? What do you know of my wishes?" Her words came out more harshly than she had intended and she was instantly contrite. Brynhild had no wish to vent her bitterness on this kindly old man. She had harmed his family quite enough. She raised her head to look at Dughall, saw him through a veil of tears as she started to sob. "What does Taranc know? I do not even understand what my wishes are, except that I wish it could all be different."

Dughall remained silent as she wept. He offered no further comment or comfort save the occasional pat on her knee. He waved away the servant who entered to tend the fire.

At last Brynhild raised her tear-ravaged face again. "You must think me very foolish."

"I think you very troubled, and I would dearly like to understand why."

Her laugh was bitter now. "You do not. You would hate me if you knew and I could not bear that."

"I could never hate you. You are as my daughter. I have come to love you and I want to help. Taranc does, also, and he will if you let him."

She shook her head. "He will not. He will think me dirty, a slut, not worthy of him. No one can help. No one can change what has passed."

"Harsh words. What have you done to deserve them?"

"I cannot tell you."

"There is someone else? A man back in your homeland, perhaps?"

Brynhild shook her head. "No. Not anymore."

The old eyes gleamed with wisdom and a lifetime of experience. "But there was. Do you love him, this other man?"

"No!" She glared at Dughall, the very notion laughable. "I… I thought I did, but I was wrong."

"Did he love you?"

Her laugh was without mirth. "No, he did not. He used me and would have hurt me. He… he tried to rape me."

Dughall frowned, his face darkening. "What was the name of this man?"

"He was called Aelbeart."

"A Celtic name?"

Brynhild nodded. "He was a slave, a thrall in my village. I fancied myself in love with him, but I was young and foolish. He tricked me, convinced me to trust him, then one night he… he… I was so frightened. My mother caught us and she was angry. She blamed me, I know she did. After it happened, Aelbeart was sold. I never saw him again."

"You must know that not all Celts are vicious beasts. Not all would act as this Aelbeart did. I am a Celt, as is Taranc. You know Taranc would never countenance such behaviour. Do not judge all Celts by the actions of one vile individual."

Dughall was right. The adult Brynhild knew it, but the frightened child somehow managed to remain in control of that part of her battered soul. It had to end, she knew it. Dughall was right. It was time to grow up.

Dughall reached for her hand and squeezed it. "Go, find Taranc. Talk to him. Tell him of this, tell him that you wish to marry if that is truly what you want. Ask his help. He will give it. You can trust him, you know that."

Brynhild nodded and closed her eyes. "I do know."

"He is on the beach, I believe, helping to land the day's catch."

Taranc would never allow others to work whilst he looked on in idleness. It was one of the characteristics of his leadership that Brynhild most admired, but she did not believe she wished to raise this matter with him in the company of the other fishermen.

"I shall wait for him at our home."

188

"Ah, yes, probably a better plan. Will you eat with me before you leave?"

On impulse Brynhild leaned forward and kissed his wizened cheek. "Thank you, Lord Dughall. That would be nice. I... I do not deserve your kindness."

• • • • • • •

After their meal Dughall walked with her to his door then remained at the portal and followed her with his eyes as she strode across the village where he had lived his entire life and onto the path leading back to Aikrig. Perhaps he might yet welcome Taranc into his family as his son, though the daughter was very different.

Dughall shook his head sadly as he turned to go back into his home. Life here had seemed so simple once, before the Vikings came.

CHAPTER SIXTEEN

She slept.

Taranc paused within the doorway, allowed the meagre light from his lamp to wash over the slender figure curled up beneath the rugs on his bed. Her breath came slowly, deeply. She appeared content.

He took but seconds to drop the bar on the inside of the door, remove his own clothing, and douse the lamp before sliding in beside her. Brynhild was naked and warm. He could not resist drawing her to him, her smooth back pressed against the hard, cooler planes of his chest.

Was she still angry with him, resentful that he had taken a switch to her again? Or worse, that he had concluded the matter between them as he had. He did not know why he had done so, but neither could he find it within himself to regret his actions. How could he feel remorse when her pussy had quivered around his digits, when she had clenched and gripped his fingers like a tight gauntlet as she moaned her release? He quirked his lip in the gloom. He would know her mood soon enough.

"You have returned," she whispered in the pitch blackness that shrouded them. "I am glad."

Ah, perhaps not angry, then.

"You are awake."

"I have been waiting for you. You are very late."

He nuzzled her hair. "I am sorry."

"No matter." She rolled over to face him, and reached to lay her palm against his cheek in the dark. "I am sorry too. I... I thought I had driven you away."

"'Twill take more than a well-aimed shuttle to achieve that, I fear."

"I shall bear that in mind, Celt."

He chuckled. "Are you tired?"

"No, not especially. I... I want..."

"What do you want, my Viking?"

"I want you. I mean, I want to talk to you. I have something to tell you. And... something I must ask of you."

He leaned up on his elbow and peered into the darkness, searching the shadows for a glimpse of her face. He could barely make out her pale features, framed by her bright flaxen hair, but what he could discern was enough to know she was sincere. And very scared.

Of him?

"You have me, little one. And I have you. Whether we marry or not, you are mine."

"Because you took me."

"Aye, and because you stayed. Fate threw us together, but I would not have it otherwise. We shall not wed if that is not your wish, but it changes nothing. You are still mine. Now, and always. You know the truth of this."

"I do," she agreed softly.

"Then we have arrived at an understanding, you and I."

She shook her head. "Not yet, though I hope that we will."

"You speak in riddles, little Viking."

"I... I am not affectionate. I am distant, cold sometimes. I would make a poor wife, you are correct on that score, and a worse lover."

"You are not cold now." He hugged her warm body to him. "And I shall determine whether you make a good lover

191

or not since I consider your judgment on the matter to be flawed." He lowered his head to brush his lips across hers, his voice rough with need when he spoke next. "I want you so much it hurts."

"I want you," she repeated. "I want all of you. But there is much to settle first."

He would have deepened the kiss but instead he drew back. He rolled onto his back and wrapped his arm about her shoulders to pull her to him in the dark.

"Once before, I asked you who had put those notions in your head, the nonsense you just spouted about being cold and unlovable. You refused to tell me. Will you tell me now?"

"I… yes, I will. I want to. I need to."

He kissed the top of her head. "Go on. We shall talk, the two of us. You will tell me what this is all about, and we shall decide what is to be done."

•••••••

"But—" Brynhild gaped at him. The past was past, there was nothing to be done.

Taranc seemingly had other ideas. "It has to end. Here, now. Whatever troubles you, it must stop. You must see this."

"It will never stop."

"When did it start?"

"What?" The sudden change of tack threw her. "What do you mean?"

"When did it start? This thing which has you tied in knots and fills you with self-loathing? If you cannot tell me about that, then tell me about the time before."

She could do that. Taranc was making this easy for her, as she should have always known he would. Brynhild drew in a deep breath, then exhaled slowly. "It was… a long time ago. I was little more than a child."

"What did you dream of, when you were a child,

192

Brynhild?"

Another question she had not anticipated. "I... I dreamed of growing up, of marrying a fine Viking warrior. I dreamed of a horde of rowdy children running about my longhouse. I would be wealthy, and beautiful, a woman of the Jarl, like my mother."

"I see. Fine dreams. You *are* beautiful, I have always thought so. Tell me more of your mother."

Brynhild closed her eyes and allowed her head to rest on his chest. She smiled as memories assailed her; the scents, sounds, impressions of her childhood. "My mother was called Solveig, and she was a fine lady. She was stern, we all obeyed her. Apart from my brother, Gunnar. He was her favourite although he was not her natural son. I... I always wanted to please her."

"I see. It is good, is it not, to strive to please your parents?"

"I failed. I disappointed her. She was angry with me. She died angry with me."

"Did she say as much?"

"No, but she must have been, after... after..."

"After," he prompted, his voice low.

"After what she saw. After she found me and... Aelbeart."

She clamped her hand over her mouth as though to ram the name back in whence it came. Until that afternoon with Dughall she had not uttered that hated, feared name for a decade, but now it hung there between them, hovering in the air like a toxic odour. She wrinkled her nose in disgust.

"Aelbeart? A Celtic name if I am not mistaken."

She nodded, no longer able to stem the flow of words. It was as though a dam had burst, and the torrent escaped, unstoppable, sweeping away all before it.

"He was a thrall, a slave in our settlement. My father purchased him, I think. I do not know, he just arrived. He was... handsome."

"I see." Taranc waited, his patience seemingly without

end.

"I… I was fourteen years old. Aelbeart would smile at me, offer me flowers sometimes. A daisy head, a rose perhaps. He told me the petals of the cornflower were the same colour as my eyes. I … I have never seen a cornflower."

"He was your friend, this Aelbeart?"

She shook her head, hard. "He was a slave, so no, we could not be friends. But, I watched him. I could not help it. He was… everywhere. Every time I left our longhouse, he would appear at my side. He helped me with my chores, told me I was pretty, and clever, and… and he flattered me. I became confused, infatuated, I suppose, but at the time I just… I just adored him."

"Was he of a similar age to you?"

"No, he was older. Twenty-five summers perhaps, maybe more. I was never quite sure."

"Ah."

"What do you mean? Ah?"

"Nothing. Please continue. Did your family know of your… interest in this slave?"

"Of course not." She gaped at him, shocked at the very suggestion. "I could never tell. Aelbeart said we must keep it a secret."

"Did he say why that was?" Taranc's tone was deceptively soft but Brynhild knew him well enough to be able to detect the undercurrent of suppressed anger. Was it directed at her? She thought not.

"He… he wanted me to help him to escape, eventually. When I was older he said we would go away together, and we would be happy."

"But running away with a slave was not your dream. I of all people should know that, and you just told me so. You were to be a lady of the Jarl, like your mother."

"A life with Aelbeart *became* my dream. I wanted it. I wanted him. I was wicked, sinful, greedy. It was all my fault."

"Wicked, sinful, *and* greedy? What happened?"

"Aelbeart wanted more than just brief and secret flirtations in the fields or around our settlement. He persuaded me to slip away and meet him, sometimes at night after the rest of my family were in bed. I did not want to at first. I was afraid… my father… But I agreed eventually. So, we would meet, walk together, talk. He… he kissed me. And I let him, because I am a slut."

"Who told you that?" he prompted.

"He did. Aelbeart. I said it was wrong, what we were doing, and that I could no longer meet him in secret. He became angry and told me I was no better than a common harlot, a slut who had teased and tempted him, only to let him down when he had trusted me. He said I was beholden to him, I owed him for the sacrifices he had made in being prepared to wait for me. He could have escaped, could have found his freedom, and he would now that he knew I did not care for him as he cared for me." She paused, remembering the heated words, the pleading as she begged Aelbeart not to leave her. "He said I must prove it, that I must prove my love for him or he would have to go. He told me that he was a Celt and that they are a passionate race. There was but one way to prove my love to a Celt, nothing less would suffice." She glanced up at Taranc, his handsome features impassive as he listened to her tale. She rushed to get the rest of it out, to lay it all before him. "I knew no better, not then, so I believed him. I went with him one night to the meadow behind the barn where the grain was stored. It was quiet there, secluded."

"You were barely more than a child."

"Even so, I knew what I was doing. I loved Aelbeart, and this was what I had to do to make him stay. He told me to lie down. He even brought a blanket…"

Taranc said nothing, but he tightened his embrace around her.

"But however much I loved him, and I did, at the time I truly did love him and I wanted to please him and make everything right, I did not like what he did to me. I did not want that. I said so, told him to let me go. He would not. He held me down. He pinned me to the ground. I struggled, cried, pleaded with him to leave me be, to let me go back home. He... he said I could never go home again. Not now. I would tell my father, and Aelbeart would be punished. My father would have had him killed, I know that to be true. I knew it then, also, but I swore I would never tell. It was no use, he would not let me go. I... I thought he meant to murder me. I still believe that he did intend that, and he would have, but for some reason he suddenly stopped and I was able to scramble away. Then my mother happened upon us."

"Solveig? She found you?"

"Yes. I have no notion why or how she knew where I was. But suddenly she was there. She was angry, I had never seen her so incensed. She ordered me to get up, to put my tunic on and to go, to run away home at once and she would deal with Aelbeart. So I ran, my feet bare on the wet grass of the meadow. I heard him yelling after me, screaming at me. He called me those names—slut, harlot, whore. That I was a cold, heartless little bitch, ugly, foul on the inside. He was yelling at my mother too, that it was all my doing and that she had borne a whore for a daughter, that I had lured him there. I was evil and corrupt and a filthy little witch."

"What did Solveig do?"

"She believed him. The evidence was clear enough. She had seen me, lying beneath him, my clothes already removed. What else was she to think?"

"Did she say that?"

"Of course not. She refused to speak of it."

"What happened to Aelbeart?"

"She had him sold, that same night. I never saw him again. He was sent to the slave auction, and we never spoke of him again. But from that night I looked for him everywhere, not in eagerness now but in dread. He had threatened to murder me. He hated me, and he had good reason. He would have his revenge. I feared him, and that fear grew. It became more than I could manage. It consumed me. I knew, deep down I knew it was a delusion, a fantasy, a dark nightmare created by my own guilt and shame and the horror of what almost happened that night but it took root and it festered. I feared all Celts. I hated them with the same passion that *he* had claimed, and I blamed them, every last one of them, for the loathing I felt every time I caught sight of my reflection in the river."

She paused, then continued, her voice now a low whisper. "I hate them still."

Taranc still held her hand in his. "No, you do not."

"I do. I—"

"I am a Celt. Dughall is a Celt. You do not hate either one of us and we do not hate you."

"But, this is not the same."

"You were a child, badly frightened and confused. It seemed simpler then perhaps, and safer, to assume that all Celts were like this Aelbeart. It was a way to protect yourself. Now, as a grown woman, you must know that not to be so. Not all Celts are evil, as Aelbeart was. He manipulated you for his own ends. He used you and he betrayed you. He would have hurt you and he deserved your hate. There is nothing irrational in the way you feel about him even now, all these years later."

"But—"

"I knew there had to be something of this nature at the root of all this. I saw, the first time I ever met you, when I knocked you to the ground to stop you from being trampled by that horse, then again in the forest. You were paralysed by fear when you found yourself pinned down. I was insensitive, I should have—"

"You were not insensitive. You were kind to me, each time, and that confused me. I... I tried to provoke you, to make you behave as Aelbeart had, as I expected you to, because that would have proved me to be correct in my fears and would have confirmed that all Celts were the same.

But you were not the same."

"No? Are we not? Did I not behave just as Aelbeart earlier, after I whipped you? You asked me to stop." He groaned. "I'm an insensitive bastard…"

"No, you are not. That was different…"

"How? How was it different?"

Brynhild took her time before she answered. She needed to think, to sift through and understand her confused emotions. "Because whatever I might have said, I wanted you. I think I always wanted you, though that terrified me at first. *You* terrified me because I was attracted to you and I feared it would all happen again, that I could not help myself. That it would be like it was with Aelbeart."

"I am not Aelbeart."

"No, you are not. And you have always taken care of me although I did not appreciate that at first." She closed her eyes, reliving the time in the forest when he had witnessed her terror and released her at once, despite the risk to himself, to his escape plans. He had not understood her fears, but he saw and he had responded.

"Yet you judge me, you judge all Celts, by the same harsh standard."

"I am sorry."

"You are forgiven."

Brynhild lay silent, considering his words. She drew in a long, deep breath. "I cannot be forgiven because I have not been punished for my wrongdoing. That is the way, is it not? You explained it to me, before, in the forest before we reached Hafrsfjord. A spanking ends the matter, and wipes away the guilt."

"Brynhild, you do *not* deserve to be punished because of this Aelbeart. The fault was entirely his, not yours."

"Not because of him. Because of Fiona."

"Fiona? What has any of this to do with her?"

"I… I was angry, hurt, scared. I blamed all Celts for what Aelbeart had done to me, and when I got the chance I took my hatred out on Fiona. And on others from time to time, but mostly on her. It… it was wrong of me. It was beneath me and I am deeply ashamed of my actions."

Taranc stroked her hair, combing his fingers through the long strands. "You need to put that behind you. It is in the past and there is nothing you can do about it. Fiona is not here, she is safe and happy with Ulfric, you did her no lasting harm."

"But I could have. How do you know? How can we know?"

"Brynhild, let it go."

"I cannot. I… everyone here is so kind to me. Your people have welcomed me and I know it is because of you, because you kept my secrets and convinced all that I am a good woman, a woman to be respected. But it is a lie. I am not like that."

"You are. You could be, if you—"

"Yes, that is what I mean, what I am asking of you. If you were to punish me for what I did, I could really start over. I would have my pride back, my self-respect. I would deserve the respect of others, including you."

"You know that you have my respect."

"I do not. How can I, when you know what I did?"

Taranc sighed, but Brynhild noted he did not disagree with her. She strengthened her resolve as he continued.

"You wronged Fiona; that is true. Therefore, it is her forgiveness you need, not mine. I have no right to punish you."

"I will never see Fiona again."

"That is probably true, though we can never know what lies ahead."

"I shall not see her again," Brynhild repeated, her tone laced with the certainty she felt. "I shall have no opportunity to set matters right with her. But… but you could act for her, on her behalf. You loved Fiona, you cared about her and wanted to protect her. From me. That is why you agreed to help my brother, is it not?"

"Yes, you know I did. And I have explained my feelings

toward Fiona."

"I know, and I do understand that. You were her friend, her betrothed. You were close to her so you could act on her behalf."

"Let me be quite certain I have understood you. You want me to act as some sort of proxy, to punish you for your cruelty to Fiona, and then to forgive you for it."

"Yes. That is it, exactly. I wish to atone for what I did. I need to find a way to redeem myself and make amends. I will accept my punishment, whatever punishment you consider fitting, and from here on I will do all I can to aid Lord Dughall in his advancing years, as Fiona would if she were here. It is all I can think of to do. Is it enough, do you believe?"

"More than enough. And just to be certain that there is no misunderstanding between us on this matter, please know that regardless of any of this you have my respect, and my admiration. You are a proud woman, I love that about you and I always have even though it drives you to do things you might later regret. But I am proud of you, and I am proud of the way you have survived the hardships and cruelty which you have endured. Although I wish the circumstances had been different, I cannot regret bringing you home with me."

Brynhild levered herself up until she knelt beside him on the bed. "So, you will help me then? You will do this thing, for me?"

"Aye, if it is your wish. But if we do this, we do it right. Your punishment will be harsh, and it will be severe. It will have to be, if you are to achieve the vindication you seek."

"I know that. I… I collected some switches on my way back from Pennglas today. They are over there, in the bucket by the door."

"Ah, such dutiful contrition, my Brynhild. That is a promising sign. However, I may have another idea, one equally suited to the gravity of the occasion. A more… intimate solution."

Brynhild's heart lurched. She had envisaged a switching, or perhaps a session with Taranc's belt. Either would hurt, she knew that well enough, but she would welcome the cleansing powers of the pain. Indeed, she was relying upon it. Now he appeared to be suggesting some other course.

"I am not sure…"

"You have asked my help, so the decision is mine, is it not?" His tone had hardened and Brynhild shivered. She recognised that timbre in his voice, the note that spoke of dominance and a man intent upon imposing his will.

"Yes, Sir," she murmured. "I am in your hands."

CHAPTER SEVENTEEN

"Tell me, Brynhild, do you have any ginger in your cooking stores?"

She knelt beside him on the bed, her expression little short of bewildered. "Ginger? I... I believe so. Why?"

Taranc allowed himself a wry smile. "Please find me a decent piece if you would. A finger at least four inches in length if you have it, the thicker the better. Whilst you do that, I shall bank up the fire since we will be glad of its warmth this night."

He watched her from the corner of his eye as he crouched beside the smouldering fire and teased the embers back into a small blaze. He tossed a couple more logs on as she returned to him, a plump but gnarled hand of ginger balanced on her palm.

"Will this do?"

"Yes, that will do very well indeed. Now you may kneel here, at my feet, and wait in silence while I prepare for your punishment." He took the ginger from her and placed it on the table, then he retrieved his woollen trousers from the floor where he had discarded them when he first came in.

"Should I get dressed too?"

"What part of kneel in silence was not quite clear to you,

Brynhild?"

He was gratified when she lowered her gaze and laid her hands on the tops of her bare thighs. So far, she seemed ready to comply though that might well change when she came to fully comprehend the humiliation he intended to visit on her. It was fitting though, since Brynhild had made it her business to humble and humiliate Fiona and the penalty to be exacted should reflect that. If his proud Viking truly did wish to make amends she would accept the justice he offered.

Taranc extracted the small dagger he always kept tucked in his belt and seated himself at the table. He did not speak to Brynhild as he sliced the thickest of the fingers from the rest and started to peel the ginger. Once he had completed that task he set to carving a deep groove all the way around it, about an inch from the end. He worked with care, taking his time as Brynhild knelt beside him. He did not glance at her, though he knew full well her eyes rarely shifted from the spicy root in his hands. The pungent aroma teased his nostrils and he knew she must smell it too.

Little did she know…

"There, I believe that will do." Taranc set the root aside and laid down his dagger. "Now, if you would be so good as to lay across my lap, I shall place the ginger where it needs to go."

"Where… where does it need to go?" Her voice shook. Perhaps she was beginning to suspect.

Taranc's tone was deliberately casual as he replied. "It is to go inside your pretty arse, my sweet Viking. So if you will just position yourself as I asked, I can get on with putting it there."

"My…? No, that is… it is…." Her eyes widened, her shock and dismay apparent. She shuffled back as though she might even now elude his punishment.

It was already much too late for that.

"Brynhild, do not provoke me further by making this difficult. I have told you what is to happen and your only task here is to submit and to obey. This is your punishment, this and the spanking you will shortly endure. The ginger will make the sensation all the more… intense, but this is what you want, is it not? This is the price of the forgiveness you seek."

"I do not understand. How…?"

"Brynhild, you will place yourself over my lap at once, and cease asking questions. All will be clear soon enough." Taranc deliberately sharpened his tone. Obedience was required, not conversation. He expected her to do as she was told, and to do it now.

Slowly, hesitantly, Brynhild got to her feet. She approached him, placed her hand on his wool-clad knee, then with a soft whimper she laid down across his lap.

Taranc took a moment to admire her slender back and rounded buttocks as they were displayed before him. Her skin was pale in comparison to his own sun-kissed torso, testimony to her Nordic heritage and to a life spent in a cool climate. He trailed the backs of his fingers down her spine, noting the way she trembled under his touch but did not squirm or wriggle. She was scared, apprehensive, but she was ready to surrender to his demands.

"This is good. Now you will reach back with both your hands and hold your buttocks apart for me."

Brynhild gasped. "I cannot. You cannot ask me to do that."

"I have not asked you, I have told you. Now you will obey."

And she did. After just a moment or two of hesitation, Brynhild stretched her arms behind her and dug her fingers into the fleshy curves of her bottom. She pulled the soft globes apart, exposing the tight ring of muscle that guarded her secret entrance, soon to be breached.

"I cannot see properly. Lift your bottom up a little more. Show me your arse, Brynhild, then ask me to place the ginger inside your hole."

Taranc's cock leapt to granite hardness as she adjusted

her position to afford him a better view. She planted her feet firmly on the rough earth floor in order to lift her buttocks higher and tip a little further forward on his lap.

"Spread your legs, too. I want to see your pretty cunny, and watch your arousal grow as I spank you."

At another time she might have disputed the prospect of arousal, but she merely widened her stance to expose her plump lower lips to his view. Despite her nervousness, and the humiliation he was heaping upon her with the promise of worse to come, her clitty was already swollen and peeking out from under the hood that sheathed it. Taranc saw no reason not to enjoy himself by toying with her for a while.

He laid the tip of his finger on her clit and circled the sensitive nub, slow at first, his touch the barest whisper. He increased the speed and pressure as she swelled and writhed, only stopping when he sensed she was close to her climax. He traced the outer edges of her entrance, his touch idle now as he collected her moisture on his fingers.

"I shall use your own juices to ease the way for the ginger because I am not a heartless man, but be under no illusion that this will be easy. The natural oils from the root will provide some help, I daresay, but they will feel as though they are burning your tender skin. This is a most sensitive place, my proud Viking, as you are soon to discover."

As he spoke he laid the tip of his middle finger against the tight pucker and started to press. Brynhild resisted, squeezing against him as though to deny him entrance. Taranc lifted his hand and dropped a sharp slap onto her upturned buttock.

"Stop that. You will allow me entry." Again, his tone was sharp, stern.

"I... I apologise. I did not intend..."

"Just relax if you can, Brynhild, but if you cannot manage that then you will submit to this anyway. Do not resist."

"No, Sir. I understand. I... oh!"

She let out a sharp squeal as he twisted his finger and it entered her up to the first knuckle. Taranc paused, allowed her a few moments to adjust, then he pushed the rest of his finger into her tight rear hole.

"Good. Thank you." He rotated his finger inside her as Brynhild panted, her breath warm against his bare ankle. "Am I hurting you?"

"N-no, Sir. It just feels very odd."

He supposed it would but saw no merit in commenting further. Instead he reached for the peeled ginger root.

"I could slacken your hole by driving my finger in and out, like this…" he demonstrated with a couple of quick, deep strokes that left Brynhild groaning on his lap, "maybe add another finger, perhaps two. On another occasion, probably, I will. But for today, I want you to remain tight, and grip the root hard to gain maximum benefit from the lesson I intend to teach you this night. It will be more painful, and more memorable for you. A true penance. Are you not delighted that I have considered so thoroughly your need for atonement, my Viking?"

Brynhild was silent, for once. That would not do.

"Have you forgotten that you are to ask me to insert the ginger?"

"I… I have not forgotten."

Taranc waited, the pungent root poised between his fingers.

"Please, Sir, would you place the ginger inside me?" Her voice was small, barely audible.

"Inside you? Where inside you, exactly?"

"In… in my arse, Sir."

"It will be my pleasure, though probably not yours." Slowly, deliberately, he withdrew the finger that had penetrated her arsehole. The pink pucker remained slightly open, quivering as she waited. Taranc placed the end without the groove against the tight entrance, and he pushed.

"Oh. Oh!" Brynhild let out a moan as the root slid into her.

Taranc paused when the first inch disappeared and

turned the ginger slowly in her tight rear channel. Her entire body trembled but she managed to maintain the firm grip she had established on her buttocks as she held them open for him, and she remained still. Taranc pressed again and the rest of the root slipped past the coil of muscle that closed snugly around the groove he had carved, holding the intruder in place.

"You may let go now, and relax. It is in."

"Is… is that it?" She sounded quite hopeful.

"Not quite. There remains the matter of your spanking."

"Of course. How many spanks will you—?"

"Until I decide you are truly sorry. And Brynhild, be assured, you will be very, very sorry by the time I am finished."

"Perhaps you should get on with it, then."

Ah, belligerent as ever. "I believe I shall wait a moment or two. Until I am quite sure I have your attention."

"What do you mean? I… oh, oh, that stings. It is burning me…"

"Ah, the ginger is starting to take effect. In a minute or so it will reach the point where you are unable to remain still or gain any relief. When you reach that point you will tell me, and I shall commence your spanking."

Brynhild whimpered and wriggled on his lap. She reached back again, as though she might grasp the root herself and pull it out. Taranc captured her flailing hands and folded them in the small of her back.

"Tell me when you are ready to start, my Viking." It would not be long now.

"I think… I think…. Oh! Ooooh!"

Right, then. Taranc started to drop slaps onto her upturned buttocks, slow at first, setting up a steady rhythm. Each spank caused her firm flesh to indent, then spring back, reshaping into its former curve, the mark of his hand a pink smudge on her pale skin. The sight was glorious, made even more so by the inch of pale golden ginger protruding from her delectable arse.

Brynhild slithered and squirmed and rolled about on his lap but Taranc held her firm, his free hand holding her wrists together against her back, and his leg slung across hers to ensure she did not roll off his knee in her agitation. He watched as she clenched and squeezed and fought to escape the burning from within, which by now must be excruciating, and all the while he continued to drop spank after spank onto her reddened bottom. Only when her squeals had risen to a volume that he feared might attract unwelcome attention from elsewhere in the village and both buttocks had darkened to a rather delicate shade of cerise did he pause.

"It hurts less if you do not clench."

Brynhild panted and sniffled as she struggled to regain some semblance of control.

"What do you mean? How can I not clench when you, when you are…?"

"Quite, and this is your dilemma. Lie still, and relax your bottom. Does the burning subside?"

A few moments passed, during which he supposed she was testing his assertion.

"Well? Does it?"

"Yes, I suppose so."

"And now clench, as you were before."

It took scant seconds for her to begin squealing all over again and wriggling against his hold.

"Oooh, oooh!"

"Settle down." He waited until she lay reasonably still once more. "So, now you know. If you keep your bottom soft while I continue your spanking, you may be able to manage the ginger. It is worth trying, is it not?"

"How can I stay soft when you are spanking me so hard?"

"And I will spank you harder still. We are nowhere near done yet, but you must have expected that. You have much to atone for, my Viking."

"I know," wailed Brynhild, and he suspected that her

gulping sobs were not entirely generated by her current predicament.

"Shall we continue?" He softened his tone and caressed her bottom gently. The heat from her flushed skin warmed his palm as she winced under his touch.

"Yes. Yes," she agreed. "Please, I need this to be over."

Taranc commenced the spanking again, but the smacks were deliberately harder now. For the most part she managed not to clench her buttocks, and he fancied the effort must be worth it as she seemed less agitated, more resigned to her fate. He started to drop slaps on the backs of her thighs too, paying particular attention to the spot where her legs and bottom met. His Viking would not sit in comfort for a while.

Brynhild cried out with each stroke, but her sobs and squeals were muffled as she pressed her face against his legs. It seemed she was no more anxious to attract attention than he was and ready to accept as much punishment as he chose to dole out. Only when she lay still against his thighs though did he slow down and finally halt the relentless onslaught.

Brynhild sobbed quietly. Taranc released her hands and she buried her face in them, weeping as though her heart was quite broken.

"I am sorry, so sorry…" she repeated, again and again, the mantra rolling from her tongue.

Taranc knew it to be true, and it was enough.

"We are done here," he murmured. "You may go and lie on the pallet, and tell me when the ginger stops burning, which should not be too long now as the effect is short-lived. I will then take it out."

He half-expected her to demand that he remove the root at once, but she did not. Obedient as a puppy, she rose unsteadily to her feet and tottered the few steps across the room to reach their bed where she lowered herself onto it. She lay face down, her punished bottom and thighs glowing in the flickering light of the fire. Taranc could not recall having seen a more beautiful sight. He sought out a lamp and carefully lit the wick, the better to peruse his handiwork.

"Take a few moments, think about what has just happened between us, and about what is to happen next."

"I… what is to happen now? I thought you said it was over."

"Your punishment is over, but it does not end there. A severely chastised woman needs to be fucked."

"I… I believe I might like that, Sir."

"I am bloody certain you will. I intend to make it my business to ensure that you do. So, the ginger…?"

CHAPTER EIGHTEEN

It took but a few moments to remove the ginger from her unresisting arse. Brynhild's modesty was entirely vanquished, it seemed, as she lay acquiescent for him. The used root discarded on the floor, he removed his trousers again then rolled her onto her side to face him as he lay down beside her.

Her eyes were red-rimmed, tears still glistened amid the azure but she managed a tremulous smile.

"Thank you," she whispered, and leaned up to brush her lips across his. The kiss was a shy one, hesitant and uncertain, as though she half-expected to be rebuffed, even now. He recalled what she had said about being cold, undemonstrative. His proud Viking had much to learn.

Taranc cupped her jaw in his hand and slanted his mouth over hers. She reached for him, twisting her fingers in his hair. He deepened the kiss, angling his lips over hers and teasing his tongue over the seam until she parted to allow him in. He tasted her, tested the warmth and wetness of her inner space, played with her as he danced his tongue over hers. Brynhild gasped, her breath catching in her throat. Slowly, uncertainly, she began to respond, her tongue tangling about his as she sucked gently.

Sweet Jesu, where did she learn such a trick?

Taranc rolled onto her, his palms now flattened against her breasts. The plump mounds swelled in his hands, nipples pebbling as he caught the delicate peaks between his fingers. He broke the kiss, intending to take her stiff little bud in his mouth, but paused when she went rigid in his arms. He glanced into her face, now more clearly visible as his eyes accustomed to the dark. She stared back at him, terror and yearning at war across her tense features.

With a silent curse at his own thoughtlessness Taranc rolled onto his back, pulling her with him so she landed on top, her nude body draped across his chest. She cried out, grabbing for his shoulders.

"What? What are you doing? I do not want to stop, I…"

"Then do not stop. Kiss me, Brynhild."

"But I do not know how…"

"You did it before. Lay your mouth on mine. We shall go from there." He combed his fingers through her hair, blessing the sweet Saviour that she chose to wear it loose when in their bed, and drew her down toward him. Her lips met his, and she softened into the kiss. He darted his tongue between her lips again and their sensual dance continued unabated.

Ah, but his little Viking was a fast learner. She scrambled further onto him, her legs braced on either side of his hips as she rubbed against him, her wetness coating his lower abdomen. She was oblivious, he knew that. Brynhild had no idea that her arousal pooled on his skin, that her readiness, her desire was so redolent he could actually smell the sweet aroma of her. He feathered his touch across her shoulders and down her spine, probing each vertebra in turn as she writhed under his hands. When he palmed her tender, punished buttocks, her kiss became more desperate, more untutored yet all the sweeter for it. He cared nothing for delicate technique and all for unbridled sensuality.

"I want… I need…" Her words were frantic, breathy. She pushed herself up on her hands to peer into his face.

"Tell me what to do."

"Straddle me," he commanded. "Take my cock in your hands and direct it toward you."

"I cannot. I do not know how."

"I shall show you."

He helped her to arrange herself as he had described, her hot quim hovering just a fraction away from the head of his cock. He took his erection in his own hand, angled it to her entrance and thrust his hips up. Her slick lips parted to accept just the tip of his cock, but he did not press home. Instead he smeared his own juices with hers, spreading their wetness about, coating her lower lips from the tight ring of her arse to the quivering nub of her clitty. She moaned as he rubbed the smooth, slick head of his cock against that sensitive button, the delicate flesh plump and trembling as he worked her harder.

He positioned his cock at her entrance, just inside, then released his grip to allow her own lips to hold him there. His hand now free, he rubbed her clitty in earnest, from side to side, then as she squirmed and panted he circled with his fingertip. She lowered her body, almost imperceptibly taking more of him inside her.

Brynhild was lost, her moans becoming more frenetic as she sought something he knew she did not really understand but pursued with an intensity she could not control. He could exercise restraint, however, and one of them must. He would not allow this to fail; it was too vital, too critical to their future together.

This had to be good. For her. She must succeed here, now, tonight.

He brought her higher, closer, his skilled fingers teasing and stroking and caressing her clitty as she soared toward her release. He lifted his hips, pressing forward, upward. Her body stretched and opened to accept him.

Brynhild gasped. Taranc paused, waited. She circled her hips, lowering herself a fraction more, working him inside her.

"It feels… tight. It will not fit."

He detected the wondering despair in her tone and was not having it.

"It is tight, gloriously so, but we fit beautifully."

"I… oh!" She let out a sharp cry as he pressed forward again.

"Am I hurting you?"

"Yes," she whispered. "Do not stop."

He buried his face in the hollow of her neck as he squeezed and tugged on her clitty. Her body quivered in his arms, trembling as her response surged forth.

"Oh, I… I…"

He knew the exact moment of her release and used the sudden, uncontrolled softening of her body as his opportunity to drive his cock fully home. She screamed, a rasping, guttural sound of pleasure laced with pain, and her cunt convulsed around him.

Taranc held still, his palms now on her buttocks to hold her in place. Brynhild was unmoving, her body reshaping to accept his intrusion. Taranc kissed her hair, murmured words intended to calm, to reassure, to thank her. Brynhild tilted her head back to meet his gaze.

"So, Celt, you are finally fucking me." Her tone was triumphant.

"'Twould seem so."

"Is this it? All that there is?" She rotated her hips in a large, slow circle.

He shook his head. "Not entirely. I prefer to take my time though. We shall go slow, and gentle, and with infinite tenderness."

"Tenderness?" She furrowed her brow. "Why tenderness? Why is that necessary? I thought—"

He kissed the end of her nose. "I know what you thought, and why. But you were wrong. There will be tenderness between us. You ask too many questions, little Viking. I have one for you though. Is there any pain still?"

She frowned all the more. "Why, no. No, there is not.

How? I mean, I thought…"

"Tenderness," he repeated, tightening his grip on her sore buttocks to rotate her hips since she had stopped. He groaned as she instinctively squeezed her inner muscles around his cock. "Oh, sweet Jesu, you feel so good."

"As do you, Celt." She clenched again and resumed the motion herself now, rolling her hips and picking up on his sensual manipulation as she moved to take control of her own pleasure and his.

Typical Brynhild, he mused. Always taking charge, always wanting to lead, to give rather than to take. He would allow it, this time, this first time because he sensed that she needed this in order to start to restore her confidence. But it would not always be thus.

Brynhild rocked her hips above him, lifted her body then sank back down to take him fully inside her. His hands on her waist helped to take her weight, but the initiative was all hers. He allowed her to play, to test and experiment, to explore what felt right and good and where the pleasure pooled. Her breasts bobbed and swayed before his eyes, the plump, rosy-tipped mounds begging to be licked. Taranc took one nipple between his lips and sucked hard. Brynhild arched toward him, thrusting her breasts at him, wordlessly demanding more.

Her second release was swift, more intense than the first, he fancied, as she shook with the force of it. Brynhild wrapped her arms about his head to hug him to her, pressing her breast into his mouth. She pumped up and down on his cock, greedy and insatiable now, demanding and insistent as she ground her body down onto his.

He could not hold out much longer, but neither would he allow himself to finish before she was done. He slid his hand between their bodies again to take her clitty between his finger and thumb and roll the sensitive nubbin. She panted, ready, straining, seeking, reaching…

Taranc reached around her with his other hand to insinuate his fingers in the seam of her bottom. He found

215

her rear hole, circled once, pressed, and slipped the tip of his middle finger inside.

Brynhild screamed. She screamed long and hard and loud, the sound barely muffled at all against his shoulder.

He blessed the foresight that had led him to bar the door as he entered. The last thing he wanted at this juncture was his mother and his aunt bursting in armed with pitchforks and torches, bent upon rescue.

His own release followed hers but scant moments later. Taranc let out his own groan of satisfaction as his balls tightened, twisted within their sack and his semen surged forth to fill his she-Viking's hot, tight channel. He grimaced into the darkness, a smile playing on his lips.

He was content.

• • • • • • •

Days passed, stretched into weeks, then months. Taranc found no cause for complaint at the bargain he had struck. Brynhild set his home to rights, assisted by Annag. His meals were wholesome, hearty, and hot. She weaved; she marched about his village, cloak billowing in the stiff northerly breeze that heralded the onset of the colder month, ordering his people about. She showed them how to salt the fish they caught, and insisted that a deep pit be dug in which to store ice in the winter. They could preserve their meat in ice, she insisted, enjoy fresh food in the depths of the harshest blizzards when it was impossible to hunt or fish. She never stopped, was always moving, always working, as though by constant movement she might stave off the need to think, to reflect upon the injustices that had brought her here.

Did she long for her home? For those left behind?

He did not know and would not ask again. He had offered, just once, to take her back to the Norseland if she so wished and he would have aided her in presenting her case to her brother; if not Ulfric then the other, Gunnar.

Brynhild had refused, insisting that she had no desire to ever see Ulfric again.

If there was one thing he could say with certainty about his lovely Brynhild, it was that she held a grudge well. She swore she would never forgive her brother for his betrayal and Taranc saw no cause to doubt it.

Privately, Taranc could find no reason to quibble with Ulfric's decision, wrong-headed though it had been. Taranc had emerged the victor.

Brynhild was happy, he was sure of that. He knew she found pleasure in managing her household and enjoyed the company of Dughall. She spent most evenings at the manor house in Pennglas, but was always pleased to accompany Taranc back down to the coastal village and to writhe with undisguised lust in his arms the moment their door was closed and barred.

She was a truly glorious lover, responsive to his touch but equally ready to initiate their lovemaking. She was inquisitive too, and inventive, a sensual creature who once awakened revelled in her own pleasure and in his. He would chuckle and insist he had unleashed a siren of old, a Nordic goddess devoted to sensuality and lust. Brynhild would laugh and assure him that the goddess Freya had far weightier matters to concern her than the state of a Celtic fisherman's cock, but she would have no hesitation in dropping to her knees before him and releasing that same swollen cock from within his woven trousers. She would cradle his erection in her hands, lick the tip, taste the juices that flowed from the slit there before taking as much of the head and shaft as she could inside her mouth. Then she would work her tongue and teeth and throat until his seed spurted forth. She would swallow hard and lick him clean, a contented smile playing about her sensual lips as she sat back on her heels inordinately pleased with herself.

Cold? Never.

Distant? Lacking in affection? He believed not though she was not even remotely demonstrative in other ways.

Always proper, always respectful toward him in public, Brynhild was quietly efficient and fair in her dealings with his people and seemed to have found contentment here at Aikrig. This was all that mattered to Taranc. He loved her. It was that simple.

• • • • • • •

"Do you have a few minutes to walk with me?"

Taranc glanced up from the timbers of the fishing boat whose hull he was coating with pitch. Brynhild stood behind him, her cloak flapping in the breeze. Her elegant features appeared tense, her skin paler than he liked. He hoped she was not sickening in this unfamiliar land, this strange climate, though surely she was accustomed to worse.

"Is all well with you, my Viking?" He rose to his feet and wiped his hands down his trousers.

Brynhild picked up a piece of rag and offered it to him. "Here, clean your hands. Yes, perfectly well. Come."

She turned to pick her way along the beach, turning just once to make sure he was indeed following her.

Taranc took a few moments to admire the tempting sway of her hips as she moved away from him. Perhaps she might not object too strenuously if he was to suggest she get herself back here right now and drape herself over the rail of the boat he was working on. She might even be so good as to invite him to lift her tunic to reveal her bare arse. He would ram his cock into her from behind, for he knew she loved it when he did that, and perhaps drop a few playful spanks on her delectable cheeks.

The notion had real merit. He opened his mouth to summon her back, but she chose that moment to pause and turn around.

"Please, hurry. I… I need to talk to you."

The troubled expression on her beautiful features dispelled his errant thoughts. He strode after her, then fell in step alongside.

"Tell me," he ordered.

"Soon. I just—"

He stopped, took her hand, and turned her to face him. "Tell me."

She tilted her chin, her jaw flexing in a defiant expression he had come to know well. Belligerence was writ across her features, as though she expected him to take her to task. What had she done?

Taranc waited, arms folded.

"I am pregnant."

"Ah." He should not be surprised, he spilled his seed into her on a more or less nightly basis. It was only ever a matter of time. Yet, he was taken aback. Perhaps it was her attitude toward this turn of events that dictated her hostile reaction rather than the news itself. "You find this to be a matter of some concern?"

"Do you not?" She stamped her foot in indignation, as though that might change anything.

Taranc shrugged. "No."

"We cannot wed."

"Can we not? Very well."

"My child will be a bastard."

"Our child will be chief of this village in due course, and my heir. I shall acknowledge and own him."

"What if it is a girl?"

"The same."

"Oh. Well, that is all right then. Thank you, Celt. I merely wished to make sure." She turned to leave him there on the beach.

Taranc watched her retreating form for a few seconds, allowed her to complete five, perhaps six paces, then he set off after her at a sprint. He caught her up, seized her about the waist and tossed her into the air, Brynhild flopped back down into his arms in a chaotic flurry of flapping cloak and kicking legs as she shrieked her outraged protest at such undignified treatment of her person.

"Set me down at once. What are you doing? You are

quite deranged, Celt, a savage. I shall—"

Taranc put an end to the tirade before she could properly warm to her theme by the simple expedient of kissing her. Brynhild went still in his arms, then curled her wrist behind his head and pulled him closer. She could never resist a direct assault on her senses. He exploited that trait without mercy, deepening the kiss as he strode with her up the beach and into the cover of the surrounding trees.

"Where are we going?" She managed to mutter the question against his lips. Taranc did not break stride, or pause to respond.

He soon reached his destination, a secluded copse ringed by a dense undergrowth. Here, the trees were less closely packed and soft meadow grass carpeted the ground. Dappled sunlight tumbled through the branches overhead, the illumination soft and pale, delicately painting the earth below. Here, Taranc set her on her feet. He spread his cloak on the ground then drew her down to her knees beside him.

"Lie down, sweetheart."

"Here? Why?"

"Yes, here." He grinned into her startled face. "And do it because I asked it of you."

She eased herself onto her back, eyeing him with undisguised suspicion. Her brow furrowed even more when he moved to kneel between her feet, but she did not protest when he lifted her skirt to her waist.

Blonde curls greeted him. Taranc bent to press his nose into them, inhaling the sweet, musky aroma of her, a scent that he loved. He fancied he could detect the slight change that denoted her pregnancy, though of course that was whimsical and she would laugh out loud were he to voice such romantic nonsense. His practical Brynhild had no time for such capricious sentiment.

He spread her thighs and drew the flat of his tongue through her folds, already damp. Her breath hitched as he eased the tip of his tongue inside her entrance, she lifted her hips, thrust forward. He pushed her knees up toward her chest, raising and opening her to him. His beautiful she-Viking, so prickly moments before, relaxed in his hands and allowed her thighs to part. She flung her hands behind her head, her eyes closed as he lapped at the sensitive button of her clitty. The delicate flesh swelled, peeped out from within the hood that had shrouded it just moments before, darkening to a deep, rich pink as her arousal built.

He could fuck her. She would love that, he knew, as would he. But not this time. This time, he had something else in mind. He scraped his teeth across the tip of her clit, then suckled gently upon it. Brynhild writhed on the ground before him, twisting her hips one way then the other as she sought to increase the intensity of sensation.

Taranc held her still. On this occasion, he would control and she would accept. There would be no coercion, just a determined and ruthless erotic storm designed end executed with deliberate intent to send her past the point of oblivion. It was time his Viking learnt the true meaning of surrender.

He brought her to the edge of her release, then retreated. Brynhild arched her back, her heels now planted on the blanket as she pressed her demanding cunt against his mouth. She tasted so luscious, so exquisite, so utterly delicious he could have wept.

"Taranc, please…" Her voice was ragged, her moan verging on desperation.

This was good, but his beautiful Nordic lover had some distance to travel yet, Taranc determined. She would beg and plead and weep for her release, and her pleasure would be all the sweeter for it. He slipped two fingers into her channel, then a third.

Her inner walls fluttered about his thrusting digits as he plunged deep. He turned his hand, angling his fingers as he sought that spot that would send her wild. He found it, smiled as she lurched under his skilled touch.

"Now. Taranc, I need you to… to… oh! *Oh!*" She thrashed her head from side to side on the cloak, her fingers now tunnelling through his hair as she sought to control the precise angle and pressure of his assault on her senses. Her efforts were to no avail, Taranc was determined upon that, but he enjoyed witnessing her futile attempts to force the pace.

He lifted his head and gazed up at her; her features were flushed now, the rosy hue spreading from beneath her cloak and creeping up her neck. Her jaw was tight, her lips flattened against her teeth. She glared at him.

"What are you waiting for? I am ready."

He splayed the palm of his hand across her lower abdomen, his thumb lazily tracing a gentle caress over the tip of her clitty. She gasped and arched upward.

"You like that?"

"Yes," she ground out.

"What else do you like?"

"You know what I like."

"Tell me. Tell me what you want, and you shall have it."

"My release. I want my release. Why are you doing this?"

"How do you want it? Tell me."

"I do not understand. You know—"

"What do you want me to do to you? How would you prefer to be touched?"

"With your mouth!" She yelled the words at him. "Your mouth, your tongue, inside me."

Taranc smiled. "Ah, not so hard after all, once you stop resisting your desires. My tongue, then…" He leaned back in and parted the lips of her cunny with his thumbs, then plunged his tongue as deep as he was able inside her quivering entrance.

Brynhild trembled. She shuddered, panting softly as he drew his tongue in and out.

"Your fingers now. Deeper…"

"My pleasure," he murmured, driving three fingers deep again. He wondered if she would have the words, the awareness of her own body that would enable her to ask him to stroke that pleasure spot.

"There is somewhere, a place where it is more…"

Ah, so she had been taking notice.

"You mean just here, my sweet?" He found the place and pressed.

"Yes. Oh… yes…"

"Is there more I might do for you? Remember, you have but to request and it is yours."

"Your mouth…"

"Again? Of course. Is there any particular—?"

"Suck me. That place. Just here…" She released her grip on his hair in order to lay her fingers over her swollen clit. "It feels good here."

"Oh, yes, I know it does. Like this, then…"

He took the plump bud between his lips and scraped it with his teeth. He watched as her eyes rolled back in her head, her entire body now shaking as he brought her once again to the very brink of ecstasy. This time, he did not retreat. This time he held her there, his fingers inside her, his mouth, teeth, tongue working on her clitty to draw every last frisson of sensual delight from her body.

He knew it, the precise moment she yielded. He knew the exact instant she gave herself over into his keeping, her pleasure his to create, to give or withhold as he chose.

He witnessed the definitive juncture when she handed him her trust and he took it into his keeping.

Satisfied he had attained his goal, Taranc hollowed his cheeks to increase the suction on her clitty, just enough to send her spiralling past the point of no return. His fingers stretched and caressed her inner walls, his tongue flicked the tip of her clit without mercy and she was lost.

Brynhild fisted his hair between her fingers and she screeched her release to the heavens.

After, she lay still, spent in his arms. He held her, enjoyed the gentle rise and fall of her chest as her breath returned to normal. His hand lay within the folds of her cloak, her breast beneath his palm. He allowed himself a private smile as her heartbeat slowed, settled to a steady, rhythmic beat.

He believed she was happy, here, with him. Or she could

be, if she could be reconciled to her past and embrace her future. Their future.

"Why did you do that?" she murmured drowsily.

He did not pretend to misunderstand. "Why, for the sheer joy of it, Brynhild. For the sheer fucking joy of it."

CHAPTER NINETEEN

Brynhild folded her hands together across the round swell of her abdomen. The baby delivered a sharp kick from inside, hard enough to halt her step. She paused to brace against a tree beside the track that led to Pennglas. She had promised Dughall that she would call to see him this day and did not wish to disappoint her friend though she found the journey on foot arduous as she entered the final month of her pregnancy.

The old man had been unwell. He had succumbed to a chill that had gone to his chest and kept him confined to his bed these past two weeks. He was improving now, and she was relieved to hear the news but would feel better for seeing him herself and watching him sip the draught of chamomile tea she intended to brew for him. It was a most efficacious cure; she had every confidence Dughall would soon be up and about again. Best to press on. Brynhild straightened, drew in a deep breath, and continued her hike uphill.

Pounding footsteps from behind brought her to a halt again. She turned. Several villagers from Aikrig scrambled up the rise toward her, their pallid faces lined in alarm. One man peered back over his shoulder then grabbed the elbow of a woman by his side. "Come, we must hurry. There is refuge to be had in Pennglas, Taranc said that it is so."

Refuge? Brynhild reached for the man's sleeve as he passed her.

"Why are you fleeing to the village? Has something happened to Taranc?"

Please let it not be so. She would offer up another fine goat to the goddess Freya, if such were needed to keep her man safe.

The man barely broke his stride. "They are back. Taranc told us to make haste to Pennglas and to warn the people there. We shall fight them this time. They shall not steal from us again, nor shall they take our people as slaves. Taranc will not allow it, never again."

"Who? Who is here?" The man she first spoke to had shrugged off her hold and was already scurrying up the hill away from her. Brynhild reached for an elderly woman, Aine, a widow she had come to know who had skills in the art of dye-making. The woman stopped.

"Ye need to be coming wi' us, lass. Taranc will want ye safe, I ken it."

"I *am* safe. What is happening?"

"We are attacked. The Vikings are back."

Her knees buckled. She clutched at Aine who wrapped her arms about Brynhild's waist.

"Let me help ye, lady. We shall take refuge in the manor house with Lord Dughall."

Brynhild gathered her wits, and with her returning senses came temper. White hot, searing anger surged through her. She staggered back, shaking her head.

Vikings? Vikings dared to come here, to her home?

Her people?

She would not stand for it.

"You go on to the village, find safety and tell Lord Dughall what is happening. Bid him see everyone safely inside, the doors barred. I shall go to the beach."

"No, ye cannot. Taranc would—"

Brynhild glowered down at the smaller woman. "I am a Viking. These invaders are *my* people. They need to know they are not welcome here, that there is nothing on this shore for them. I shall stand beside Taranc and tell them as much."

There were more protests, more pleading that she look to her own safety and that of her child and accompany the fleeing villagers, but Brynhild was no longer listening. She gathered her cloak about her and started back down the hill, her step brisk and purposeful as she headed for the beach and for Taranc. Together they would face down these Nordic raiders and send them back into the sea.

She encountered others as she went, others from Aikrig, all dashing headlong up the narrow lane in search of safety. She caught snatches of conversation as the villagers rushed past.

"I remember him, the tall one with the yellow hair."

"He was here before, the other time…"

"Lady Fiona… was it really she? It looked like—"

Heart in her mouth, the truth only now beginning to dawn, Brynhild burst through the barrier of trees that shielded the beach from view. She stopped in her tracks, barely able to take in the scene before her.

All the Celts but Taranc had fled. He, alone, stood on the damp sand face to face with the tall Viking warrior who stood proud at the helm of his dragon ship as the vessel bobbed on the waves.

Ulfric.

Her brother. Here.

Brynhild beheld the tableau, unable to breathe for several moments. Taranc's confident tone rang across the beach.

"What is your purpose here, Viking?" He spoke in the Nordic tongue.

"Ah, now on that matter I would like to talk with you. May we come ashore?"

No! Every fibre of Brynhild's being screamed 'no!'

Taranc was seemingly not of similar mind. "You may, Viking. And Fiona, naturally. Is that your boy I see there?"

Her brother inclined his blond head respectfully to the village chief before him. "Aye, my family is with me."

"Indeed." Brynhild could not fail to recognise the note of sardonic amusement that now laced Taranc's tone. "This promises to be quite the reunion then."

Ulfric appeared unsurprised at the enigmatic response. "She is here? And well?"

"Of course, though I would caution against paying your respects, Viking. Your actions were not well received."

Brynhild had seen, and heard, enough. She strode forward, incensed. "How dare you show your treacherous face here? You claim to be a brother—you are nothing more than a self-serving worm. If my husband does not fell you where you stand, I shall do so myself."

She marched down the beach to take up her stance beside the man she had refused to wed but now claimed as her husband, the man she had chosen to spend her life with, the man who had saved her. Taranc had given her very existence meaning, a purpose. He had put a child in her belly, taught her to enjoy her body, to take her pleasure as she now knew she deserved, yet he seemed ready to betray her without a second thought. For reasons she could not start to fathom Taranc was about to welcome Ulfric onto their soil. It was not to be borne.

Silence descended. The Vikings who had remained on board the dragon ships with their leader gaped at her as recognition dawned. Their faces betrayed their utter confusion. Fiona, too, clutched at Ulfric's sleeve as though demanding some semblance of explanation. It seemed she was to be disappointed, at least for now.

Ulfric was first to speak. He angled his head toward her and plastered a broad smile across his duplicitous features. "Ah, sister. You appear... well." His assessing gaze travelled over her distended belly and his eyes narrowed. "Much has happened, I see, since last we spoke." His next words were aimed at Taranc. "Yours, I presume?"

Taranc's nod was abrupt and curt. He reached for
Brynhild's hand and squeezed it briefly before she managed
to snatch her fingers out of his grasp. He met her gaze, his
expression calm but not without a hint of warning, then he
turned and strode up the beach in the direction of the house
they shared.

He did not look back again. His final words were flung
over his shoulder, and she assumed they were intended for
Ulfric. "Are you coming then?"

Brynhild hurried after Taranc. "You cannot permit this.
I do not want him here. I want none of them here."

"It seems you are to be disappointed, my sweet, since he
is following us up the beach. I trust we have food to hand,
ale a-plenty? Where is Annag? Murdina?"

"I do not know. Everyone fled to Pennglas on your
orders. I shall not feed them."

Taranc shrugged. "Your brother has said he wishes only
to talk. If that is all, and I see no cause not to believe him,
we can hear him out and he can be on his way."

"But—" Brynhild whirled to face her brother and the
woman he had chosen over her, the woman who had lied
about her actions that fateful night and caused Ulfric to cast
his sister from her home. She marched forward to punch
her brother hard in the centre of his chest, bringing his
progress to a halt.

"Now, Brynhild, I only want to—"

"Shut up. Why would I care what you want? Did you
care about *my* wishes all those months ago when you plotted
to have me abducted, carried from my home by force?
When you cast me out to make room for your... your..."

"Brynhild." Taranc's tone was low, a warning. In time,
Brynhild recalled that the woman who stood before her was
Dughall's daughter, and for that reason alone she would
hold her tongue.

"You are not welcome here. If you are not gone from
these shores within the hour I shall gut you and leave your

entrails here on the beach for the gulls and crabs to feast on."

"I am not convinced such a welcome would find favour with the rest of the Nordic horde waiting on the longships," observed Taranc, his customary sardonic smile returning. "Perhaps we might be a little less brutal in our approach, less bloodthirsty?"

Brynhild cast a baleful glance his way, her tone scathing. "You may find peaceful solutions if you feel so moved. I just want them gone. All of them. I shall go to Pennglas. I expect to find no dragon ships on our beach when I return."

• • • • • • •

Dughall found her in her usual spot, curled in the window seat beneath his hall.

"Is it the truth? My daughter is here? Fiona has returned?"

Brynhild raised her tear-ravaged features to regard him as a pang of irrational jealousy pierced her. Yet again, she would be set aside in favour of the Celtic woman. "Yes, he has come and he has brought her with him."

"Where are they? I must see my daughter."

"I left them at Taranc's house in Aikrig." She swiped the moisture from her eyes and managed a wan smile for her old friend. She could not be ungenerous, even now. "I know that Fiona will not leave without seeing you."

Dughall nodded. "And your brother? Did you speak with him?"

"I did, briefly. I invited him to turn his ships about and leave at once or I would scatter his entrails upon the beach."

"I see. 'Twas not a joyful reunion, then."

"He betrayed me. He believed Fiona's lies and… and…"

"Why would he not believe my daughter? She is not a woman given to spouting falsehoods." Dughall's voice remained level, but his resolve was clear enough. He would not hear criticism of his beloved child.

"I…" Brynhild clamped her mouth shut. What was there left to say?

"My lord, Taranc approaches. The Viking is with him."

Dughall murmured his thanks to the servant who had scurried in to announce the imminent arrival of their visitors. Brynhild noted that he did not call for refreshments, for ale or mead or platters of fine food to welcome their guests. He laid his hand upon her shoulder and gave a gentle squeeze, then turned to follow the servant out of the main door.

Brynhild remained where she was, her face buried in her hands.

Long minutes passed. Voices drifted in from outside: Dughall's, raised in anger; Ulfric, calm. Taranc occasionally, also quiet, reasonable, unperturbed.

How could her gentle and caring lover greet her faithless brother like a long-lost friend? How could he show Ulfric even the slightest degree of respect, invite him into their home? It was quite beyond her.

Even as she pondered this conundrum the outer door opened again and Taranc stepped through, Njal clinging to his hand. The lad caught sight of his aunt and squealed in delight. He ran the length of the hall to fling himself against her skirts, then scrambled up onto the window ledge beside her. Brynhild enfolded her beloved nephew in her arms and surrendered to more uncontrolled weeping.

"I missed you. I missed you so much." She gulped the words through her tears. "I never expected to see you again."

"I love you, Aunt Brynhild. I'm so glad we found you. Why are you angry that we are here?"

"It is not that. I…"

Taranc eased himself into the seat alongside the pair. "Your aunt has had a shock. She is not angry. At least, not with you."

"She is angry with my father," observed the boy, "and with Fiona." He turned to fling his arms about Brynhild's

231

neck. "Please do not be angry. If you are, Taranc says we will have to go away again, and I want to stay here."

Brynhild was stunned. "Stay here? But—"

"My father wishes to remain here. He has asked Taranc." The boy looked to the Celt for confirmation. Taranc had the grace to shift in his seat.

"What... What have you said?" she whispered.

Unflinching, Taranc met her gaze. "The idea has merit."

"It is madness. It would never work. They are our enemies, they cannot be trusted."

"I think—"

Further conversation was curtailed by the door swinging open again, this time to admit Ulfric, Fiona, and Dughall. Her brother entered, and sauntered across the hall, pausing just feet from where she sat. He actually smiled at her.

"Brynhild? Sister?"

"Brother? Bastard?"

Ulfric was undeterred by her hostile welcome. "I am sorry..." he began.

Her temper flared again. She glared at him. "Do not bother. Save it for one who cares what you think, how you feel. This one, perhaps." She levelled a glare at Fiona. "I hear you are wed to your little—"

Taranc cleared his throat. "Do not say it, Brynhild. Not in front of her father, and the lad."

He was right, of course. Brynhild nodded and hugged Njal to her as though the boy might offer the shield she needed. Still, the words of anger, of recrimination could not be contained. Her anguish was too great, the hurt buried for too long not to surface now.

"For her? You sent me away, for her? I was your sister, your own kin. I cared for your home, your son, yet you threw me aside. I loved you. You and Njal were everything to me. How could you do it?"

At once Taranc's arms were around her. Brynhild clung to his woollen cloak as though her very life depended upon his solid presence. She curled her fingers in the sturdy fabric, her sobs loud and gulping as she gave vent to grief and pain too intense to contain a moment longer.

His palms traced large, soothing circles on her back as he held her against his chest. "You have your family back, now, sweetheart. All of them and more besides. They are to stay here, with us."

Taranc's words did nothing to dispel Brynhild's agony. If anything, her weeping grew louder, more unbridled as a fresh wave of despair washed over her.

She had survived the ultimate betrayal, not once but twice. She had rebuilt her life, again, only to have all she had worked for swept away once more by circumstances she could not control. She would lose everything—her precious haven, Taranc, her fragile standing in this alien place she had decided to call home.

Taranc shifted. Brynhild fought to hang on to him but he loosened her hold and stepped back, murmuring words she did not entirely catch about grief and pain and about giving her time. New arms gathered her in, familiar scents assailed her nostrils, the aromas of wolf skin cloak, leather, the sea, so uniquely Viking.

Past caring now, Brynhild wept in her brother's arms. He held her, his lips on her hair, murmuring apologies she had no desire to hear, explanations she would never accept. But as he did so, even as his meaningless words drifted about her, something shifted in her troubled, shattered soul.

It hurt. It hurt so much, *too* much, but the pain had become excruciating to hold on to. She had no choice, no alternative if she was to survive a third time. She had to let it go.

So she did. Brynhild the pragmatist, the survivor, the resilient, efficient mistress of her own destiny surrendered the dam of anger and bitter disappointment she had nurtured all these months and that had festered to bring her to this moment. She found release.

· · · · · · ·

"Why are you here?" Brynhild faced her brother across the oak table in the home she shared with Taranc. Fiona and the rest of the family continued to enjoy Dughall's hospitality at Pennglas but she had felt the need for solitude and had made her excuses. In his usual bull-headed manner Ulfric failed to grasp that she needed a respite from him.

He grinned at her, seemingly oblivious to her desire to be alone. "I was concerned for you, going off on your own, and in your condition. Taranc too. He would have come, but I said—"

"No, idiot. I mean why are you *here*? In Scotland? Why are you not at Skarthveit? And what was it that Taranc said earlier, about your intention to remain here?" She vaguely recalled mention of this but had been too distraught at the time to seek clarification. Now, her head clearer, she demanded an explanation. "What of your settlement in our own land? Our people there?"

"Most of our people are here now, or at least all who chose to accompany us across the North Sea."

"You have brought everyone? But… why? Where are they?"

"Most remained on or close to our longships, until such time as I could speak with Taranc and with you. I had no desire to create panic here by coming ashore with dozens of Viking warriors at my back. That would have created quite the wrong impression." He paused, then, "As to why… you will recall Olaf Bjarkesson."

"Of course. He would have been my kinsman had Eirik lived. Yours too."

"Aye, but he became my enemy when Eirik and Astrid died. You know he blamed me for their deaths."

"Yes, he was wrong, but…"

Ulfric's expression was grim. "The feud continued, grew worse. Olaf's attacks became more frequent, more deadly. His men set upon Fiona and Njal when they were out of our village on one occasion, and followed that skirmish with a vicious assault on Skarthveit itself. We managed to repel them with the help of our thralls, though I had to promise them their freedom in exchange for their aid."

"You freed the thralls? All of them?" Brynhild could barely comprehend her brother's actions.

"I did. Fiona can be most persuasive when she sets her mind on something. And in truth, I had little option if I was to defend Skarthveit successfully as we were seriously outnumbered. But it was just one battle, one attack fought off. There would be more and I might not always prevail. I have my family to think of, my people. We need to live in peace on our own shores if we are to thrive and prosper, to grow crops and raise our families. It was obvious that Olaf would never relent. So I decided to leave."

"You just gave up? Gave him Skarthveit?" She could not conceal her shock, her dismay that her childhood home was lost. "You allowed him to drive you out? To drive all of us out?"

"The settlement is just longhouses, a few crops, and a half-built harbour. Olaf was busy destroying our farms in any case, and we can rebuild our houses elsewhere. I had no stomach for the life we would have had there, so I decided to move on and invited all who would to follow me."

"So you came here?"

"Of course. Where else?"

"Anywhere. You could have gone anywhere else."

He shook his head. "No, it had to be here. I had to see you, to know that you were well and content. I believed that Taranc could make you happy, that he would take care of you. I would not have entrusted you to him otherwise. But until I saw for myself..."

"So you are here for me?"

"I am. I had to come after you."

"How did you know we would be here at Aikrig?"

"I didn't, not for certain. But I suspected, and where else would he go? This is Taranc's home. And now it is mine too. Ours."

"Taranc has agreed." It was a statement, not a question.

"He has, and Dughall also, who will tolerate me and the rest of our people for the sake of his daughter. But I would know I have your welcome too. Despite everything."

"It appears I have little choice in the matter." She stood, intending to fetch ale from the barrel she kept close to hand.

Ulfric caught her elbow as she passed him. "Perhaps not. But you do have a choice over how you respond. Will you welcome me? My family? Fiona? Will you welcome all of us as we make our home here?"

Brynhild regarded him for several moments, her beloved elder brother, the one she had relied on all her life... until Taranc. Her decision was made. It was made earlier as she had wept in his arms in the great hall at Pennglas.

Slowly, she nodded. "You are welcome here, brother," she whispered. "You and yours."

The words were easy. Now, she must work at making them a reality.

• • • • • • •

"I shall send for Fiona. She has some skills with herbs, perhaps—"

"Aagh!" Brynhild seized Murdina's hand and squeezed hard as a fresh wave of agony caused her distended abdomen to contract. She panted in the half-light of the house in Aikrig, perspiration beading across her forehead as she laboured to deliver her child into the world.

She shook her head. "I do not want her here. Oh... Taranc! Where is Taranc?"

"I am here." He came to kneel beside the bed and took her other hand in his. "It will not be long now." He looked to his mother as though seeking confirmation.

Brynhild groaned, her usual stoic courage in tatters. "It has been a full day, and a half. I am scared..."

"All is well," insisted Murdina. "I have attended many births in my time, and see no cause to worry. The babe will be here soon."

Taranc tried again. "Perhaps a soothing draught would ease the pain somewhat. Fiona might—"

"No!" Brynhild dragged herself to a sitting position as another contraction seized her. She screamed as her belly twisted, the sound ragged, her voice hoarse now. Her futile cries of agony bounced off the timbers of their dwelling, echoing in her ears as the child stubbornly refused to shift.

She sank back against the bolster that Murdina had jammed behind her shoulders, despairing that this ordeal would ever be over. The next contraction was upon her almost before the last had receded. How much more? How much longer before her body split in two?

Suddenly, almost without warning, the pain arrowed down, now settling at her very core. Brynhild let out another guttural moan, then a startled yelp. The urge to push was beyond overwhelming. As both Taranc and Murdina urged her on she bore down with all that was within her, forcing this determined, obstinate little being out into the light.

"I see the head." Murdina peered between Brynhild's thighs. "One more good push, with the next contraction…"

"Aaagh!" Pain gripped her again, and Brynhild tightened her crushing grasp on Taranc's hand. Even in her own tortured misery Brynhild could not miss the grimace that flickered across his features. He did not pull away though.

"So close, my Viking. You can do this. Just one last push…"

He was right. Brynhild bore down again, and her baby slithered into Murdina's waiting hands.

"A boy," announced the older woman. "A fine, yowling lad who looks the very image of his sire."

As though to add his own contribution, the child chose that precise moment to open his mouth and bellow his displeasure to the heavens. His thin, high cries now filled the house as Brynhild sagged back against the pillows. Murdina hastily wrapped a blanket about the squirming child and laid him on Brynhild's chest. At once he ceased his bawling, instead starting to root among her garments. Brynhild opened her shift and pressed his tiny mouth to her nipple, though it took a little experienced intervention by Murdina to see the child properly latched on and suckling hard.

Satisfied that all was well, Brynhild submitted to Murdina's continuing ministrations. As the older woman cleansed her spent body and dragged the soiled bedding away, Brynhild spared a look at Taranc. She noted the glistening in his forest-green eyes. On closer inspection of the downy head at her breast she knew the baby shared his brown hair, though the infant's eyes had yet to take on the brilliant hue of his father's irises. Or maybe he would take after her. In that moment it did not matter. Nothing mattered save that her baby was here, safe, healthy.

A boy. She had a son.

"What name shall we give him?" Brynhild looked to Taranc for guidance. "A Celt name, since he shall be chief here and lead his people. Our people."

"Then Morvyn. That was my father's name. If you are agreeable?"

She nodded. "Morvyn is an excellent choice. I believe our son shall make a fine chief."

Taranc merely nodded.

CHAPTER TWENTY

"Is the lad well?" Lord Dughall sat at her board, a mug of Brynhild's fine mead before him. It was rare that the old man ventured so far from Pennglas, but he had made the journey today. "Does he thrive? Taranc tells me he does, but I wished to see for myself. You visit me so rarely these days."

The faint thread of admonition could not be ignored. And it was true. Her visits to Pennglas were infrequent.

"I have been busy. The baby..."

"I miss you. I miss your conversation, your ready wit."

"But you have your daughter. I am sure that Fiona will see to your comfort."

"Indeed she does, and I am glad of her presence. And the lad. Njal is a fine boy. You raised him well."

"He is Fiona's to care for now."

"He misses you too. Why do you not come to see us?"

Brynhild cuddled her son close. "You know why. You must know. Fiona has told you why Ulfric sent me away."

"Yes, I have heard the story. Of the stocks."

"Well, then—"

"But I know you, and I know Taranc. He has assured me that there was a mistake, some sort of misunderstanding. Is that not correct?" The old man turned to greet Taranc who had entered as they spoke.

"Aye, that is the only explanation," confirmed Taranc as he helped himself to a mug of ale. "But if we are all to live here together we should seek to establish what really happened."

"Everyone believes Fiona's account," observed Brynhild bitterly, her baby nestled against her chest. "What is the point of reopening the wound?"

"Both Dughall and I believe that Fiona is telling the truth as she understands it to be, but we cannot accept the implications of that. There has been a mistake, a misunderstanding." He reached for her hand. "You are a good woman, a fine, brave woman, not a coward. I know that you would not do this thing. I have always known."

"Then why does Fiona insist that I did?"

"I do not know. That is why I want you to ask her."

"Lord Dughall could ask her."

The old man flattened his lips. "I have, and she says she is certain of what took place. I do not think she is telling me false, but equally I am convinced, as Taranc is, that it cannot be as she says."

"Yes," urged Taranc. "*You* must speak with her. You must discern what we are all missing because no one else can do it. Only you and she were there that night, the truth lies between the pair of you. You must settle this, my Viking, for yourself, for Dughall, for me, and for our fine wee laddie here."

Brynhild sat in silence long after Taranc returned to his duties in the village and Dughall left their house to make his way back up the hill in the small cart he had used for the journey down to Aikrig. As the sound of the metal wheels clattered into the distance leaving just silence behind, she heaved a long, frustrated sigh. But she could not fault Taranc's words.

He was right. It was time this matter was settled.

• • • • • •

She found Fiona in the lord's solar at Penglass, retching into a bucket. Brynhild had chosen this morning to make her approach as she knew both Ulfric and Taranc were off hunting, and Dughall had assured her they would not be disturbed. She held her baby on her hip as she regarded the other woman from across the room.

Fiona must have sensed her presence. She called for a damp cloth and some water with which to refresh herself. Brynhild glanced about and spotted the pitcher of cool water that had been left in readiness on the low table. She dipped the cloth that lay beside the vessel and wrung it out, then placed it in Fiona's flailing hand.

"Thank you, Hilla." Fiona had mistaken Brynhild for the servant who usually attended her needs. She wiped her lips, then turned to face the servant. Fiona's eyes widened, whether in alarm or annoyance Brynhild could not be sure. Without doubt, though, her presence here was neither expected nor welcomed.

"Brynhild!" Fiona rose to her feet, but her upright stance proved to be short-lived. She sank to her knees with a groan and retched again into the pail.

"'Twill pass. Does Ulfric know?" Brynhild recalled her own misery in the early stages of pregnancy. Her sympathy was grudging, but genuine.

Fiona nodded. "Yes, but no one else, yet. It is very early."

"I wish you and the babe well."

"Thank you." Fiona eyed Brynhild with undisguised suspicion. "I had not expected to see you here today. Is there something I can do for you?"

Brynhild chose to ignore the cool note of dismissal. She had come here for a purpose and would not be dismissed.

"Yes, there is. I want you to know the truth of what happened that night in Skarthveit, the night of the stocks."

Brynhild stood her ground as Fiona glared at her. She

did not anticipate this to be a conversation the other woman would relish. That could not be helped. It was happening anyway.

In the days since Taranc had convinced her that this must be done, Brynhild had devoted considerable thought and planning to her mission. It was ever her way to do so, but on this occasion it was vital that she succeed. Taranc was correct, they had to reconcile this if their families were to thrive together.

Brynhild was convinced the key lay in convincing Fiona, and then Ulfric, that she had become distracted that night rather than deliberately abandoning the Celtic slave to her fate. Fiona was perfectly aware that Njal had been ill. Indeed, she had rushed to fetch a pail. But for some reason she refused to share this crucial detail with Ulfric. Brynhild was determined to know why.

Unfortunately, Fiona had other ideas. "I have no wish to discuss it further. Now, if you will excuse me, I have matters to attend to." She offered Brynhild a polite nod and made for the door.

"Wait." Brynhild did not intend the commanding note that laced her tone, and it was clear that neither did Fiona. Nor did the other woman care for it.

Fiona's eyes hardened. "If you will excuse me…" She was leaving.

"Wait… please. I would have you hear me out." She did not come here intending to beg, but Brynhild was not above doing so if that was what it took.

Her plea was sufficient to give Fiona pause. The other woman halted, looked back over her shoulder, then gestured to a seat. Fiona set about making herself comfortable.

It was a start, enough, thought Brynhild. She settled beside Fiona and concentrated on steadying her breathing. Never usually one to balk at a difficult conversation, she found herself terrified now. She must pick her words with care for she was unlikely to find another opportunity to set out her case.

She came straight to the point. "I wronged you. I am deeply sorry for it."

Fiona cast her a sidelong glance. "It is in the past, and we need not—"

Brynhild rushed on. Now that she had started she needed to get the words out quickly. "When I arrived here, started to make a new life for myself, I realised how badly I had behaved. I had my reasons, I suppose, but they were not good ones and did not concern you. My actions were beneath me. I wished to apologise, to make amends. But I could not, I did not expect to see you again."

"And now you have. You have had months in which to apologise if that was your wish."

"I know. I should have. But, you should also know that Taranc punished me for what I did to you. I asked him to. I asked him to act on your behalf and he did so. It… it was a serious spanking, the worst he has ever given me."

"Taranc *spanked* you? For me?" Fiona turned to regard her, wide-eyed.

"Yes, he did. And he forgave me, on your behalf, but now that you are here I realise that you may not consider the matter settled. I would understand that. I am ready to apologise to you, and—"

"He spanked you? Actually spanked you? Bare bottom and, and everything?"

"Yes. Bare bottom and, and…" Could she actually tell Fiona the whole truth of what Taranc had done to her? She supposed the other woman was entitled to know, since it was done on her behalf. "He put ginger inside my bottom too, and spanked me whilst it was there. It was very unpleasant."

Fiona gaped at her and actually blanched. Brynhild wondered if she needed to fetch the pail again.

"Ginger? Oh, my…"

"Yes, so you see he took his responsibility toward you most seriously."

"I can tell that he did. But you and he are… you are … happy together? Despite the ginger, and the spanking?"

Brynhild nodded. "We are. He is a good man."

"I always thought so."

"So, now that you know, I must ask you if you are satisfied that the matter is settled. I am deeply sorry for the hurt and fear I caused you, and if I could undo what took place between us I would do so. I hope you can accept my apology."

Fiona regarded her for several moments, then gave a slow nod. "It is finished. Let us speak of it no more." She made as though to rise but Brynhild laid a hand on her arm. "There is one more thing I need to talk to you about. It concerns that night of the stocks."

"Yes?"

"It was not my intention to leave you out in the cold all night."

Fiona raised one doubtful eyebrow, her expression speaking for her.

Brynhild pressed on. "I was distracted, by Njal's illness." She explained quickly about the loss of Astrid, the shock and fear this tragedy had instilled within her, and her concern that her beloved nephew might be snatched away just as quickly. "My fears were groundless, but I was not to know that then. I instructed Harald to remain with you and to release you after a short while. You saw me speaking to him? Just before I returned to the longhouse?"

On this, at least, they seemed to concur. Fiona nodded. "You spoke to him under your breath. I did not hear what you said."

Brynhild knew a pang of guilt. That had been spiteful of her. "Yes, it was my intention to frighten you so I did not allow you to hear me tell Harald to release you after thirty minutes."

Fiona frowned. It was clear this was indeed news to her. Brynhild went on to explain that she had returned to Njal's bedside and had completely forgotten the drama outside.

Her concern had been wholly for the little boy in her care and she had given no thought at all to Fiona. She met the Celtic woman's gaze and held it. "I am ashamed to say that I forgot all about you. I should not have, but that is what happened."

"But—"

Brynhild continued as though Fiona had not interrupted her. "It was only when Njal at last slept that I realised that neither you nor Harald had returned indoors. I came at once to seek you out but as I left the longhouse my brother charged past me with you in his arms."

"I know. You have said all of this." Fiona seemed exasperated, and weary. Brynhild could not blame her. She had told her nothing new and the other woman was no closer now to believing a different version of events than she had been a year ago in Skarthveit.

Brynhild opted to try a different tack. "Forgiveness is precious. I know better than to ask it of you for I treated you very badly. I would have your honesty, however."

Fiona glowered at her, indignation writ across her features. "Honesty? I have always been honest in my dealings with you, and with Ulfric."

Brynhild shook her head. "Ulfric does not believe my account of that night because he insists his son was not ill. Njal was quite recovered by the following morning when Ulfric next saw him so I can readily understand why he believes it to be so. But you know, do you not? You remember?"

Brynhild could have wept with relief when Fiona slowly nodded. She pressed on, seeking to press home the small advantage.

"I was cruel to you, but I did not intend you to die that night. You would not have. I would have freed you had my brother not already done so. Harald had his instructions, my commands were quite clear. He knew he was to bring you back inside after a short time had elapsed."

"He left me," breathed Fiona. "A woman, in one of the

longhouses…"

Brynhild gave a snort of disgust. She never could abide disobedient thralls and Harald's dereliction of his duty had cost her dear. "He had no business leaving you unattended in order that he might dally with some wench. He should have stayed, he knew that." Brynhild had no doubt that the slave's disappearance the following morning owed much to his knowledge of his own culpability. Harald had no desire to face her, or Ulfric, to account for his actions.

Fiona still appeared confused. "You did not instruct Harald to stay. I would have heard…"

"I did, but not in your hearing." Brynhild was emphatic; much rested on this point. "Harald knew, and I knew, but I could not prove it. I still cannot, but I swear that it is true."

"Why should I believe you now?"

Brynhild tilted her chin up. Pride would not allow her to grovel, not yet. "Why should you not? I would not lie about this. Njal *was* ill, events could have been as I say."

Silence stretched between them. Eventually Fiona nodded. "Very well. Let us leave it at that, then."

Brynhild clutched at her sleeve as Fiona made to rise. "No, you must tell Ulfric."

"Ulfric knows. We spoke—"

"About Njal. You must tell him about Njal. He does not know that, so you must not have told him or he would believe you. He would believe *me.*"

Fiona considered for several moments, then inclined her head slowly. "Very well, I shall tell Ulfric what I remember of that night. All of it. He still may not—"

"It will be a start. The truth is important, there can be no reconciliation without it."

Fiona sighed, but did not disagree. She appeared quite spent. On a sudden impulse Brynhild offered to prepare a chamomile tea for her. "It may settle your discomfort," she advised.

Fiona tottered over to the bed. "I believe I may stay here for a while. The tea would be… most welcome."

Brynhild paused at the door, Morvyn now fretting in her arms. "We are sisters now. Perhaps, in time, we might be friends."

She slipped out the door and closed it behind her, then leaned against it, breathing heavily. She had made her peace with Fiona and had succeeded in enlisting her help. It was a start.

• • • • • • •

The weeks slipped by, and a peace of sorts descended upon the communities of Aikrig and Pennglas. Ulfric had listened to Fiona, and Brynhild thought that perhaps the other woman had worked on her behalf for which she was grateful. In any case, her brother had accepted Brynhild's account of the incident with the stocks and offered his apologies for the misunderstanding.

Brynhild accepted his apology, though that had never been her main concern. For her it had always been about the truth, and about her self-respect and the regard of those about her. Those were restored and she found herself less and less interested in raking over the ashes of what was past.

Further, she was no fool. Even she could see that had events not unfolded as they did, she would still be at Skarthveit, wallowing in her own fears, living out her days in her brother's household. Instead, here she was, mistress of her own home, forging a life with a man she adored though she found it quite impossible to share that nugget with Taranc for fear he did not feel the same.

He was affectionate, loving even, especially in their bed, but otherwise theirs was not a demonstrative union. Still, she had no complaints, they got along well enough and Brynhild was happy. She had her home, a community where she was respected, and she had her precious little boy who was now starting to crawl about their house and babble his first words.

Life was fine, she concluded as she worked at her loom.

Life was just fine.

"Where is Taranc?" Ulfric burst through the door, his cloak flapping around his broad shoulders and his sword drawn. Rarely had she seen him so fierce.

"He went to Castlereagh, with Murdina and Morag. They have a cousin who is ailing…"

"Castlereagh. Where is that?"

"A village up the river, perhaps an hour from here, on horseback. They… they took Morvyn with them."

"I shall send for him to return at once. And you, you should make haste to Pennglas. Dughall is there, and Fiona and Njal."

"Why? What has happened?"

"Dragon ships are sighted, three miles up the coast and headed this way. We are under attack."

"No!" Brynhild splayed her palm over her pounding heart. "Surely, no…"

"Whatever their intent, they will think again once they spot my ships on our beach. They will not wish to take us on, but if they do try to land here my warriors and the Celts we have trained and armed will soon see them on their way. Have no fear, sister, we can and we will defend our home from these raiders."

"Why? Why would Vikings come here?"

Her brother shrugged, his jaw set. "Go to Pennglas. I will deal with this."

As the door slammed in her brother's wake, Brynhild reached for her own cloak and secured it around her shoulders with an ornate pin. She hurried from her house, but did not turn in the direction of the larger village. Instead, she ran along the coastal path leading to the beach. Already she could see the dragon ships skimming the waves and fast approaching their shore. Her brother's confidence was misplaced; these Norsemen were headed straight for Aikrig.

The ships reached the beach. Brynhild stopped, panting, and shaded her eyes to watch as the leader leapt into the shallow foam and waded ashore. She squinted into the low sun, the glare reflecting back from the surface of the water.

Surely that was not...

It was. As she managed to focus on the lone figure now striding up the sand there was no mistaking the dark leather attire, the huge wolf skin cloak, those ebony locks.

"Gunnar," she breathed.

Even as she watched Ulfric confronted his brother. Words were exchanged, but from the stiffness of their broad shoulders, the tense set of Gunnar's jaw, Brynhild had no illusions regarding the nature of this particular reunion. Gunnar was livid and had come here seeking blood.

"You. Yes, you. Help me, if you would." She summoned the assistance of a serf hovering close by. "Come with me to the well. Be quick."

Under her direction, the man aided her in drawing two full buckets from the fresh water well that served their village. Brynhild took one by the handle and hefted it up, trying not to spill too much. "You, bring the other pail. Come with me." She hoped the water was bloody cold as she strode off in the direction of the confrontation unfolding on the beach.

By the time she arrived the fight was in full swing. Her brothers brawled like cornered wolves on the golden sands of her adopted home. Brynhild had never been more ashamed of them. Was this disgraceful display the way a Viking chief earned the respect of his karls, his peers? She thought not. No indeed!

The pail of water was satisfyingly cold, she noted, as she flung the whole lot over both their idiotic skulls. Gunnar let out a roar of outraged bewilderment and shook the torrent from his dark locks, but not before the second bucket was emptied over him. Ulfric fared no better. The pair of them lay gasping and flapping on the sand, drenched, peering up at her. They reminded Brynhild less now of wolves and more of a pair of drowned rats. Her contempt for them plummeted to more or less the same level.

"Get up, the pair of you. Do you never learn? Grown

men, brothers, brawling in the sand like a pair of rabid dogs." She glanced about, not best pleased at the audience that had gathered to witness the spectacle. Celts and Vikings alike sniggered and smirked at their bedraggled leaders. Had these Freyssons no pride, no dignity at all? Their mother would be mortified.

"Ah, Brynhild. I was hoping to run into you." Gunnar offered her a lopsided grin, the scar that ran the length of his cheek doing nothing to soften his expression.

She refrained from kicking him in the ribs, but that would only reduce her to their level. Instead she gathered her cloak about her and adopted her most haughty expression.

"Were you? Well, now you have, and you can at least do me the honour of standing to greet me properly."

She had the satisfaction of seeing him ease himself painfully to his feet. It served him right, the imbecile. She fervently hoped Ulfric had come out of the encounter in similar discomfort, and was gratified to note that it was so. Gunnar's Celtic wife—Mairead, she seemed to recall—hovered about the pair issuing words of gentle concern and offering poultices. Brynhild shook her head in exasperation. She would be minded to let them bleed, but this Mairead appeared to be of a rather kinder disposition.

Even now the brothers bickered and taunted each other, and violence seemed ready to erupt anew at any moment. Brynhild had heard and seen enough.

"Shut up, the pair of you. Come with me." She glowered at each of them in turn, offered what she hoped might pass as a polite nod of welcome to the sister she barely knew, and turned to lead the dishevelled party from the beach.

CHAPTER TWENTY-ONE

Taranc leapt into the saddle of the horse he had commandeered, his tiny son tucked within his cloak, and galloped hard for Aikrig. The warrior sent to summon him had barely slipped from his mount in the rutted track that ran the length of Castlereagh and passed for the main street and delivered the tidings of the imminent attack before the Celtic chieftain had seized his horse and turned the animal in the direction of his home. Taranc dug his heels into the horse's flanks and prayed he would be on time.

He could not lose her... could not lose the fragile family he had worked so hard to build, to keep.

Fucking Vikings. Why could they never keep their thieving hands to themselves? Still, he blessed the fact that his friend and now brother of sorts, Ulfric, would be his ally in defending their village. His Viking warriors would help to protect the Celts and their homes. They would not be taken as slaves, their crops destroyed, their property seized. Never again.

His heart sank when he thundered into Aikrig at a flat gallop and saw for himself the three dragon ships that sat proudly on the beach, as well as those Ulfric kept in plain view. Seemingly the deterrent had not worked.

251

"Where? Where did they go?" he demanded of the nervous serf who ran to greet him.

"There was a fight, and…" The man gestured up the beach, toward the track leading to Pennglas.

"A fight? Are people hurt?"

"Only the Vikings, lord. Lady Brynhild—"

"Brynhild? She was here? Is she injured?" *Please, please let it not be so.*

"No, but she was very angry. She… she threw water at them."

"She…? Water?" At a loss, Taranc nudged the horse into motion again, this time a more sedate canter. "They are at Pennglas?"

"Aye, I think that is where they went." The serf called out to Taranc's fast-retreating back. "Your lady told them to follow her, so they did."

I bet they did, he thought grimly. *I bet they bloody did.*

He arrived at the manor house in Pennglas a few minutes later to find Njal and Donald seated upon the steps before the main portal, chatting happily. About them, Celts and Vikings gathered in groups, voices low as they regarded each other with bewildered suspicion. Taranc noted that several of the Norsemen were strangers to him; they had clearly arrived with this most recent influx from across the seas. He narrowed his eyes, his fist curled around the hilt of the sword he had taken to carrying of late, challenging any who might feel moved to confront him.

No one did. He dismounted, arranged Morvyn against his hip, and paused before the two boys on the steps. "It is good to see you again, Donald."

The lad grinned up at him. "My mother is inside, and my new papa is with her. He has been fighting with Uncle Ulfric and his face is bloodied."

New papa? This was a turn up. Taranc ascended the steps slowly and pushed the door open.

Dughall's hall was teeming with people, most of whom he recognised. The lord himself, of course, was seated at his high table, Fiona by his side. Brynhild stood at the end of the table, her spine stiff and her expression little short of murderous as she regarded her two brothers. Taranc winced. They had without doubt laid into one another and he was not sure if he could determine who had emerged the victor. He abandoned the attempt. Mairead, too, hovered beside her husband, her expression more fearful. Servants bustled about, Celtic serfs and Viking thralls scurrying back and forth but with no obvious purpose.

His Brynhild was slipping.

"What brings you here, brother?" Brynhild's voice was icy. He remembered well that tone, which he swore could freeze the very fires of hell itself.

"I am here to take you home." Gunnar's imperious tone rang out.

Taranc's heart sank. There was no reason at all why she should not return with her brother, should not reclaim her former status in her homeland. No reason apart from the fact that he loved her and could not bear to lose her now.

Brynhild's jaw tensed and she appeared to be considering the offer with the utmost care. Taranc held his breath.

"Thank you, brother. Your concern is noted. But you mistake my meaning. How did you know to come here in search of me?"

"He," Gunnar gestured contemptuously at Ulfric, "he left word for me of his intentions, his decision to abandon Skarthveit, and where he would go. He also left word of his actions toward you. As soon as I learnt of your fate I had to come. I would not leave my sister at the mercy of savages, alone in a hostile land."

Brynhild regarded her brother down the length of her aristocratic nose. "Again, I thank you and I am sincerely glad of your concern. However, your aid is not needed. Had I desired to return to my homeland I am quite certain that my husband would have taken me there."

Taranc exhaled and stepped forward, a determined grin

plastered upon his face. He moved to stand beside Brynhild. Her face lit up with a smile nothing short of beatific when she spotted his approach.

"Husband?" spluttered Gunnar, his battered features comical in his amazement. Taranc wondered if perhaps the Viking's handsome nose was broken as well as bloodied. He schooled his own expression into the friendliest demeanour he might manage. It would not do to smirk.

"Yes, my husband," confirmed Brynhild. Taranc believed she had never seemed more magnificent to him. "Ah, here he is. Taranc, come and greet my brother. You will remember Gunnar, I am sure."

"I do, yes." Taranc draped his free arm across Brynhild's shoulders and bent to kiss her. He was gratified that she returned his greeting with equal warmth and a tad more enthusiasm than was arguably proper, given the public nature of their current circumstances. "I am sorry I could not be here to greet our guests earlier, but as soon as I learnt of their arrival I made all haste to join you." He juggled Morvyn awkwardly before handing the child to his mother. "Needless to say, Morvyn was not cooperative. Our son is demanding his next meal, my love."

The barb found its mark. Gunnar peered in astonishment at the squirming child and Taranc could not doubt that the Viking had rapidly arrived at the obvious conclusion regarding his parentage. He opted to press his advantage, since he had surprise on his side.

"I expect you have questions. Ah, I see you and Ulfric have already started your own discussions." He performed an exaggerated wince as he peered into the Viking's ravaged visage and drew in a hissing breath. "Never mind," he continued merrily. "Shall we be seated and perhaps we can deal with the rest over a mug of ale and some food." A hefty dose of goodwill would do very nicely here, he surmised, and in any case the Vikings were marginally less likely to throw more punches if they were seated, or so he hoped. "Fiona, do we have the makings of a feast to welcome our visitors?"

Ever quick on the uptake, Fiona bobbed to her feet. "Of course. I shall see to it."

As she trotted off in the direction of the kitchens, Taranc thrust his hand out at Gunnar, daring the other man not to accept his greeting. Gunnar shook hands with all the enthusiasm he might have felt for grasping a hissing adder by the throat, then moved to take a seat opposite his brother. As he passed before Dughall, the old man struggled to his feet. Gunnar Freysson paused before him as the elderly lord peered up into his scarred face.

"You. I recognise you." Dughall's tone was bitter, furious even. Taranc gave a brief shake of his head, a silent plea to his overlord not to reopen hostilities now.

Gunnar, too, appeared content to allow peace to reign. He muttered polite words regarding Dughall's kindness to Brynhild whilst she had been at Pennglas.

Dughall was not to be gainsaid. "You were here before, that other time, on the steps of this very house."

Taranc looked to Brynhild, then to Ulfric for some sort of explanation. None was forthcoming. Gunnar was equally uncommunicative, though from the pained expression on his features Taranc had no doubt he understood the old man's point well enough and did not relish the coming confrontation. The assembled company stood in awkward silence, and Mairead chose that moment to bend double with an ear-splitting shriek.

Gunnar sprang into action, sweeping her into his arms and demanding that he be directed to a place where his pregnant wife might lie down and rest. Brynhild was equally quick to respond. Still with Morvyn squirming at her hip, she ushered the pair from the hall into Dughall's solar and slammed the door behind all four of them.

Taranc, Ulfric, and Dughall regarded the dark oak of the door for several moments. No one spoke. Dughall shook his head, muttered something which Taranc could not quite catch, then gestured for his manservant to assist him from the hall. He followed his daughter in the direction of the kitchens.

Taranc sank into the seat opposite Ulfric. "What was all that about?"

Ulfric scraped his fingers through his tousled blond locks. "I am not entirely certain, though I could make a wager."

"Adair?"

"Aye. Adair. Fiona's brother died in the raid, when we took the slaves from here. Dughall saw him slain, right at the foot of those steps outside."

"Gunnar?" Taranc knew, even as he uttered the name, that it had to be so. There was no other explanation.

"I never asked, but I expect so. Dughall remembers, he will denounce him."

"Shit."

"It was a battle…"

"An unequal one. You cannot seek to defend what your brother did here that day."

Ulfric hesitated, then shook his head. "I know that. At least, not if I wish to retain Dughall's regard, not to mention that of my wife."

Taranc cocked his head toward the solar. "So, she is pregnant? Mairead? Does he treat her well?"

"'Twould seem so. And aye, he does. He is besotted. Gunnar will want to remain here over the winter, to see the child safely delivered. Will you permit that, given…?" The Viking raised his hands in a gesture of bitter frustration that encompassed all about them.

Taranc pondered that question for several moments. He could find little to commend Gunnar Freysson to him thus far, but he knew Brynhild had always claimed to be close to her youngest brother and would doubtless enjoy his company. And Taranc wished no ill will to Mairead. Still, the decision was not his to make.

"I will not go against Dughall in this. Or Fiona. If they refuse him their hospitality, he must leave."

Ulfric waited for several moments, then nodded. "Let us hope it does not come to that."

The door from the solar opened and Gunnar emerged. Both men regarded him from their vantage point at the high table.

Taranc heaved a resigned sigh. "Your brother has vented his displeasure upon you most effectively. I daresay he is even angrier with me for the part I played in Brynhild's fate." He stroked his chin thoughtfully, wondering in what condition the Viking might seek to leave it. For certain, he would not make the matter simple for the Nordic warrior, not this time. He started to rise. "I suppose we'd better get this over with."

Ulfric grabbed his arm and pulled him back into his seat. "Wait. See what transpires. If my brother seeks to take issue with you, I believe my sister will actually kill him."

Taranc's derisive snort was his response. "And I fear that you are quite deluded, my friend. She would more likely offer to hold his cloak."

"She loves Gunnar. She will be glad enough to see him here, however equivocal her greeting just now. She and I… well, she has not entirely forgiven my actions though we get by. But you? My sister adores the very bones of you. And Morvyn, of course. She has chosen you as her husband and she will protect you with her life. It is simply the way she is—the Viking way."

Taranc wished he could believe that.

"Is that also the Viking way?" Taranc nodded to where Gunnar had paused on his way over to the high table where they sat to speak with Donald. The lad had burst through the outer portal and run headlong the length of the hall, his expression distraught. The dark Viking stopped his flight and ushered the boy into the vacant window seat, then sat beside him. Their heads were bowed together, their conversation low but, to Taranc's mind, intense.

"The last time I saw them together, as far as I recall, your brother was purchasing the lad from you as a slave. You drove a hard bargain."

"Aye. A decent purse of silver. I knew he wanted the lad, or more to the point he wanted the mother and the lad came as part of the deal. He was never going to further distress Mairead by haggling over the price he was prepared to pay for her son, so I took advantage. Trade is trade, after all."

Taranc chose not to dignify the remark with an answer. "That does not look like a master talking to a slave," he observed.

"I tend to agree."

They watched as Gunnar stood, ruffled the boy's tawny head and sent him on his way. The lad took a few paces toward the door, then turned to rush back at the tall Norseman. Donald flung his arms about Gunnar's waist and hugged him.

"Maybe your brother has something to commend him after all. We shall see."

Taranc used his foot to slide a chair out from the table with a raucous scrape. He gestured to Gunnar to join them then reached for the pitcher of ale and poured a liberal measure. A generous drop of goodwill might go a long way.

• • • • • • •

"That is the second time you have introduced me to one of your brothers as your husband." Taranc made the seemingly casual observation over their late evening supper. He and Brynhild had returned from Pennglas an hour earlier, the sleeping Morvyn in his father's arms. Now the lad lay in his own cot beside their bed, wrapped in brightly coloured blankets.

Brynhild shrugged. "It seemed easiest, on both occasions. My brothers hold... traditional views on such matters."

"And you do not?"

"You know why we are not wed. You yourself believe we are ill-suited. And you are right. It is better as it is."

He might have once harboured such a foolish notion.

"We are happy, are we not?" continued Brynhild.

"I am, certainly." He scratched his nose and tilted his head thoughtfully. "Gunnar wishes to remain here for the winter."

"Yes. He said as much."

"He killed Adair."

She gaped at him. "Are you sure? How do you know this?"

"Ulfric believes so too. Dughall saw what happened that day. He recognised your brother."

She nodded, and he knew that she had not missed the significance of the brief exchange before Mairead was taken ill, though that had turned out to be little more than a ruse to interrupt proceedings that the Celtic woman considered had taken an awkward turn. He was fast coming to appreciate that the timid and homely little Mairead was far more cunning than she appeared at first sight.

"Dughall will not permit him to remain here." She stated the obvious conclusion, pain and disappointment evident in her features. "I… I had hoped…"

"We must respect Lord Dughall's wishes on the matter." He wished it were otherwise, that he could make this thing right for her.

"I know that. Even so, I wish…"

"You know, you could return to your homeland, with Gunnar, when he goes back."

"That is not what I meant. I will not leave. I intend to remain here." Her tone was emphatic as she met his gaze.

"That is your wish? Your choice?"

"I have said so. Do you not believe me?"

He chuckled. "I know better than to doubt your word, my Viking."

"You should, by now. But perhaps I should demonstrate my resolve in this matter even so."

He raised an eyebrow. "How do you propose to accomplish that, little one?"

Without another word she slid from the low bench beside him to kneel at his feet, and shuffled between his spread thighs. Her nimble fingers worked the fastenings of his trousers and within moments his hard cock sprang free. She gazed at his erection for a second or two, then smiled up at him. "May I?"

He stroked her pale blonde head and nodded.

Brynhild took his cock between both her palms and drew her hands the length of the shaft. She rubbed the heel of her right hand over the smooth head, smearing his juices over the slick, shiny crown as she cupped his balls with her left. She weighed them in her fingers, squeezing, the pressure light at first then firming.

Taranc let out a low groan. "God, I need to fuck you..."

"Hmmm, perhaps. Soon."

Perhaps? He growled his intent.

"First, I shall do this..." She bobbed her head forward and parted her lips to take the crown of his cock into her mouth. Taranc sank his fingers deeper into her hair and twisted a hank of it in his hands. He resisted the urge to thrust, to fuck her face hard, but it was a struggle and he believed he might yet lose the fight.

Brynhild moved forward, angling her head to take more of his cock into the warm, wet pocket of her inner cheek. She scraped her teeth around the sensitive ridge that circled the head, then traced the same course with the tip of her tongue. She rolled his throbbing, aching balls in her hand and with the other she gripped that portion of his shaft she could not take into her mouth and she pumped her fist up and down his length. She kept the strokes slow at first, leisurely, taking all the time in the world as she sucked on the head with the cultured daintiness of the highborn lady he knew her to be.

Brynhild Freysson was complex as the stars that adorned the heavens, and as simple as the back of his own hand. He knew her utterly, yet not at all. She exasperated and enchanted him in equal measure. Quite simply, he loved her.

"Brynhild, I—"

She hummed against his cock, sending a frisson of vibration trembling through him. Taranc closed his eyes and allowed his head to drop back. He would spend in her mouth in mere moments unless…

He tightened his grip on her hair and eased her head back. "I want my seed inside you."

She acquiesced, her submissive nod and quiet smile sending a bolt of pure lust arrowing straight to his balls. *Christ, this would be quick!*

He scooped her up and stepped past the small pallet where their son lay sleeping. Gently Taranc laid his Viking on their nest of blankets and tugged at the ornate brass pin that held her skirt in place. The fastening released and her lower body was bared to him. He paused for a moment, always more than ready to admire her long, slender legs and the triangle of pale blonde curls at their joining. Brynhild herself made short work of her tunic and the thin cotton leine she wore beneath.

"Are you warm enough?" Annag had tended their fire whilst they were at Pennglas but he could always throw another log or two on the flames.

"Yes, perfectly. Hurry…"

He kicked off his trousers and boots, and divested himself of his knee-length tunic. She was already spread out for him as he moved over her.

"I died a thousand times on the ride back from Castlereagh. I did not know if you… if you…"

"I was safe."

"I did not know that." He buried his face in her neck. "I could not bear to lose you."

"You will not lose me, my Celt. I am yours."

"Mine," he agreed as he thrust his cock into her slick heat.

Brynhild gasped and arched under him. Her fingers closed about his shoulders and she hung onto him as though afraid he might yet slip from her. She rolled her hips as she squeezed her inner muscles about him. She was tight as ever, all heat and wetness and warm, willing welcome. Her breath came in ragged pants, hoarse and more laboured as her arousal built. She was close, he knew. So was he.

He altered his angle just a fraction, but it was enough to ensure every stroke caressed and teased that sweet inner spot. She needed more, he knew it, so he bent his head to take one turgid nipple between his teeth and bit down lightly. Brynhild groaned. He bit harder and she squealed.

Ah, just right then.

He withdrew his cock, held there for just a few moments, the head just piercing her entrance as she squirmed and quivered on the tangled blankets, clawing at his shoulders and begging him to fill her. His balls ached, he ground his teeth and flexed his jaw as he forced himself to wait, to make her wait.

She screamed when he at last relented and drove his cock deep again. The sound reverberated about their house and Morvyn whimpered in his sleep. Taranc spared a glance over. The child settled again, though the mother did not. Brynhild wrapped her long legs about his waist and hooked her ankles together in the small of his back. She abandoned any semblance of restraint and ground her hips against him as her release took her. His beautiful, sensual Viking clung to him and sank her perfect teeth into his shoulder as passion overwhelmed her. Taranc drove his cock into her body, again and again, each stroke long and deep and demanding her total response.

He had it, all of it. She convulsed about him, her cunt contracting to grip him like a fist. Moments later he tumbled into his own release with a hoarse cry of triumph, then collapsed, limp, on top of her.

He fell asleep still buried within her, his Viking nestling within his arms.

• • • • • •

Two months had passed, and still Gunnar Freysson remained at Aikrig. He and Mairead had moved into the tiny one-roomed fisherman's cottage she once occupied with her husband. It was a squash, especially with the two children, and Taranc had offered them the use of a larger dwelling. Gunnar refused. He insisted theirs would not be a lengthy stay, he merely sought a place to remain for the colder months until it was safe to make the crossing back to the Norseland with his fast-growing family. He had endured far sparser accommodations on the battlefield and could make do.

Mairead and her children were content to be wherever Gunnar was, so that seemed to settle the matter.

Dughall had made no further reference to the question of his slain son, at least not in Taranc's hearing. He was not certain if Gunnar and the elderly lord had discussed the heir's death, but assumed they must have since neither was a man to allow an issue of such import lie unresolved. Taranc would not ask. It was between them.

He knew that Brynhild was enjoying the company of her brothers, and he was proud that she even managed to forge friendships with their wives. He was under no illusions regarding the effort she had made to build those relationships. Her natural reserve made it difficult for her to reach out, though she was ready enough to accept that she had wronged Fiona deeply. She was doing what she could now to make amends, and Fiona's natural generosity of spirit worked in her favour. They got by, and Vikings and Celts continued to thrive together.

And now, his own family was growing. Brynhild was pregnant again. She hoped for a daughter. He hoped she would have her wish. A feast was planned at the manor house to celebrate the good tidings and to invite the blessings of both Christian and Norse deities down upon the coming babe. Taranc much preferred this approach to the sacrifice of fine livestock, though he suspected a goat would yet be called for even so.

CHAPTER TWENTY-TWO

Brynhild gazed the length of the table, and could still not entirely believe that she found herself here, at the heart of this noisy, laughing family. Vikings and Celts alike drank to her health, and that of her unborn child. A solicitous Fiona kept the bucket close by, ever mindful of the inconveniences of these early weeks. The chamomile tea Brynhild swore by was in copious supply and Mairead offered her own recommendations from her basket of herbal remedies. The love and support of other females was something Brynhild had missed as she grew to womanhood herself and now she basked in its comforting warmth. Murdina and Morag were kind and caring, they had welcomed her to their family. Annag was her rock and staunch ally, and the younger woman's wicked sense of humour a source of endless amusement to Brynhild.

Her little boy brought her joy, as did the other children who scampered about the hall. Njal and Donald were raucous, though they tended to spend most of their days with their Viking fathers. Little Tyra, however, was invariably at Brynhild's house in Aikrig with her mother and was into everything, ably abetted by her devoted little helper, Morvyn. The tiny pair ran Annag ragged.

"So, little sister, another babe. Who would have thought it?" Ulfric raised his tankard yet again, his grin infectious.

"Aye. We shall have another feast in the summer, to celebrate the birth," announced Gunnar. "A fine Viking festival and I shall make sure I am here for that. I wish I had been here to celebrate your wedding, sister. I would have been, had our brother not seen fit to have you whisked off without so much as a word to me. I missed all the festivities whilst I languished in Gunnarsholm in total ignorance."

The Celtic contingent exchanged perplexed glances. Murdina called for more ale to replenish barely depleted mugs and Dughall demanded to know where the musicians had got to. Had he not left specific instructions that a piper be on hand to entertain them? There was to be dancing, was there not?

It took but one sidelong glance at her brothers to know that they were not fooled at all. Ulfric and Gunnar exchanged a look, then her eldest brother turned to meet her gaze.

"Brynhild? What is this?"

"What? What is what?"

"This…" Ulfric swung his hand toward their hosts. "Why the sudden interest in music and sploshing ale into already perfectly full cups. What are all of you trying to hide?"

"Hide? Why should we be hiding anything? You are speaking in riddles, brother, and I do not care for it. I believe I may be feeling somewhat ill…"

Fiona rushed to bring the pail closer. Ulfric was undeterred.

"Gunnar mentioned that he missed your wedding celebrations. Why should that cause such a flurry, I wonder?"

"Yes," agreed Gunnar. "Perhaps you could tell me of that glorious day. I would like to know the details since I could not be present. Tell me of the guests, the feasting, the flow of fine ale and wine."

"Do not be ridiculous," snapped Brynhild.

Gunnar shrugged and turned his attention to Taranc. "Perhaps you might enlighten us then. Were there musicians? Games? Was the ceremony in the Christian or Nordic tradition?" He balanced his elbow on the table and planted his chin in his hand. His smile was unwavering as he waited for an answer.

"There was no ceremony." Taranc stated the plain truth, bald and undiluted. Brynhild considered reaching across the table and slapping him.

"No ceremony?" Ulfric repeated the words, as though checking he had heard correctly.

"No ceremony," confirmed Taranc. "We are not wed."

"A babe almost a year old, another on the way, and you are not wed? Might I trouble you for an explanation?" Ulfric's tone had hardened.

"We did not choose to wed. We are not suited." Brynhild slapped the table, sending her own mug clattering to the floor. "And it is none of your business in any case."

"I beg to differ." Ulfric now fixed his steely gaze on Taranc. "Do you love her?"

"What?" Taranc glared at his tormentor.

"Is the question too hard for you, Celt? I seem to recall you asked me much the same thing once."

"And you did not answer me then."

"I did not, but you will answer me now. Do you love her?"

"Aye, of course I love her. She knows that."

"And she loves you. We all know that," put in Gunnar. "So, why…"

Taranc shook his head, his expression stony. "She does not love me. She does not wish to wed, and I will not force the issue. We are happy, though, and we shall remain as we are, for as long as we choose to be."

The dark-haired Viking let out a derisive snort. "Thor's balls! How did you two get into such a mess? Brynhild, tell the man, will you? You love the very bones of him."

"I—"

"Tell him."

"I love him."

"There, I told you so." Ulfric got to his feet. "Now, we will be needing that piper for we are to have a wedding."

"We will require a priest," suggested Fiona.

"Yes, and more food, and tables out in the courtyard, for we shall invite all to celebrate with us." Mairead, too, warmed to their theme. "We could have a priest here by tomorrow, and…"

"No!" Brynhild stood, her face ashen. "I cannot. I mean, we will, but not yet. Not so soon. I must… I am not ready…"

Taranc reached for her hand and pressed her cold fingers to his lips. "Does this sudden reticence concern Aelbeart?" he murmured.

She sank back into the chair she had just vacated, the breath leaving her lungs in a soft exhale. "It is not… I mean, it does not seem fitting that I…"

"We need to leave him in the past, where he belongs. It is time to move on."

"I…" Tears streamed unchecked across her cheeks. She was at a loss. Relief mixed with absolute horror as it sank in that not only was Taranc privy to her deepest, darkest secret but soon all would know what happened. She could no longer hold it within. The truth was about to burst forth, uncontrolled, ugly, brutal in its stark nakedness. She was not ready, would never be ready.

"It is time." Taranc's steady, calm voice cut through the roiling emotions to reach her. "I shall help you. You are not alone, Brynhild. You have your brothers too. And your sisters, those who love you."

Even as her mind recoiled, Brynhild knew he was right. She managed a tearful nod, swiping at her face with her fingers as though she might dry her tears that way. Fiona produced a kerchief and moved to perch on the arm of Brynhild's chair. She ignored the protests, the stiff reserve that was ever Brynhild's natural response and simply took the Viking woman in her arms and rocked her against her chest.

"It cannot be that bad, surely. If Taranc says it will be all right, you must know that it will. You trust him."

Brynhild could only nod her agreement. She heard Taranc bid Annag and Morag take the children from the hall, then he dismissed the rest of the servants. By the time she collected her senses sufficiently to face the gathering again the only people still at the table were her brothers, Fiona and Mairead, Dughall, Taranc, and Murdina.

"So," began Taranc, his smile warm. "Shall I start?"

"Yes, if you please." She had never been more grateful to anyone.

"Very well. This is a story which Brynhild told to me some months ago. I shall try to relate it as faithfully as I may, though she may wish to correct me on some points." He paused, then, "It starts when she was fourteen years old, growing up in her father's settlement in the Norseland…"

Those present listened in near silence as Taranc presented the account of what had transpired between Brynhild and the Celtic thrall. Gunnar interrupted to swear softly and declare that he recalled the cur, a slimy weasel of a man given to laziness and thievery. Ulfric concurred. He was convinced their father would have been rid of Aelbeart soon enough in any case since he was of little use. Both men's eyes narrowed, their handsome jaws flexing as the details unfolded.

"He did what? He actually touched you? The bastard laid his hands upon you even though you told him—"

"He did," confirmed Taranc. "Brynhild has said that it was so."

"Our father would have hanged him, had he known."

"I… I did not want that. Everyone would have known about what he had done, what *I* had done. I was ashamed…"

"He deserved to hang, or worse." Gunnar got to his feet

to pace the length of the hall. "Where were we when this all took place? I do not recall anything…"

"You and Ulfric were away, with our father, raiding." Brynhild had found her own voice at last and was able to fill in the details. "You arrived back at Skarthveit perhaps three weeks later, and by then our mother had had Aelbeart sold. He was gone."

Ulfric nodded. "Aye, I remember now. I was glad to see the back of him and did not ask any more questions. Thralls did tend to come and go in our father's time since he was at heart a trader. I thought nothing of it."

"Our mother knew what he had done to you, you say, yet she said nothing? Not to our father, not to us?" Gunnar seemed incredulous.

"She said we would not speak of it. I… she blamed me."

"Why would she blame you? Solveig was not stupid."

"It was my fault. I was foolish, gullible. If she had not arrived when she did…"

"That was fortunate indeed, but none of what you have told us was your fault. You were a child." These words of comfort came from Fiona. "You have said you hope for a daughter of your own next. Would you not believe her in the same circumstances? You would never blame your child, hold her responsible for the wicked actions of a cruel and self-serving man."

"He was a slave, I was of the Jarl. I should—"

"He was a predator, a beast. He should have been punished for what he did to you. He got off lightly, in my view. Solveig was never usually so tolerant, except with him." Ulfric jerked his thumb in Gunnar's direction. "I do not understand why she did not have this Aelbeart put in chains to await our father's justice, whatever the shame that brought on you. I do not wish to cause you any additional distress, little sister, but our mother was never one to pander overmuch to our finer sensibilities as I recall. She would do her duty, do what was right."

Brynhild shook her head, her tears welling afresh. "I

know. I know that. That is why, deep down, in her heart, I know she held *me* responsible, not him. If she truly believed me to be blameless, she would not have let him go, would never have let him live to do such a thing again elsewhere. She would not have left me wondering if, when, I might next turn a corner in the marketplace and come face to face with him once more."

Silence descended upon the hall as those present digested the truth of her words. Neither of the Freysson brothers disagreed with Brynhild's assessment of their mother's character.

The clearing of a throat in the doorway to the kitchens brought eight pairs of eyes swinging in that direction. A tall Viking thrall stepped forward, bowed to Gunnar, then to Brynhild. "Jarl, lady… I believe I may be able to be of some assistance."

"Weylin? What are you doing here? Eavesdropping?" Gunnar scowled angrily at the man.

Brynhild peered at the slave, and thought she remembered him. He had been her father's thrall first, then the man left with Gunnar when her brother set up his own settlement at Gunnarsholm. The thrall was older now, and had a hardness about him she did not recall though she had barely known the man. It seemed strange to her that Gunnar would bring a thrall with him on this visit since it was not customary to take slaves on Viking raids, but she had not questioned it.

"I asked to come, and you allowed it, Jarl. I… I believed I might be needed."

"Yes, you did. An unusual request but I assumed you had a hankering to see your homeland again and I saw no reason not to permit it. Your service has been loyal over the years."

"My home is some distance to the south, Jarl. I… I wanted to be here for this. You see, I was there, that night. I saw what happened. Or some of it, at least."

"Did you, indeed?" Gunnar's tone was dangerously low.

"Then I think you had better share your knowledge with us now. And whilst you do, I shall be trying to make some sense of the fact that you have chosen not to share it before."

The thrall swallowed, his throat working hard as he sought to control his nerves. Brynhild knew her brother to be a tolerant and lenient Jarl. His thralls fared well enough, better than most, but he demanded loyalty and would punish dishonesty harshly. Weylin would do well to quake in his shoes.

The thrall rallied under his Jarl's stern glower. He cleared his throat again, and began. "I... I shared the thrall barn at Skarthveit with Aelbeart. He arrived there about half a year after I did. We were friends, at first, of an age."

"Go on," Gunnar prompted when the man stopped.

"He complained. All the time, he complained. Always moaning, always finding fault. He sowed discontent all about him. Soon we all became tired of his peevish whining. The life of a thrall is hard, it is natural to be... resentful, especially at first, but eventually we all must settle to our lot and find our place. Aelbeart would not, and he would not allow anyone else to either. He was unpopular and soon found himself isolated among the rest of the slaves. That... that is when he turned his attention to the wee lady. The Jarl's daughter."

"What do you mean?" breathed Brynhild.

"He used to boast about befriending you. He would tell the other thralls that you followed him about, like a puppy, though in truth it looked to be the other way round to the rest of us and we would laugh behind his back at his delusions. He would watch for you, find ways of making sure his duties brought him close to where you might be— at the river, in the meadows, in the granary. He was a pretty enough fellow so it was not a surprise, perhaps, that you liked him. He could make himself very amiable, could Aelbeart, when he chose to make the effort."

"So, you think he made a fool of me? Is that it?"

"I would not say that, exactly. Though he did flatter you and he took advantage of your youth. You were confused, I daresay…"

"That sounds like a fair enough description." Gunnar leaned one hip against the edge of the table. "So, that night? What did you see?"

"I knew that Aelbeart had taken to meeting the wee lady in secret. He bragged about that, too. I told him he would regret it, that as soon as the Jarl found out—and he would—it would end in disaster for him. He laughed in my face. He was arrogant, believed he could not be stopped. He intended to use you, Lady Brynhild, to make his escape. You were to steal food and valuables for him and aid him on his way, then he would abandon you once he had no further need of you."

"Bastard," murmured Ulfric under his breath.

Weylin nodded. "Aye, I thought so too. I… I followed him, that night. I saw him slipping out of the barn, a blanket rolled under his arm. It did not take much to work out what he intended to do. It was too much, he went too far." The thrall paused as though collecting his thoughts together. "I knew that the Jarl was away, as were you and your brother. But Solveig was at Skarthveit. Her finest sow had just farrowed and produced a litter of fine piglets. She was well pleased with them. I… I opened the gate to the pen as I passed and the wee things scattered across the village. Of course, it was not long before their squealing attracted attention and your mother was quick to respond. She came from the longhouse threatening to take a switch to whichever fool left the gate unfastened, but she soon had most of them rounded up again."

"So what has this to do with Aelbeart?" Ulfric glared at the thrall.

"Solveig knew she had piglets still missing and was determined to find them all. She set off to search further afield, where squeals and scuffling could be heard by the old granary. I went with her. She found another pig on the way there and grabbed it, then handed it to me to take back to the pen. She continued on alone."

"You. It was you who brought her there." Brynhild could only stare at the thrall who twisted his hands together nervously. "She did not arrive by chance."

"No, not entirely. I am not certain what happened next, but I heard a shout, a man's voice I thought, and more squealing from another of the loose piglets. I shoved the one I had back in the pen and ran back in the direction Solveig had taken. You passed me on the way, lady, running hard. You were crying and you did not see me."

"No, I did not," agreed Brynhild.

"There was shouting, at least at the start, all of it from Aelbeart. With all that din it was easy enough to find them, but by the time I got there, he was dead."

"Dead? He was dead?" Brynhild gaped. "Are you certain? How…"

"A knife wound to the chest. Solveig's dagger."

"She killed him."

"Aye, it looked to me as though she did."

"She told me she had him sold."

"I daresay she preferred not to reveal the truth of what happened, in order to protect you."

"She killed him. For me. You actually saw this?"

"No, I arrived after. But someone did see. There was another man there when I arrived. He and Solveig were talking. He offered to help her dispose of the body."

"Who? Who else was there?"

Weylin shrugged. "I do not know. It was a stranger, a Celt, but not from our village. I had never seen him before. I wondered, after, if it was he I heard shouting as I returned the loose pig to the pen but I had no opportunity to ask."

"It probably was." Taranc regarded the group from his seat next to Dughall. "I recall I did yell something, to gain the lady's attention."

All eyes turned to him. "You?" breathed Brynhild. "But how…?"

Taranc inclined his head. "Aye, it was me. I was the stranger who happened upon to be passing that night and became embroiled in the altercation."

"But it was ten years ago, and in the Norseland. How could you have been there?"

"Ah, my Viking friend." Taranc grinned at Ulfric. "Do you suppose you were the first raider to ever arrive on these shores? I was taken by Vikings once before, though not from here. I was caught up in a raid on a village to the north of here. I was knocked unconscious, and when I woke up it was to find myself on a longship bound for your fair land. I was every bit as dissatisfied with my lot then as I was the second time your hospitality was forced upon me, and far less inclined to bend to the Norseman's whims. I escaped on the second night I was there and started to make my way down the coast in search of a boat.

"Naturally, I avoided villages and settlements, but I had eaten nothing save a few sour berries for over a day and I was hungry. From the brow of a hill I saw a village. I spotted the barn, set apart from the rest of the village, and the livestock in pens. It was dusk, so I settled down to wait for a couple of hours, intending to help myself to a chicken once the village was asleep. When it was full dark I crept closer, heading for the barn in the hope there might be something stored there which I could eat.

"I heard voices, so I hid in the shadows. The couple passed close by but I could not see them. They went behind the barn and soon I heard the scuffles and giggles that suggested some sort of tryst was going on. I made to move away, but before I could do so the sounds changed. I did not understand the words as I had no knowledge of the Norse language, but it was clear to me that the girl was no longer a willing participant. I turned about and soon found them. He had pinned her to the ground and she was crying. At the same time, all sorts of commotion was starting up in the village itself. I could hear shouts, the squealing of animals—pigs, it sounded like—people running about. Not that any of this seemed to matter to the man who was attacking the girl. He was oblivious to all of it. The more she struggled, the more brutal he became.

"There was a woman. I could see her silhouette in the moonlight. She was trying to round up the loose pigs and headed toward the couple on the ground, but she stopped and seemed to turn away. I shouted, then, to get her attention, but it seemed she would still be too late. The bastard had his hand over the girl's face, to stop her from crying out. I had no alternative. I stepped out of hiding and landed my boot in his ribs. It winded him, enough to allow the wench to get free of his clutches. Then the woman was suddenly there. She confronted the attacker, and never even saw me as I slid back into the undergrowth. It was my intention then to slip away and continue my journey, but I could not simply leave her."

Taranc paused and allowed himself a wry chuckle. "I need not have worried. The man continued to rant at the woman in the Norse tongue but she had nothing to say to him at all as far as I could tell. She simply waited until you had left, Brynhild, then she stepped forward, her dagger in her hand, and she gutted him with it."

Brynhild could not breathe. She gaped at Taranc. "She... did what?"

"It was quick, I grant you that. I doubt he felt much, nor even saw it coming. One moment he was on his feet, haranguing the lady, the next he was in a crumpled heap at her feet. I do not think she believed his delusional ravings, and she certainly did not allow him to live to repeat his lies to others."

"So it is true. He *is* dead? All this time, he has been dead?" Brynhild whispered.

"Yes, sweetheart. He is dead."

"Are you sure?"

"I am. I could see that she could not dispose of the body without help so I showed myself and offered my aid in exchange for food and clothing, a weapon. The lady was agreeable to my terns so I carried the remains to the cliff edge and flung the worthless bastard into the sea. He was dead all right, you may be quite sure of that."

Brynhild sank back in her chair. "She did not let him go? She was not tolerant, not lenient with him?"

Taranc shook his head. "Oh, no, that she was not. She killed him on the spot for what he did to you. Of course, I did not have the opportunity to know her well, but the impression I had was that Solveig loved you very much and would do anything to protect you. She was not disappointed in you, my Viking, and she blamed the one who was responsible. She was no fool, and you take after her. She would be very proud of you."

"Why did you not tell me of this, when I first told you about Aelbeart?"

"I did not see the girl clearly. She was never more than a shadow, and I had never been to Skarthveit before so did not recognise the place. It had changed a great deal by the time I was there next. The barn where all this occurred was gone…"

"Yes, my father had it cleared and built a new one."

"And you never saw me. You never even knew that another Celt was also there."

"No," agreed Brynhild. "But it was because of you that Aelbeart lost his grip on me and I was able to escape. Because you attacked him, distracted him for a moment until my mother arrived. Even then, when you did not know me and you might have been captured, you still helped me."

"I could not let him hurt you. Had Solveig not arrived when she did, I would have done more."

"I can't believe I never knew, never realised…"

"Why would you? Why would any of us? Solveig was dead by the time I returned. I am sure I would have remembered her, though there have been moments when I almost recognised her in you. When you told me the story you said your mother believed Aelbeart and had him sold at the slave auction so I had no cause to question that. I certainly did not connect it to the killing I witnessed, the body I helped to dispose of. But Weylin's account, along with yours, brought everything together. The picture was complete, the truths along with the falsehoods, and at last it made sense."

"She believed me. And you saved me. All those years ago, you were there and you saved me. I assume my mother kept her side of the bargain?"

"She did. Two hours later she returned to the place we agreed to meet and brought me food, clothing, a sword. She even provided me with a hammer and showed me how to remove the shackle from my ankle, though she made me swear not to do it until I was well out of earshot of the settlement. With the supplies Solveig gave me I was able to continue on, and soon found a small boat moored in a cove. I stole it and managed to make the crossing back to Scotland. Naturally, I hoped not to encounter Vikings again, though the good Lord saw fit not to bless me in such a manner. Still, I should not complain…"

"I am glad you were there. I wish I had known…"

"I am glad too. Glad also that the truth is out now, and complete."

"Aye, there is much to be said for having the complete picture," observed Dughall from his seat at the head of the table. "Much to be said. Life is indeed a complex tapestry and we can never know quite how all the threads will be intertwined. Now, I believe we were discussing arrangements for a wedding."

EPILOGUE

Four months later

"I shall miss him." Dry-eyed, Brynhild stood beside a weeping Fiona at the graveside. "He was as a father to me, also."

Mairead flanked Fiona on the other side and between them they offered their friend and sister such comfort as might be had.

On the opposite side of the still open grave Taranc, Ulfric, and Gunnar stood in silence, each contemplating their own recollections of a man who had profoundly touched their lives.

Lord Dughall of Penglass had passed away three days earlier, having fallen victim to a brief but virulent fever. In the end his death was peaceful and Brynhild fancied he met his Maker with a smile on his face. She did not share the Christian faith that prevailed in this land, though she understood enough of it to appreciate the hope that by offering prayers to the saints and Blessed Virgin to intercede, the old man's soul would not be delayed overlong in Purgatory. She would contribute a sacrifice of her own, naturally, since it could do no harm. She had already selected the calf.

The priest summoned from Balseach to perform the burial rites ceased his intonations and shuffled back from the head of the grave that would be Dughall's final resting place on earth in the plot of consecrated ground on the edge of their village. The new coffin had been placed on top of that which held the remains of Adair, and Brynhild liked to think that the pair might be reunited. Certainly, Fiona and Mairead believed this to be so, once their prayers were answered by the Almighty and his host of blessed saints and Dughall was ushered to his eternal reward.

No one was more deserving, she thought.

Taranc moved around to take the spot where the priest had stood. He cleared his throat and all eyes turned to him.

"I knew Lord Dughall of Pennglas my entire life. He was ever a fine and just lord…" A chorus of murmured assent echoed from the villagers gathered about them, Celts clustered here to bid their farewells to the man who had been their overlord for more years than most could recall. Vikings, too, swelled the ranks to mark their respect for the fine leader they had come to know.

Taranc gazed about him, seemed to take a few moments to collect his thoughts, then continued. Her husband had been named as Dughall's heir, though it was generally assumed that Ulfric and Fiona's baby son, named for the old man, would eventually succeed his grandfather. She had never felt more proud of her husband of just three months than she did at this moment. Taranc stiffened his spine and resumed speaking.

"I have been acquainted with Dughall my entire life, but I believe I only really came to know him in this last year or so. In recent months I have witnessed him deal with profound grief, sadness, heartache, as have we all. He led our people in our darkest hours, comforted us in our anguish even as he suffered the agony of loss himself." He spared a glance at the two Viking chieftains who each had the grace to bow their heads, then hurried on. They had discussed the words he would say and Brynhild knew that it was not Taranc's intent to rake over the ashes of the past. It would not have been Dughall's wish either. "He was an example, a mentor, a man admired by all who knew him."

More murmurings of agreement.

"But I believe he was a greater man than even he knew. Dughall of Pennglas was a man of compassion, of mercy, and of forgiveness. A pragmatist, yet a man of deep principle. A visionary, a man able to learn from his past, and look to the future with hope and an unshakable belief in the goodness of people and the power of kinship to heal even the deepest wounds. He welcomed into his home those who had wronged him, those who had been his enemies, and he made friends and allies of all. He put the needs of those he loved before his own grief, set aside his own anger for the greater good. That cost him dear, but he did it because he cared for those who relied upon him and would never fail to do his duty. I hope I can be a worthy successor. I shall endeavour to hold his legacy safe, and to pass it on in time to those who will follow all of us here."

Taranc moved back to stand between the two Viking chiefs, nodded to each in turn, then at the priest who stepped forth to resume his stance at the head of the grave.

"Let us offer up a mass for the soul of our brother," intoned the cleric, his arms aloft.

Vikings and Celts alike joined him in prayer.

THE END

Made in the USA
Coppell, TX
23 April 2022